LEGALLY BOUND

MASTERS OF MARQUIS
BOOK 5

GOLDEN ANGEL

1

Tugging on the bottom of her corset, Camille tried to feel like the powerful woman she had once been and not the beaten-down wreck she felt like right now. It wasn't easy. She'd thought putting on the clothing would help her get into the right headspace, but instead, she felt like an imposter. Like a kid playing dress up rather than an adult getting back in touch with herself.

Was it possible for someone's personality to fundamentally change?

"You look fabulous. Stop it," Julie said, elbowing her in the side. The petite Asian Domme barely came up to Camille's shoulder with both of them in heels, but that didn't stop her from trying to boss Camille around. It wasn't personal. Julie tried to boss everyone around.

"I feel like a poser," Camille muttered but let go of the corset, if only to keep Julie from elbowing her again.

The look she got back from her friend was steely. The kind of look Camille had once been capable of bestowing. She wanted to give back as good as she got, but she didn't think even her best effort would match Julie's. She didn't really *feel* it. Her glare felt fake, and therefore was weaker, which made her feel even worse.

Woman, snap out of it. You are spiraling.

"You are not a poser. You've just… lost your way a bit. That's why you're here tonight. To find a sexy man who will worship you and remind you of who you really are. Who you were before you took that damn job." Julie's tone sharpened.

Camille knew Julie didn't approve of her working for the Donaldson Law Group, but they'd been hiring and paid well enough for her to keep her mom in the expensive nursing home to get the care she needed. Dementia was a nasty disease. As an only child, with her dad gone, and her mom's sister also not in the best health, it was up to Camille to take care of her mom. The job was the reason she'd slowly lost her confidence, not to mention her personal life, over the years.

All issues that she really didn't want to think about tonight.

"I thought I came here to forget about my job." She raised her eyebrows at Julie, attempting to put a little more 'oomph' in her eyes. It must have worked. Julie smiled and nodded in satisfaction. Camille just wished she felt it more.

Fake it till you make it.

"Good. Let's get started then." Julie opened the door to the room she'd reserved for Camille… well, the inner door. The bedroom connected to a themed kink room—the Dungeon Room—which let out into the hallway. They were on the second floor of Marquis, a popular restaurant in downtown D.C. The regular patrons didn't know above the dining room there was what basically amounted to a kinky hotel.

There were erotic shows on the second floor as well, but she wanted to be a participant in a scene, not a voyeur. Julie wasn't wrong about the beating her mental state had taken since she started working for Donaldson. Handling divorces all day long was difficult enough, but Donaldson's clients tended to be grade-A assholes, and the partners were all cut of the same cloth. She knew money didn't necessarily turn someone into a bad person, but Donaldson's partners and clients were among the worst examples of of snobbish entitlement.

She'd worked there for almost five years and felt as though she'd completely lost her way in life. Lost sight of the things she wanted for herself. Lost who she was at her core.

Julie had finally convinced her to come to Marquis to try to reconnect with her old self. She'd even reserved a room in Camille's name, so if she met someone she wanted to scene with, she could. If nothing else, it was nice to have a place to change, so she didn't have to worry about running into anyone she knew out on the street.

Sure, her coat would have covered everything, but *she* would have known what she was wearing underneath, which was very little.

The light green corset dress she'd chosen complemented her dark skin, which pushed her breasts up to impressive heights, and there was a lot to push up. The corset pulled in her waist, and it had been a bit of an adjustment remembering how to breathe in one, but she did feel more comfortable now. The hem of the skirt flared out from her hips and flirted around her thighs.

She'd let her curls do their thing, and they'd actually cooperated, the tight coils standing out around her head, as if they were enjoying their freedom rather than the ruthless smoothing she usually did when she pulled them back into a bun for work. It really did help her be more herself.

Taking a deep breath—well, as deep as she could with the corset —she followed Julie through the dungeon portion of the hotel room into the hallway, down the stairs to the first floor of Marquis. The restaurant had been shut down for a 'private event,' which was only open to the kinky members of Marquis and its sister club, Stronghold. The room was already packed with people, drinking, eating, and generally having a good time.

The curtains were tightly drawn across the front windows, and while no one was in full fetwear, she wasn't the only one in a corset, and there was an awful lot of leather on display. The smell went right to her brain, and she felt some of her muscles untense as good memories washed over her.

She'd only had one serious kinky relationship, but it had been a good one until Jay had decided he wanted to go deeper into kink. Not that she wasn't deep, but a twenty-four seven power exchange wasn't for her. Despite her sadness at losing him, she'd wished him well and sent him on his way, then played more casually until she'd started working for Donaldson.

Moving herself and her mom closer to D.C. when she started work had been the end of her playing. Driving out to the house parties in Baltimore was just too much effort at the end of the day, and the idea of making new friends in D.C. had been too daunting. At least until Julie had moved here and decided to drag Camille out of her house for the New Year's Eve party at Marquis.

Julie was a good friend.

"Okay, let's get ourselves a drink, then I'll start pointing out possibilities to you," Julie said seriously, crooking her finger in indication that Camille should follow her. A drink sounded good, though it would only be the one if Camille did find someone she wanted to scene with.

Alcohol and kink did not go together well.

After being introduced to the bartender, Shane, Julie pulled Camille through the crowd, introducing her to a few people along the way before they finally ended up with a small group of Julie's Dominatrix friends. The two couples were warmly welcoming, happy to meet any friend of Julie's, and their immediate acceptance made Camille feel both better and worse. Better because they were treating her like one of their own, and worse because there was still a part of her that didn't feel like she deserved it. That didn't feel like she belonged.

"Oh, look, Sam and Q are here! That turned out even better than I expected," Olivia said. The redheaded Domme was apparently also the manager of Marquis, and Julie had called her 'bossy but fair.' Which in Julie speak meant that when Olivia spoke, Julie actually listened. Not an easy task to accomplish.

Turning her head, Camille looked at the couple who had just walked through the door, along with everyone else. The handsome black man had his arm around a curvy blonde who was nearly as tall as he was, and from the way they were looking at each other, they were completely smitten. Her heart melted a little at the sight, the same way it had been all evening when she'd seen happy, kinky couples.

It gave her a bit of hope.

"You're lucky that worked out," said Luke, Olivia's boyfriend and submissive, shaking his head. Just as tall as she was, even in her heels, he was a good-looking, muscular guy. Camille was rather envious of the easy way the two of them had with each other. That was what she ultimately wanted. "I really thought they hated each other."

"They did." Olivia was more than a little smug. "But that didn't stop the sparks from flying. Forced them to deal with each other and get past their issues, and all those sparks were able to catch fire!"

"Olivia likes to think of herself as a matchmaker," Lisa said, laughing as she curved her arm around her girlfriend, Sharon. The pretty blonde was actually the second Sharon Camille had been introduced to—the other had been petite, with black hair and a wide smile. Other than the smiles, the two Sharons were complete opposites. "It's kind of hard to argue with her results."

By which Camille assumed Lisa and Sharon had benefited from Olivia's matchmaking.

"Who would you pair me with?" she asked curiously. Olivia's eyes immediately lit up with interest, her entire focus zeroing in on Camille. The intensity in her grey eyes was uncomfortable, and Camille fought the urge to look away.

Next to her, Julie sat up straight, a scowl marring her delicate features.

"Don't you dare." She pointed a finger at Olivia. "I already have someone picked out for her."

This was the first Camille was hearing about that.

"You do?"

"I do." Julie sighed. "I didn't want to tell you because you almost didn't come tonight. I thought if I told you there was someone specific I wanted to introduce you to, you would dig in your heels even more."

"You don't know that I would have done that," Camille retorted as she crossed her arms over her chest. Yes, she probably would have, but she still felt the need to defend herself. Julie didn't know everything.

Julie rolled her eyes.

They both knew that Camille's automatic response to someone telling her what to do tended to her doing the exact opposite. Which was partly how she'd ended up at Donaldson when everyone she talked to told her that she shouldn't accept their offer but didn't want to talk about why. It was also something she didn't get to do very often since she had to follow the partners' directions at work... even when they were inane.

"Uh huh. Well, I'm not going to tell you who I picked. I'm just going to point out the options, and Olivia is going to stay out of it." Julie lifted her chin, shooting Olivia a defiant look. The other Domme smiled like the Cheshire cat, as if she was enjoying Julie's challenge.

"Maybe I can pick for myself." Camille looked around the room and caught the eye of an absolute giant standing on the other side. He was a cutie. "What about him?"

The big man stared back at her before his eyes dropped to Julie and lingered for a moment before he looked away.

"That's Connor, one of our shyer Doms," Olivia replied, running her fingers over her chin. "He's a total teddy bear, but I'm pretty sure he's not going to be interested in what you're offering." Teddy bears didn't really do it for Camille, but he was a big cutie. She might have been willing to make an exception. "I think you'd like Freddy."

Julie glared across the table at Olivia.

"She's not going to choose anyone you try to pair her with." Julie shook her head.

"You don't know that." Camille spun around in her chair. "Where's this Freddy?"

"He's here somewhere. I saw him earlier," Olivia said, waving her hand. "I'll point him out to you. There are a few others here you might like better, though. Don't go for Freddy just to spite Julie."

Nodding, Camille looked around as Olivia and Julie started giving her a rundown on the possibilities, with Luke, Lisa, and Sharon adding in their own thoughts about the single submissive men who were present.

***

FREDDY

As the champagne was passed around, Freddy smiled, hiding his feelings of discontent. No one wanted a party pooper. It was no one's fault that he was single—again—for the new year. Out of the corner of his eye, he saw Emery snuggled up with Mistress Red, the two of them practically glowing as they looked at each other.

"You sure you don't want to find someone other than me to kiss?" Steve asked, looking nervous.

"Hey, I thought we agreed we'd rather share a kiss with a friend than kiss no one at all," Freddy teased, before becoming more serious. "But it's okay if you don't want to. We can wait."

Steve hadn't been 'out' as a gay man for long. Realizing he was gay *and* kinky *and* submissive had been a lot for him, so Freddy had taken the other man under his wing. He usually watched out for the club submissives, anyway, but Steve was a special case because he was also the younger brother of Freddy's good friend, Chris, and because he was so new to every aspect of his sexuality.

Although Freddy was bi, he wasn't sexually attracted to Steve, but he didn't mind being there for a friend. Sure, he'd rather be kissing a hot Dominant at midnight, preferably a Domme, but this wasn't so bad. It was better than last year when he'd kissed his champagne flute at midnight.

The countdown started.

"Ten!"

Movement caught Freddy's eye, and he turned his head to see Master Eric headed for him and Steve with a determined look on his face.

"Nine!"

No, not toward him and Steve. Toward Steve. Oh, oh, oh! Freddy had told Steve that he thought Master Eric was interested!

"Eight!"

Steve had insisted it was just a training relationship for the class. Didn't look like that from the expression on Eric's face.

"Seven."

Master Eric had his eyes trained on Steve and was moving like a man on a mission.

"Six!"

Stepping back, Freddy pivoted and pulled Steve with him, so he was facing the right way.

"Five!"

"Freddy, wha—?

"Four!"

Master Eric was in front of them, hands coming up to cup Steve's face.

"Three!"

"Say no if you don't want me to kiss you." Master Eric's voice was low, rough.

Freddy sighed out loud. It was like a moment straight out of a movie.

"Two!"

"Yes," Steve whispered.

"One! Happy New Year!"

Okay, well, if he wasn't getting a kiss of his own, at least Freddy was getting a front-row seat to some of the juiciest gossip—and one of the hottest kisses of the night. Damn. Master Eric looked like he was going to devour Steve, and Steve seemed inclined to let him.

Apparently, last year's midnight did predict this year's. He'd be sharing a kiss with his champagne again. He brought it to his lips while he watched Steve rub himself all over Master Eric.

Envy pulsed through Freddy, which he hated, but he knew it was normal. Seeing so many of his friends pairing off made him more and more aware of what he ultimately wanted, what he wasn't getting, and what he didn't know how to get. He'd played with just about every Dominant at Stronghold and Marquis yet had never sparked with anyone.

Not the way Eric and Steve were sparking with each other right in front of him.

Considering he wasn't picky about what gender he ended up with, he should have more chances than the heteros, yet here he was.

Someone tapped his shoulder, and he turned, holding back his sigh, expecting to see another of his friends there, someone who would want the gossip, but it was a woman he'd never seen before. Freddy blinked, his mind automatically running through his mental catalog of members. No, he had definitely never seen her before.

He would have remembered.

She was about an inch shorter than him, but a quick glance confirmed she was wearing high heels, putting her another couple of inches shorter. Curvy as hell, she was packed into a light green corset dress that barely contained her breasts, which were threatening to spill over at any moment. Medium brown skin, dark brown eyes, and black curly hair styled naturally in a riot of springy coils that stood out around her head.

She looked like a goddess, and Freddy locked his knees against the instinct to drop and worship her.

"Hello, I'm so sorry. Do I know you?" The urge to keep babbling about how he knew everyone at the club was strong, but he held it back.

Her lips curved in a stunning smile, and Freddy's knees trembled.

"I'm Mistress Camille, Mistress Julie's friend."

That's right. She'd been on the guest list, but Julie hadn't been sure she'd actually come. Freddy assumed she must have just arrived because he would have definitely noticed her walking around earlier.

"I'm Freddy. I help run the front desk and well, all sorts of other things." *Do not babble. Do not babble. Do not babble.* He couldn't remember the last time a Dominant had had this kind of effect on him.

Mistress Camille's smile widened.

"So, I was told. I was hoping you could help me out with something."

"Yes, of course." *Anything.*

She leaned in, and he bent his head forward to make sure he'd be able to hear her, his heart thumping faster in his chest as she shifted closer, so they were almost touching.

"I don't have anyone to kiss for New Year's. Can you help me with that?"

2

———————

Camille

Determined not to show her nerves, Camille waited for Freddy's answer. He was a handsome man, tall and fair, with blond hair and blue eyes. His shoulders filled out the bright blue button-down shirt he was wearing, which matched his eyes exactly, making them appear almost electric.

Had she chosen him just because Julie had insisted she wouldn't pick Olivia's recommendation?

Maybe a little.

She'd also been intrigued by the way he'd lit up when he'd realized the man he was standing next to at midnight was going to be claimed by a Dom. Olivia had mentioned that Freddy was bisexual but tended to date women, and it had seemed like maybe he was couple-y with the other man, right until the Dom had come along and swept the other man away, leaving Freddy looking both happy and envious.

It was the happy that had drawn her in from a few feet away, where she'd been seriously contemplating going to bed on her own, without approaching *any* of the men who had been pointed out to her.

The happy now showed through as a slow smile spread over his lips, his eyes glowing from within.

"I would be happy to help you, Mistress Camille." Despite his words, he didn't move forward, waiting for her to make the next move.

Relief, anxiety, and arousal rose up inside her. Damn, but it had been a long time since she'd had a man who was willing to wait for her, one who didn't try to push his own agenda or desires. At the same time, it was a reminder that it had been a really long time since she'd taken control of a man.

Hell, it had been a really long time since she'd had the opportunity.

Stepping forward to bring them closer, she reached up to grip the top of his shirt, right at the front where the collar met, and gently tugged him down. He wasn't much taller than her, just enough that she had to tip her head back a bit, despite her heels. He came willingly, eagerly, and it felt as though something was blossoming inside her.

Some part of her had been dormant, hibernating during a long winter, and was finally seeing the sun... the need, the yearning, burst forth. Pressing one hand against his chest, she moved it up to his shoulder, using her other hand to pull him even deeper into the kiss. His hands came to rest on her hips, present but undemanding. Her inner muscles clenched so hard, it almost felt like a cramp. It wasn't just that he was a good kisser—he was—it was the way he let her take the lead.

She moved, he followed.

Yes, every inch of her body screamed. *This. This is what I've been missing. This is what I've been aching for.*

When she pulled her lips away, he followed for a moment, then straightened again, his hands dropping away from her hips. There was something about the way he stood that gave the impression of active waiting, not passively standing. No, he was too focused on her. Too ready to leap into action to be called passive.

But he *was* waiting.

She studied his expression, wondering if she was about to make a really good or a really bad decision. It had been a long time since she'd scened. Scening didn't necessarily mean sex, and sex didn't necessarily mean emotions. This didn't have to be complicated.

They could start off the new year with a bang, then see what happened from there.

"Is there anything else I can help you with, Mistress?" he asked, his voice husky, his gaze fixed on her lips.

It felt good to feel wanted. Desired. She was starting to realize it hadn't just been her kinky side she'd shut down. It had been her whole self as a sexual woman. She'd been through the longest dry spell of her life. She spent all of her time doing things for other people, most of whom didn't appreciate how hard she worked for them. The only one who did appreciate it was her mom, and only when her mom was having a good day.

Would it be the worst thing to have a night completely for herself? That was what Julie had intended when she'd set this up. Camille just hadn't believed it would actually pan out.

But here was a handsome, eager man ready and willing to submit to her. From everything Julie and her friends said, he was an *experienced* submissive. One who wasn't out of practice, like she was. Which should actually make everything easier.

"I have a room," she said. Somehow her voice came out cool, calm, and collected. Some of the unruly emotions inside her settled when she realized she'd made a decision. "If you don't have any plans for the rest of the evening, I do believe I could use some help getting out of this dress."

She could have managed on her own, with a lot of undignified wriggling, but having help would be a lot more efficient.

And fun.

Freddy's eyes lit up again, his smile brightening.

"Yes, Mistress."

FREDDY

Following Mistress Camille back to the overnight rooms, Freddy tried not to look too much like an eager puppy. He felt like one but didn't want to come on too strong. It would be all too easy to fall at her feet and worship her like the goddess she was, but she hadn't asked him to. Yet.

He really hoped she would.

There was a slightly nervous air about her, which might have worried him if he hadn't happened to look over at Mistresses Olivia and Julie on his way out of the party. Both of them had grinned and given him a thumbs-up. Well, Mistress Olivia had grinned. Mistress Julie had smiled, but for her that *was* like grinning.

Mistress Camille took him to the Dungeon Room. He walked in after her, a willing sacrifice. One-night stands weren't often his thing, but since this was his first time meeting her, if things went well, he could always hope for more than a single night. He was wearing his favorite shirt and a pair of slacks, so if she let him stay the whole night, he'd be able to leave tomorrow morning without looking out of place.

The fact that he was already thinking about staying the night was exceptionally unusual, but so was the attraction he'd felt flare to life between them. He hadn't had this kind of immediate spark with anyone in years. Chemistry couldn't be controlled.

"Sit down," Mistress Camille said, gesturing to the spanking bench in the center of the room. It was the only place to sit other than the Queening Throne against the wall. "Let's have a talk before we get started."

If he hadn't already seen Mistress Olivia's and Julie's approval, that would have set him right at ease. Clearly Mistress Camille was not only experienced, she was a conscientious Domme. Freddy relaxed further as he sat on the bench, facing her while she moved into the space.

Rather than seating herself on the throne, she leaned against the frame set up not far from the bench, which was closer to him than the throne would have been. Clear brown eyes examined him thoughtfully, her expression neutral, and he couldn't help but wonder if she was having second thoughts.

He hoped not.

If she did, he'd leave now, then see if he could talk Julie into bringing her to Stronghold or Marquis on another night. One when he was free.

"It's been a while since I've scened," she admitted after a moment, releasing some of the tension in his shoulders with the explanation for her hesitation. "It's also been a while since I've... well... I don't usually move this quickly, but Julie was kind enough to secure me a room for tonight. I wasn't going to use it until I saw you."

That was flattering. Freddy smiled encouragingly, waiting to see if she had more to say. Not only because she was the Domme, but because he'd learned sometimes people would say more to fill a silence than they would to answer a direct question.

She ran her hand up and down the frame.

"I'm not a hardcore sadist," she said after a moment, meeting his gaze. "I prefer domination, bondage, and sensation play to pain play. I do like a bit of pain play, but the main thing is knowing I'm the one in control. How does that match up with your needs?"

"Pretty well, Mistress," Freddy replied easily. Unlike her, it hadn't been a while since he'd last scened, and he had his introduction spiel down pat. It had been a while since he'd had sex, but he wasn't sure that was on the table tonight, though he could always live in hope. "I'm a service sub, I prefer sensation play, though I'm a bit of a masochist, but I don't do anything hardcore. When I first scene with someone, I request a lighter introduction, so they can get used to my pain tolerance."

That had happened after he'd had a few too many Tops—mostly the men, though there had been one woman—try to go straight into the rougher stuff. A bit of genital torture, once he was deep in a scene, was one thing, but that was not a starting point for him. Anyone who balked at the request was someone he didn't play with.

Not something he needed to worry about with Mistress Camille. She smiled, and he thought he detected a bit of relief on her face.

"That's fine, Freddy. Like I said, it's been a while for me, and I plan to ease my way back into things. Do you have any favorite implements, positions, toys…"

Freddy brightened even more. It wasn't a requirement that a Dominant ask such a question, but it made him think even more highly of her than he already did. Not asking didn't make a Dom a bad Top, but asking was an indication of a good one. This was going to be a good night. It didn't matter that she had been out of the scene for a while. She clearly knew what she was doing, and he was going to have no trouble giving himself over into her care.

"Floggers, the thuddy ones, are always a favorite. On the edgier side, I enjoy wax play and some breath play. For toys, cock rings, plugs, or wands. When I'm deep in a scene, occasional cock-and-ball torture, though no stomping or crushing." That was one of his hard limits. "And for a good sensation play scene, blindfolds are a particular favorite." He loved not knowing what was coming, being completely controlled and completely in the dark, every touch, every sensation a new surprise and delight.

Some of his preferences had made it hard for him to find a relationship in the past. There were a lot of stereotypes around what submissive men wanted, and some of them were stereotypes for a reason. Freddy had found that a lot of the assumed molds didn't fit him. He didn't want anyone to stomp on his balls. He didn't mind crawling, but it wasn't a turn-on for him, and he didn't become aroused from insults or humiliation.

He'd eventually accepted that about himself after years in the community, but at first, he'd struggled with feeling like an imposter because he wasn't hardcore. Funny enough, that had led to him being seen as something of a mentor by the other submissives as they went on their own journeys of kinky self-discovery.

Mistress Camille nodded thoughtfully.

"Then let's get started, unless you have any objection?"

Freddy immediately shook his head. His excitement and anticipation jumped, happiness billowing through him.

"Good. Strip for me, then fold your clothes and put them next to the door to the bedroom. I'm going to find some toys to play with." With that order given, she smiled beatifically at him and turned, heading for one of the cabinets.

Grinning, Freddy got to his feet.

Tonight was turning out to be so much more than he would have ever hoped it could be.

3

Camille

With her back to Freddy, Camille took several slow, deep breaths, trying to calm her racing heart.

This felt easy. Too easy? Or was she just distrustful because everything had been such a struggle for so long? Or maybe it felt easy because she was finally able to relax and be herself. To embrace her dominant side and let it free again.

Hearing the rustle of clothing behind her as Freddy followed her instructions, she smiled and opened the wardrobe. She'd looked in it earlier, so she'd known it was full of toys, but she hadn't looked too closely. Part of her hadn't believed she would need to know what it contained.

The assortment was vast. Clamps of various sizes and tensions, insertables of all shapes and sizes, an entire basket full of lubes, cock cages, oils, masks, restraints... pretty much any of the standard equipment a Dominant could ask for. Julie had told her if she had special requests—things for edge play like fire or needles—she would need to call in to the front desk. Just like a regular hotel, except they delivered so much more than toothpaste.

She was fairly certain it was also for safety reasons, which she approved of.

Despite the temptations the wardrobe offered, she kept her choices judicious. She and Freddy had just met, and she still needed to get a feel for his likes and dislikes, his turn-ons and tolerances. Not because she thought they were going to play again, necessarily, but she never wanted to push a sub past what they could handle, and that was impossible to know during a first scene.

Was she playing it a little safe? Absolutely. If things went well, the next time she'd let loose a little more.

Next time?

Yes. Definitely.

I'm not going back.

The thoughts slid through her head in the background, an acknowledgement she'd reopened a door she hadn't realized she'd closed, and it felt too good to go back through it. One night of being herself wasn't going to be enough. Maybe she had to close herself off and shut herself down at work, but she could come to Stronghold or Marquis when she was done for the day.

She didn't have to *live* like that.

And she didn't want to anymore.

"Insertable toys are okay?" she asked.

"Yes, Mistress." There was no mistaking the eagerness in his tone, so that answered that.

Holding the package of a brand new anal probe—Julie had explained that any packaged toys opened would be charged to her card—and a small tube of lube, Camille closed the wardrobe door and stepped to the side to pick up one of the floggers hanging on the wall. The long, thick leather strands were knotted at the end and should give Freddy the 'thuddy' sensation he said he liked.

When she turned around, Freddy was completely naked and kneeling next to the spanking bench, where he'd previously been standing. Seeing his legs spread, hands resting palm up on his knees, his cock standing at attention, with his head bowed, waiting for her... something clicked in her head, like a puzzle piece locking into place.

This was what her life had been missing. What she'd been craving. What she'd needed. She felt right, in a way she hadn't in months. Years.

No, I am definitely not losing this part of me again.

Julie had been right. This was exactly what she needed. And they hadn't really gotten started yet.

"Good boy," she said, calming even more as she drank in the sight of him—a man willingly kneeling at her feet who meant it. Not something easy to find, though it was admittedly less difficult when in a kink club, but not guaranteed. "I like seeing you waiting there for me. You have a very nice pose."

"Thank you, Mistress."

"I'm on birth control, not that we'll necessarily have sex tonight. Is there any other reason for protection?"

"No, Mistress. I'm tested regularly and I haven't scened sexually with anyone since my last test."

Maybe it had just been way too long, but she swore Freddy glowed more than any other sub she'd scened with. He described himself as a service sub, so she would have acknowledged any task well done, but his reaction made her want to pile on the compliments. His reaction to her words gave her both a sense of power and peace.

"I think we'll start with the spanking bench. You may get up and put yourself in position."

He might be the most graceful man she'd ever seen, even among other experienced subs. Freddy didn't just stand. He flowed to his feet, muscles rippling the whole way. He had a very nice physique, with lots of long lean muscles that looked just right on his swimmer's frame and those fun little notches men got at their hips.

He'd mentioned wax play, and she had the sudden urge to get out some candles and matches and fill those notches up...

Maybe another time... if he wanted to play again after tonight. So far, she hadn't seen anything that would indicate otherwise. Despite being experienced and obviously practiced, he was eager to play with *her.* Which gave her another boost of confidence. It was one thing for the other Dominants to accept her when Julie had introduced her as a Domme. It was another for a sub who was literally putting his body, his pain and his pleasure, into her hands.

Padding silently around the bench, Freddy draped himself over it. Whoever had last used or positioned it had set it up for someone Freddy's height. Dammit. Five bucks Freddy was who Julie had picked out for Camille. She had the sudden suspicion she'd been played.

But that wasn't Freddy's fault, and really, could she fault Julie's choice? No. No, she couldn't.

"Very good," she said, putting the probe and lube on a nearby table. Those were for later, after she finished the flogging. Walking over, she ran her hand down Freddy's back, and he sighed with enjoyment as she ran her palm over the curve of his very cute ass.

She loved a man with a good butt.

The flogger hung down at her side. The spanking bench wasn't the ideal setup for flogging, but it worked for both of the things she wanted to do, and she didn't feel like moving around too much.

Easing back into things.

This way, she wouldn't have to mess around with restraints or anything else.

"What's your safeword?"

"I use the stoplight system, Mistress. Green, Yellow, Red."

Camille nodded. Not everyone used a special safeword, and she liked the stoplight system. Some subs would push it if they only had a word for 'stop' instead of also being able to request a slowdown or a pause. Since she and Freddy were new to each other, she felt that having 'yellow' was a necessity.

He sighed happily as she stroked her hand down his back and buttocks again.

"Very good, Freddy. Let's get started then."

Stepping back, she lifted the flogger.

FREDDY

Thuddy delights rained down on Freddy's skin as Mistress Camille flogged him. He groaned with pleasure, flexing his shoulders. This wasn't the first time he'd been flogged while being bent over, but most Dominants preferred a standing position. There was something nice about not having to keep his feet while the stingy, thuddy pleasure of the leather stroked his back and ass.

The knots on the flogger could have hurt, if she'd been swinging hard enough, but she was starting off light. He didn't object. The build felt nice.

After about thirty seconds, she paused. He heard her coming closer, then her hand rubbed over his shoulders and back again, touching skin much more sensitive than it had been before. Shivering in reaction, his fingers tightened on the grips as his cock jerked where it was trapped between his body and the leather padding of the bench.

"How are you doing, Freddy?"

"Very, very green, Mistress. Please don't stop." There was a small plea in his voice. While he appreciated her caution, he could take so much more.

He wanted so much more.

She chuckled, changing her touch so it was her nails against his skin—not hard, but enough to send another shiver up and down his spine. The new sensation crawled over him, and he rolled his shoulders in response.

Then she stepped away, and he heard the swish just before the flogger landed again. It thudded against his skin, the knots hitting deep, and he sank into the sensations. Yes, it hurt a little, but in the way a really good massage hurt, and he could feel himself relaxing further and further. Without the imperative to keep himself on his feet, with the bench taking the entirety of his weight, he was able to completely let go.

He was aware of her pause, then she stepped forward to run her hands over his freshly flogged skin, checking in with him again, and her conscientiousness allowed his brain to relax, too. This was bliss.

By the time it stopped, he wasn't quite in subspace, but he wasn't far off. His body hummed, the backs of his shoulders and his ass exquisitely sensitive. She'd done a fantastic job of avoiding his lower back, keeping the thuddy strands in all the places it was safe to flog.

Something cool and slick pressed against his anus as her warm palm came to rest on his lower back. Freddy whimpered at the slight stretch. Too small to be a plug and not tapered enough—she must be using a wand or a probe. The small sting of insertion didn't compare to the pleasure as his nerve endings tingled to life, the feeling of fullness spreading as the probe pushed deeper.

Then she turned it on, and he cried out as the vibrations hit. His muscles clenched around the slim shaft, hips rocking forward and rubbing his cock between him and the bench, adding to the hot pleasure. The relaxed bubble of bliss he'd been floating in popped as pure erotic ecstasy burst inside him. The wand went in deeper, then pulled out, the vibrations sending him into spasms as he tried to fight back his need to cum.

"Good boy," Mistress Camille purred. "Cum for me, Freddy. You've been so good. You deserve it."

Praise kink activated.

If compliments were a kink, they were at the top of his list. Knowing he'd done a good job at something always made him feel good, and when it was sexual and the praise was coming from a Dominant, it was the biggest turn-on there was.

Gasping, Freddy let himself go, shuddering as she moved the probe back and forth inside him, the vibrating tool rubbing against his prostate with each movement. He cried out, hands braced on the grips, as warmth flooded beneath him, the spurts of cum coating the leather bench and his lower stomach where his cock was trapped.

Mistress Camille kept moving the probe, sending wave after wave of rapture spiraling through him until he almost called 'yellow.' Just before he hit the point where he couldn't bear it any longer, the vibrations ceased.

Freddy sagged on the bench, panting for air. As the probe slid out, he shuddered again, muscles clenching one last time.

Every part of his body was extra sensitive.

"That was lovely," Mistress Camille said, running her hand over his back again. "Very good boy."

She was going to kill him. It was as though she'd dug into his psyche and figured out every one of his highest pleasures.

That or we're just really *well matched.*

That was also a possibility, and it made him ache. They'd just met, and he didn't know whether it was wise to get his hopes up. He didn't know what she was looking for.

However, he did know he didn't want this to be finished.

Lifting his head, he looked over his shoulder at her. She was still wearing the dress she'd asked him to help her out of.

"Please, Mistress," he said, his usually silver tongue feeling oddly thick in his mouth. "May I service you?"

* * *

*C*AMILLE

May I service you?

Truthfully, she'd intended to give him aftercare, then send him on his way, but the way he'd phrased that question... she wasn't sure she could turn him away. He'd said he was a service sub, and he was asking to service her, to give her the same pleasure that she'd given him.

One-night stands weren't her thing, but she'd started this, and she should finish it the way he deserved.

The way they both deserved.

From the way he'd made his request, she was pretty sure Freddy wouldn't feel completely satisfied if he wasn't allowed to bring her to completion.

And I would really, really, really like an orgasm.

Sure, she'd figured there were plenty of toys she could use on herself after he left—she was practically dripping, she was so aroused —but why deny both of them what they really wanted? She didn't have a good reason.

"Stay here. I'm going to get a cloth to clean you up, then we'll talk about what you can do for me."

If she hadn't already decided she was going to let him do *something* for her, the smile he gave her would have made up her mind. No, she definitely couldn't take that pleasure away from him, especially since it was what she wanted, too. That was the whole point of tonight, indulging in what *she* wanted. Getting what *she* needed.

If she was being perfectly honest with herself, Freddy wouldn't have been the only one unsatisfied if she gave him aftercare right now, then sent him on his way.

"This doesn't have to mean anything," she murmured to herself. Or it could be the start of something.

Not a decision she had to make right now.

After dampening the washcloth with warm water in the bathroom, Camille returned to the front room where Freddy was patiently waiting. For a moment, she thought he might have fallen asleep, but then he turned to look at her, and eagerness lit up his expression. Yes, despite having had his own orgasm, he was clearly not done for the night. He wouldn't be until he'd made sure she'd climaxed as well.

"On your feet," she said, though not harshly, and held out the washcloth. "You can use this to clean yourself and the bench."

He wasn't quite as graceful getting to his feet as he had been before but still moved fairly fluidly. It felt odd to stand by and let him do the cleaning, even though she'd had similar moments with Jay. It had been so long since she'd had anyone to help her out, anyone to do even the smallest chore. She could see it gave him pleasure to follow her orders and was pretty sure he would have protested if she'd tried to do it for him.

Once both he and the bench were free of the shiny, sticky fluid, Camille turned around and peeked at him over her shoulder.

"I assume you know how to undo a corset?"

"Oh, yes, Mistress." Freddy smiled at her. He didn't have the same energy as earlier in the evening, but it still lit up his eyes from within. "I would be happy to help."

4

___

Freddy

Lacing and unlacing a corset was something Freddy could do in his sleep. Over the years, he'd helped numerous people in and out of their corsets, both platonically and non. He really hoped this particular instance would be non-platonic. It was completely up to Mistress Camille, of course, but Freddy was dying to show her how well he could please her.

How good he could make her feel.

Especially since she'd said it had been a long time.

The service sub in him was aching to give her everything she needed. He could see how much good the scene had already done her. She was more relaxed, her gaze more confident and flirtatious, her entire demeanor more self-assured. She'd needed this. Which, in turn, satisfied him.

Tugging on the laces, he freed them from the bow and began loosening the corset. She sighed with happiness, taking in the automatic deep breath everyone did when their laces were loosened. Freddy had worn a few corsets himself, designed specifically for his body type, so he had some inkling of how good it felt, though he suspected the sensation was doubled or even tripled for anyone with breasts.

"Oh, that feels good," Mistress Camille said, slumping slightly within the stiff boning. "It's been way too long since I've worn one of these."

"How long, Mistress?" Freddy asked softly, pulling the laces to their loosest, hoping she would answer.

"Years." There was something in her voice, but he couldn't quite figure out the emotion. Then she was lifting her hands up in the air. "Pull it up over my head."

"I would have never guessed," he told her honestly as he obeyed, freeing her from the garment.

"Well, that's good to know." Giving her body a shake, she turned around. "Back down on your knees, boy, while I figure out what we're doing next."

Freddy dropped obediently to his knees, taking the time to admire her now mostly naked body. Her breasts were completely uncovered, the soft flesh imprinted with the boning design from the corset, as were the curves of her sides and stomach. The lacy black underwear she was wearing showed enough for him to know that she shaved some of her mound, but not all of it.

His fingers itched to soothe the imprints on her skin where the boning had left its mark—she'd be tingling and sensitive there—but she hadn't asked him to, and since she'd admitted how long it had been since she'd scened, he wanted to let her take the lead completely.

"Hmm... I think this."

Peeking, surprise flowed through him when she came to a stop in front of a bondage chair rather than the Queening Throne. It was meant for submissives, as was made clear by the number of restraint options attached to it. As he watched, Mistress Camille slipped off her underwear and turned around to sit on the chair.

It was slightly tilted back enough that when she put her legs on the rests, she was in the position a lot of Tops preferred for their bottoms, with her thighs spread wide open to show off the glossy arousal coating her pussy lips. Freddy's cock stirred at the sight. He'd been right about her hair. Soft curls adorned the top of her mound, shaped into a neat triangle, but she clearly shaved everywhere else. Or waxed.

She pointed at the spot between her thighs.

"Come here, Freddy, and show me how well you can service me."

Excitement fizzed through him. He didn't mistake what she wanted. She might not have sat on the Queening Throne, but that didn't change her intent. It was just a different position.

Though she hadn't asked him to, he crawled to her, ignoring how hard the floor was on his knees. It was a short distance and the look in her eyes more than made up for any discomfort. If that had been a test, he felt sure he'd passed.

Coming up between her legs, he didn't immediately dive into her pussy, despite how tempting it was. Brushing his cheek along her inner thigh, he took his time, letting his lips drop on the middle of her thigh for a brief kiss before turning his attention to the other leg. His tongue traced a small line along her flesh, and she sighed, leaning back against the comfortable padding of the chair while one of her hands dropped down on his head.

Twining her fingers through his hair, she didn't pull him into her, letting him do as he pleased, but her grip reminded him she was still in charge. He moved closer and closer to her pussy, inhaling the delicate scent of her sex as he approached. Moaning, she gripped his hair a little harder, the tug a pleasant sensation that went straight to his dick. Satisfaction surged through him as he made his way to the outer lips of her pussy and finally let his tongue delve between them, tasting the ambrosia gathered there. It was pure heaven on his tongue.

Camille

Despite his slow approach, which she'd rather enjoyed, Freddy had no hesitation about diving into her pussy and feasting like a starving man. His tongue danced over her sensitive folds, tasting, and exploring. Quick suction against her clit retreated, then returned, over and over, teasing her but driving her pleasure higher.

Leaning back in the chair, she regripped the silky strands of his hair. This was the reason she'd chosen this chair rather than the Queening Throne in the first place. She loved the feel of a man's face buried between her thighs, not just under her, loved to hold his hair and direct him if he needed it.

Freddy didn't need it.

She still liked having a hold on him, and he seemed to be enjoying it as well.

There wasn't much he needed to be told to do.

The joy of an experienced submissive.

Giving herself over to the pleasure, Camille shuddered as she let him worship her orally, his tongue delving and pushing, the suction on her clit growing greater with each pass. He ate her out as though she was his favorite fucking delicacy.

Hot pleasure curled and curled and curled inside her, winding tightly about her inner core like wool being spun. When his mouth closed over her clit and began to suck and tongue relentlessly, she felt as if she was going to levitate.

"Oh God... yes... right there..." Her hips surged up, rocking her pussy against his mouth, and Freddy's blue gaze lifted to watch her. The intensity in his eyes, the sheer pleasure he was getting from giving *her* pleasure, sent her over the peak.

Throwing her head back, Camille let herself rock against him as wave after wave of ecstasy crashed over her, fulfilling her in a way that none of her toys ever could. Freddy suckled her clit, wringing every last drop of erotic rapture from her body she could give.

Releasing his hair, she smoothed it back, and he moved with her hand, falling back and panting from his efforts, his eyes shining with happiness.

"*Very* good boy," she said breathlessly. Taking a few deep breaths, she gathered herself. Boneless and satisfied, she wasn't ready to let that go yet. "Come on, let's go get in bed." Aftercare was still necessary, but it was getting late, so she wanted them both comfortable just in case.

For the first time, Freddy hesitated.

"Are you sure..." His voice trailed off as she gave him a look.

She wouldn't have made the invitation if she wasn't sure. Part of her appreciated his attempt at chivalry, but another part of her...

"Don't make me spank you for questioning me," she said mildly.

To her surprise, Freddy grinned.

"Don't threaten me with a good time. Mistress."

Laughter bubbling up inside her, she shook her head as he helped her to her feet.

"Come on." Keeping his hand in hers, she led him to the other room, stopping to scoop up his clothes on the way. "You don't have to sleep over, but you need some water before you go at the very least, and I would like to cuddle if you don't object to that as part of aftercare."

"Consider me your personal teddy bear."

He was funny. And submissive. Both qualities she liked in a man.

Now that the scene was over and her hormones were quieting, she couldn't help but wonder if he might be interested in... more. Maybe a date? If not a date, maybe more scenes in the future?

It felt fast, but then again, so was everything else she had just done.

Was she trying to make this into something other than a one-night stand to make herself feel better? No, she decided after a moment. She wouldn't have scened with him if she hadn't felt a spark and wouldn't be interested in a second round if it hadn't been fantastic.

The fact she liked the bit of his personality she'd been able to see so far was just icing on the cake.

She just barely managed to stop herself from going to get the water. Instead, she let go of his hand.

"The water is in the mini fridge. Please get us each a bottle," she said, tempering her tone to make it a request rather than an order now that they weren't in the scene anymore. Freddy's amused glance made her realize, of course, he knew where the bottles were—he worked here. Oh, well.

She busied herself pulling down the sheets on the bed and crawling in. Freddy came back with the bottle and handed it to her. Cracking it open, she patted the spot next to her, and he willingly climbed on, both of them taking long swigs of the water.

Kink was thirsty business.

The sheets were cool, but Freddy was warm, and she wasted no time grabbing her silk cap from where it was waiting on her nightstand and tucking her curls into it so she could snuggle up to him. The room wasn't cold, but it was cool, which was how she preferred it when she was sleeping.

"Come here," she demanded, as soon as she was on her side. Chuckling, Freddy set his water down on the nightstand on his side of the bed and scooted under the sheet, wrapping his arms around her.

He made a pretty good teddy bear, with a nice cozy nook between his arm and his chest. Camille sighed happily, snuggling up to his warmth and enjoying the feeling of lying in bed with someone else. She'd missed this more than she'd realized. Not just the kink but having someone. Resting her hand on his chest, she could feel it moving with his breath, the steady thrum of his heart a reassuring beat in her ear.

"I have to admit," Freddy murmured, his fingers tracing little circles on her shoulder, "I thought this New Year's Eve was going to be another disappointment. Instead, it turned out being the best one I've had in years." He yawned.

"Me, too," she admitted. "Julie pretty much dragged me out here."

"I'm glad she did."

"I'm kind of surprised someone hasn't already snatched you up." It was the only question circling her head about him. As far as she could see, he was pretty perfect.

Freddy shrugged, moving her head slightly, and she smacked his chest, which made him chuckle.

"I've scened with a lot of the Dominants at Stronghold, but

nothing ever really clicked quite right. Sometimes, they wanted more hardcore pain than I do, some of them wanted a poly relationship or a harem, and I'm monogamous. Some of them wanted a slave... there was always something." The tired note in his voice made her ache for him.

Sure, she'd been going without kink or sex, but what would it have been like to be so close, yet unable to find the thing you really wanted? Like craving Chipotle but being surrounded by Taco Bell.

"There's always something," she murmured in soft agreement, closing her eyes for just a moment to rest as exhaustion creeped over her. She'd get them both moving again in a few minutes.

She just needed a moment to enjoy this.

Just a moment.

5

———————

Waking up next to someone wasn't unusual, but it wasn't the norm for Freddy. Yawning, he cuddled closer to Camille, who was still asleep. She was a _very_ cuddly sleeper, and he had no objections. Not that he was touch-starved or anything, but he was also a big cuddler. Too much so, according to some people. In one of his previous relationships, he'd gotten most of his cuddling time with other subbies because Mistress Vi had not been a cuddler, which had been fine. That wasn't why they hadn't worked out, but it hadn't helped either.

Unfortunately, cuddling up close to her had the sad side effect of waking her up.

"Oomph. You're still here." She sounded surprised.

"Still here." Freddy couldn't help but laugh. "I hope that's okay."

"It is, sorry, I just... it wouldn't be the first time I fell asleep with company and woke up to a note on my pillow." She made a face. "There's a reason I don't usually do this."

He didn't know whether to be outraged on her behalf or pleased that he came off looking good, but he was leaning towards outraged. He didn't want to look good just because the bar was on the ground.

"Well, to make up for the previous men who lacked character, may I treat you to breakfast? They're having a special one downstairs."

For a moment, her expression lit up before it dimmed.

"I can't, I'm sorry... I have plans. With my mom."

The little knot that twisted his stomach when she said she had plans released as soon as she clarified who it was with. Not that he thought she would cheat, but he would have absolutely believed there was competition somewhere. Last night, he'd thought about asking how it was possible she was still single, then he'd realized it likely had a lot to do with how long she'd been out of the kink community.

That wasn't something someone could just turn off, though people tried. And if she had once embraced her kinky side, it would be even more difficult. Add in that she was sexually dominant and a black woman, he could only imagine the difficulties in finding a compatible partner.

"Well, if you would like to see me again, I'm happy to give you my number. Or I'm almost always reachable here at Marquis."

Yes, he was pushing things, but he'd warned her he was only submissive in the bedroom. Outside of it, he was happy to serve in other ways and follow his partner's lead, but if there was something he really wanted, he didn't hesitate to try to get it. It was better to be up front about that, rather than leaving it as a surprise. Some Dominants preferred to be in control all the time, which was fine. It just wasn't for him.

Thankfully, she smiled with happy relief, not at all insulted that he was being so forward.

"I would like your number, and to see you again, though I'm not sure when I'll be able to make it back out to Marquis." She ran her hand over his chest and sighed. "I have to get running though, or I'm going to be late."

As much as he wanted to protest or try to cajole her to say a little longer, Freddy bit his tongue. They'd just met the night before. Their attraction was off the charts, but they didn't really *know* each other. Just because he'd happily spend the time until check-out in bed pleasuring her didn't mean she wanted the same thing.

And she needed to go meet her mom.

Didn't want to make a bad impression on mom.

Yes, he was already thinking that way and had no shame about it. He was in his early thirties and wanted to find a lasting relationship, which meant he wasn't going to spend time somewhere he didn't at least see the possibility. Was it soon? Sure. But he and Camille had a connection, and he liked the little he already knew about her.

Plus, both Olivia and Julie had given him the thumbs-up. While he wouldn't have expected it of Julie, he knew damn well Olivia was a meddling matchmaker. If she wanted to help him find a match, he had no objections.

"I'll get out of your way then," he said.

She made a few noises of protest that he didn't have to leave right away and seemed reluctant to see him go, but he could also see the relief there. Much better to leave while she was still sad to see him go than to overstay his welcome and make her late. Besides, they exchanged phone numbers before he walked out the door, which meant he was walking with an extra spring in his step.

———

CAMILLE

"I met a man, Momma." Camille smiled when her mom's head lifted. She didn't talk much these days, and Camille was never entirely sure how much she understood, but she usually seemed to remember that Camille was someone she cared about. The mention of the man getting her attention was so like the days before dementia started stealing her mind, it gave her some hope that there was still plenty of her mom left in there.

Camille squeezed her mom's hand.

"He's kind. Funny. And a very pretty white boy."

Her mom snorted, which made her smile. Her mom had always snorted over the idea of a pretty man, but it was true. Freddy was very pretty.

"If things keep going well, I'll get a picture of him for you."

Bobbing her head, her mom hummed under her breath, her gaze unfocusing, and Camille sighed inwardly. She kept talking, and her mom's gaze kept settling on her before drifting again as they talked. That was the norm now, and it made her heart hurt, but at least her mom was present some of the time.

After lunch, Camille headed up to the front desk to check out.

"Happy New Year," Lucy, the woman who worked there, said,in smiling. "I'm so glad you could stop in today. Your mom always does better after a visit from you."

"I just wish I could visit more." It was rare she had any extra time. In fact, this afternoon, she would be working. She had a fussy client, and tomorrow would be the first meeting with his soon-to-be ex-wife and her counsel. Camille was hoping things could be worked out in mediation, but she had a feeling this one would go to court.

Nicholas Alexander III was a classic example of the entitled grade-A assholes her firm tended to represent. He'd cheated on his wife multiple times and was now throwing a tantrum that she was leaving him. It didn't help that their prenup wasn't airtight, leaving several places where he could quibble over the language, even though the intent was clear. He was determined she get absolutely nothing if she left him, because—according to him—she wasn't supposed to divorce him over a few meaningless affairs.

From the way he talked, Camille was pretty sure in Nicholas' world, someone else was always the problem. He also hadn't been entirely happy she'd been the one assigned to him until one of the partners had pointed out to him that having a woman as his lawyer would help the optics of some of his wife's claims against him in case it went to court. Mr. Donaldson had said it right in front of her, which had made her grind her teeth, but she also knew he was right.

At least Mr. Alexander came with a *lot* of billable hours, thanks to being a prima donna.

She'd become a divorce lawyer partly for the money but also with the idea she would help people through one of the most difficult parts of their lives. Her childhood best friend had gotten divorced after marrying too early when Camille was still in college, and she'd seen how Nina had leaned on her lawyer and how much help the lawyer had been.

There were probably some law firms where that kind of job was still possible... just not hers. It wasn't just the firm policies. It was also the clientele they picked up. More than once, Camille had felt as if she was on the wrong side of the negotiating table.

Sure, it took two people to make a divorce happen, but it seemed like a lot of the people sitting next to her took the cake for 'biggest asshole in the relationship.' When they didn't, it was because both parties were massive assholes.

She was not looking forward to tomorrow. So far, she'd gotten the sense Nicholas Alexander III wanted to stick it to his wife.

The feeling of depression that hung over her at the mere thought of working on his case followed her all the way out of the home and on the drive home.

FREDDY

New Year's Day was usually one of Freddy's days to rest and relax. Unfortunately, he had some work to do today. Tomorrow, he'd be meeting with his newest client for mediation. Hopefully, they'd be able to work things out without going to court. Brittany was a sweet woman who he suspected of being a bit submissive, though not all women who ended up in abusive relationships were submissive. He thought she might be, though.

Her soon-to-be ex was a real piece of work, according to Brittany's sister, who had come with her for support to the first meeting. From Brittany's quiet demeanor and the way she kept starting to speak up in defense of him only to catch herself, it didn't take much for Freddy to get the picture. She was determined to leave him, though, so he didn't think there would be a reconciliation.

The fact the man was making the divorce contentious instead of the seamless process it could be made Freddy think he was doing everything he could to keep Brittany under his thumb. He wouldn't know for sure until tomorrow when he met the man himself. It was always possible he had misinterpreted the situation.

He liked to be prepared for anything.

While he was sitting and working, his text message notification sounded. Picking up his phone, he glanced at the message.

Lexie: *Happy New Year! Where are you?*

Shaking his head, he quickly swiped a response.

Freddy: *I have to work today.*

Lexie: *It is a national holiday. Get your butt over here. Olivia told me you had a hookup last night. I need deets!*

Frowning, Freddy resisted the urge to tell Lexie it wasn't a hookup because he knew she would read all sorts of things into that statement. He also didn't know for sure that it wasn't a hookup. He just hoped it wasn't.

Sighing inwardly, he called her.

"Hello? You're coming over, right?" The sounds of multiple people in the background clued him into her location. He'd almost forgotten that Adam and Angel were having people over for New Year's Day.

"No, I told you I have work to do," he repeated, doing his best to keep his amusement out of his voice. She would consider that encouragement.

"But I want to hear about your night last night," she whined. "I didn't get to meet Mistress Camille. I had to hear about her afterward from Olivia."

"Well, hopefully, you'll get the chance in the future," he said, keeping his voice even as he tried not to let his own hopes bubble over. "She said she would be coming back to the clubs, and we exchanged numbers this morning."

The happy screech that came through the phone nearly blew his ear drum. Yanking the phone away, he shook his head but couldn't help smiling. Lexie had often despaired of finding a match for him, considering how long he'd been around the clubs without finding someone. It hadn't stopped her from hoping, though.

She might be even happier than he was.

Probably was since she had all the hope with none of the trepidation.

"It's a good thing I didn't need that ear," he teased when he got the phone back in place.

"Sorry!" She didn't sound sorry at all. "I'm thrilled for you. You deserve all the happiness, Freddy. You're going to eat a million black-eyed peas today, right?"

Freddy rolled his eyes. He wasn't a fan of black-eyed peas or kale, but Angel had dropped off a container of Hoppin' John yesterday afternoon since he'd told her he wouldn't be making her party today. Supposedly, the black-eyed peas were for luck and the kale was for money in the new year. Put them together with ham, rice, and seasonings and they weren't the worst tasting things in the world.

"Yes, I will eat the Hoppin' John Angel made me for dinner tonight," he said patiently.

He would, too, because even if it wasn't his favorite food, he figured he needed the luck. Plus, it meant he didn't have to cook.

"Good boy," Lexie replied.

It definitely didn't have the power of Mistress Camille's accolades.

"Is that all?" He didn't bother to keep his amusement out of his voice.

"For now. Happy New Year, Freddy."

"Happy New Year, Lexie."

Bemused, he hung up the phone and looked down at his computer. Did he kind of wish he'd gone to Angel and Adam's to hang out with everyone? Yes, but he'd known he would have work to do. And even though he was friends with all of them and would have had a lot of fun, he never really felt like he was part of them.

That was how he was at the club. Friends with everyone. Besties with no one. He had twenty people he could call who would come running at the drop of a hat if he needed them, yet no one to hang out with. It was a very odd place to be.

Besides... he had work to get done.

Then, hopefully, a Domme to win.

6

———————

The second day of the year was going great so far, which made Freddy feel a little hopeful his afternoon meeting wouldn't be as difficult as he feared.

Lexie had texted him first thing that Mistress Camille had put a membership application through to the clubs, which meant he would definitely be seeing her again. Soon, hopefully.

Since he'd gotten so much done yesterday, his morning flowed smoothly right until lunch time, when he was meeting Morgan. He liked to check in on her at least every other week, if not more, to see how she was doing, especially now that she'd moved in with Master Brian.

Not that it was a romantic relationship. It wasn't. It was a bunch of overprotective Dominants deciding she shouldn't be living on her own. Yes, Morgan's past made the Dominants extremely protective of her, but she would have to spread her wings sometime. She truly might not have been ready yet, though, and her living situation and Master Brian's living situations happened to be changing right around the same time, so they moved in together platonically and shared Master Brian's house. She had her own bedroom and studio for her work, and they were nothing more than friends.

Though the move had caused a bit of consternation around the club.

"Hello, beautiful," Freddy said, bending down to give Morgan a kiss on the head before sliding into the booth across from her.

As always, she was stunning. Red curls flowed over her shoulders and down her back, and her wide green eyes were expertly emphasized with makeup and the green turtleneck she was wearing. She looked like Ariel from the Little Mermaid had come on land and decided to set up shop with the regular humans. Sometimes, Morgan was just as naïve as Ariel had been, too.

"Hey! Happy New Year!" She beamed at him.

"Happy New Year."

Morgan's energy was infectious. She'd changed a lot in the past year, having gone from an unintentionally judgmental and wary woman to someone who was excited and happy about every new discovery in her life. And there were a lot of new discoveries.

"They have corned beef hash on the menu. I always wanted to try corned beef hash."

"Do you know what corned beef hash is?" Freddy asked. He wouldn't deter her if that was really what she wanted, but Morgan sometimes had some odd ideas about things.

"No," she replied happily. "Not really. But they talk about roast hash in *How the Grinch Stole Christmas,* and I figure it's kind of like that, right?"

Watching Morgan discover and immerse herself in popular culture had been a fascinating social experiment.

"I always assumed they were the same thing," he confirmed, smiling at her excitement. Being around Morgan made him remember how lucky he was. Sometimes, life got him down, sure, but he'd never had to go through what she had.

"Then that's what I want." She put her menu down, folding her hands atop it. "Freddy..." Her voice had an odd note, drawing his full attention. Morgan only sounded like that when she needed life advice.

She'd needed a lot of life advice at first, thanks to being sheltered as a child by parents who homeschooled her, so they could control her. Then they basically sold her to a Dom, who kept her as a slave with only the barest sense of consent when they needed money. Patrick's cousin had found out about her situation at a play party and rescued her, bringing her to Maryland to get her away from that scene and everyone there who knew her. Unfortunately, they hadn't been able to bring the Dom in question up on charges, but he'd been kicked out of the community, which was all they could do.

"What do you need, love?" he asked, reaching his hand across the table to put it atop hers.

"How can you tell if someone is a bad friend?"

Oof. She could never ask the easy questions, could she?

"Hey, y'all, can I get you something to drink?"

Saved by the server gave Freddy some time to think while they put in their orders for both drinks and food since they were ready. Once the server had bustled away again, he met Morgan's gaze.

"Why do you ask?"

In the beginning, her questions had often been very general, but over time, they'd shifted to become more specific. She hadn't had any questions about friendship in a while, not since she'd made her first set. Granted, they weren't the friends Freddy might have chosen for her, but they'd done her good in terms of confidence.

"I've been spending a lot of time with Sam and Noelle," she replied, fiddling with the edges of her napkin.

"I know," he said, smiling encouragingly and hiding his wince. Her second set of friends weren't much better than her first. The majority of her first group of friends were heavily disliked by a lot of the other Stronghold submissives. Carolyn and Marissa were catty and often mean, but Amy was a total sweetheart, so when they'd pulled Morgan into their little group, he'd done his best to counteract Carolyn and Marissa's influence while encouraging her to spend as much time as possible with Amy.

Lately, she'd been hanging around a lot with Sam and Noelle. Sam, otherwise known as Mistress Samantha when she was feeling her 'top' side—as a switch, she both topped and bottomed—was wonderful, but Noelle... he was pretty sure Noelle was going to be more bad news. So far, she'd been on her best behavior at the club, but he could feel tension gathering there like an oncoming storm.

"I don't think Noelle likes us very much. She does all the things you said a friend is supposed to do, but sometimes..." Morgan sighed. "I don't know how to describe it. It's probably nothing."

"It's not nothing," Freddy replied immediately. Morgan was showing good instincts, and he wanted her to trust them. This was definitely growth since she had a tendency to take situations and people exactly as they appeared and not look any deeper. "You should trust yourself. What does your gut say about Noelle?"

"That she's not very nice. Which is odd because she's nicer than Carolyn and Marissa are sometimes. All the things she says are nice, but..." Morgan made a face. "It's... I don't know. She says the right things, but somehow, sometimes, the way she says it makes it sound like she's saying something else. I don't think she likes me very much."

"Honey, I'm not sure she likes anyone very much," he said truthfully.

"But Sam likes her. So do Amy, Carolyn, and Marissa."

Ah, which explained why Morgan was second-guessing herself. She was still learning a lot about friendships and people, so since all her other friends liked Noelle was making her question her intuition. What Freddy found fascinating was she had figured out Noelle but still seemed perfectly happy being friends with Carolyn and Marissa.

"So far, she's been a good friend to them, so there's no reason not to, I guess. That or maybe they don't get the same vibe from her that you do, but that doesn't mean your vibe is wrong." In fact, he was pretty sure Morgan was one hundred percent right in this instance, but he also knew he was biased.

He was friends with Noelle's old roommate, and while Noelle hadn't been able to evict Iris, she'd done the next best thing and ended their lease without giving Iris any warning. From what Freddy had gleaned, Noelle hadn't liked that Iris had made new friends. She seemed insecure to the extreme and incredibly selfish.

She was being given a chance at Stronghold, at Iris' insistence, because Iris was too damn nice.

Freddy often considered himself the protector of the submissives, and he would absolutely protect Noelle from an importuning Dom, but he also wanted to protect the other subs from her.

"She seems very unhappy," Morgan said after a moment. "It's sad."

"You can't make her happy," Freddy reminded her gently. "She has to do that on her own."

"I'll just hang out with her when the others are there. I don't have to hang out with her on my own just because we're part of the same group of friends, right?"

"Right." The arrival of the drinks caused a minor distraction, then he asked the question he thought he'd be discussing today. "How is it living with Brian?"

"Ma— I mean, Brian," Morgan quickly corrected herself before calling him 'Master Brian,' "has been great. He's very careful. Too careful sometimes. I'm not going to fall apart just because he has a preference or asks me to do something around the house." Her brow furrowed grumpily as she took a sip of her water.

"Has he asked you to do anything around the house?" He could understand why Brian would want to be careful with that. Morgan had basically been a twenty-four-seven sex slave and housekeeper to her last master, but she also wanted to do some things for herself.

"No." She huffed the word out, obviously annoyed. "He keeps trying to do things for me. I am *not* his babygirl. And if I was his baby-girl, I should at least be getting some sex out of it."

"Uh... here you go." The server had appeared at their table at exactly the wrong time and was blushing hotly. Putting their food in front of them, she quickly fled.

Morgan looked a bit contrite.

"Oops," she mouthed, giving Freddy a little shrug. He shook with the effort to hold back his laughter.

"We'll give her a really good tip," he reassured her, grinning widely.

She smiled back, her shoulders relaxing.

"That's the other nice thing about going out with you. You don't insist on paying like I don't have my own money or something." She stabbed at her salad with a fork, spearing the lettuce as though she had something against it.

Interesting. Rebellious Morgan was out in full force today, and personally, Freddy was happy to see it. When Morgan had first joined Stronghold, they'd come up with a 'cover story' for her so she could fit in better with the other submissives and because she hadn't been sure she wanted everyone to know her past. Unfortunately, because she also came with a ton of baggage—not to mention misconceptions about the lifestyle—she'd managed to alienate some of the other submissives.

It hadn't helped that the Doms were constantly fussing over her and giving her attention the other subs didn't understand.

Freddy was still annoyed he hadn't been consulted about that decision. He could have told the Doms it was a bad idea to have all the Dominants clued in and none of the submissives. It set Morgan apart right from the beginning. She'd had some really odd and stereotyped ideas about Doms and subs, thanks to how sheltered she'd been and had been trained to be competitive with other women.

The first time she'd met him and found out he was a sub, she'd assumed he was gay, and when he'd corrected her and told her he was bisexual and preferred women, she'd been utterly confused. It didn't matter what year it was; in Morgan's world, women submitted to men.

She'd also made a lot of assumptions about who was what based on their appearances.

Talk about a hot mess. She'd gone along with it because the Doms told her it was the best thing for her. Much more well-intentioned than the previous assholes she'd been involved with but with disastrous results. Freddy was still doing clean-up around that, although Morgan was slowly becoming more open about her past with the other submissives. She wanted to tell them on her own terms, though, which meant there were quite a few who were still in the dark.

"Has Brian been paying for everything?" he asked mildly, doing his best to keep his opinions out of his voice.

"He's trying to." Morgan's eyes glinted and her chin lifted. "I'm going grocery shopping after this. I took the list off the fridge this morning."

"Good for you. I'm proud of you."

"Thank you." She beamed at him. "So... enough about me. How was your New Year's Eve?"

She hadn't been at the Marquis party, none of her group of friends had other than Sam, who had come with Q. Caroline threw a New Year's Eve party every year with her husband, and Morgan had gone to that instead.

"It was great. I actually met someone." He grinned as Morgan perked up. Despite everything she'd been through, she still believed in love and happy endings. "She's a friend of Julie's, and she's amazing."

"Is she a member?"

"No, but I think she's interested in becoming one. Either way, we exchanged numbers."

"Oooh, have you called her yet?" Morgan's interest was partly on his behalf and partly because she was still trying to figure out 'the rules' of dating.

"No, it's too soon. Plus, I tend to try to let the Dominant take the lead for the first call." He grinned at her.

"So, they get all the control over contact?" she asked thoughtfully.

"No." Freddy shook his head. "I still get to decide whether I pick up or call them back. If they make me wait too long, I might decide they weren't worth my time, but I would probably answer to find out why it took them so long to call."

"How long is too long?"

"As a rule of thumb? I know there are some people who think you're supposed to wait three days. After three days, I start to feel a little insulted." He chuckled.

"That's what I read," Morgan said, nodding happily. She'd been reading a lot of romance blogs lately, trying to figure out the 'rules.' Freddy kept stressing to her not to take them too seriously, but as long as she was enjoying herself, he wasn't going to tell her not to read them. She was probably getting a better idea of what a healthy relationship could look like from the blogs than she had from her parents or her ex.

"I prefer it when people contact me sooner rather than later. If she calls tonight, I'll be thrilled." Mentally, he crossed his fingers. With his anticipated afternoon, he would love something nice to end the day, like a call from Mistress Camille.

Even if all she wanted to do was scene again.

They'd been so well matched, he would happily scene with her, though, truthfully, he was already hoping for more.

7

———————

Camille

Today was going to be terrible.

Her year had ended pretty well, and if she counted those early hours of the morning with Freddy, then it had started out pretty great, but everything had been pretty much downhill from there.

Yesterday's visit with her mom had been fine too, actually. It was work that had frustrated her. Going through the Alexanders' prenup with a fine-tooth comb had given her a headache. Whoever had given the Alexanders the advice to sign it had been a total hack. More than one section was unclear.

Granted, things could go either way, but she wasn't sure it would go Mrs. Alexander's way, even though she was likely the more deserving party.

You're not supposed to be thinking that way. Mr. Alexander is your client, not her. You're supposed to be saving him as much money as possible... so that he can pay it all to Donaldson and some of it will come to you.

Right.

Sometimes, she felt like this job was sucking the soul right out of her body.

At least she had something to look forward to for the end of the day. Her reward to herself for getting through this afternoon was calling Freddy. During her lunch hour, she'd also sent in the application for membership to Stronghold and Marquis. In some small way, she was claiming some of herself back.

"Ugh, this is going to be such a waste of time." Nicholas Alexander III, all six feet of him, was slouched in one of the conference room chairs. At first glance, he was handsome enough. In his late forties, he still kept himself in shape. He had dark brown eyes and matching dark brown hair sprinkled with just a touch of salt. At second glance, it was impossible to miss the petulant set of his mouth and the arrogant unhappiness emanating from him like a bad smell.

Well, it was impossible for her to miss. She knew Rachel, the receptionist who had escorted him into the conference room, hadn't noticed his flaws. She had been all smiles and giggles as Mr. Alexander smirked and flirted with her.

Thankfully, he didn't try that with Camille.

"Do you want me to call the meeting off?" she asked. Mrs. Alexander was due any minute, along with her counsel from Addison, O'Shane, and Smith, and Alfred Johan. AOS, as they were known, had a reputation for representing women like Mrs. Alexander, who had ended up married to rich assholes who didn't want to pay their alimony.

They made a lot of money making those rich assholes pay out the ass.

Personally, Camille would like to see nothing more. Professionally, it was her job to thwart their intentions. According to him, she was supposed to keep him from having to pay anything at all, which was why they were going to court.

She was pretty sure he'd hoped Mrs. Alexander wouldn't be able to find representation or that she'd decide it wasn't worth going to court and would just quietly go on her way. Camille had tried to explain to him that wasn't going to happen as soon as she knew who Mrs. Alexander's representation was, but Mr. Alexander had dug in his heels, and now here they were.

Which meant trying her best, knowing if she succeeded, she was going to screw some poor woman out of money she was rightfully owed, or her own client, and therefore, her firm, were going to be unhappy with her. This morning, she'd figured out the reason the partners had passed Mr. Alexander off to her. They knew the chances of winning were fifty-fifty, and they didn't want him unhappy with any of *them*.

Worried it would ruin their golf game or something.

"No," Mr. Alexander said after a long minute, straightening in his seat and tugging his suit jacket down so he didn't look so rumpled. "No, I'm not going to let that bitch get her hands on any of my money. Not when she's trying to fucking leave me."

Camille really hoped Mrs. Alexander actually was a bitch. Then she wouldn't feel so bad about having to represent this asshole. She didn't bother to point out the reason his wife would get his money was because of the prenup *he'd* signed.

There was a knock on the door before she could respond. It opened and Rachel smiled as she walked in. The knock had just been to give them a quick heads up that the other side had arrived.

"Right this way. Ms. Sinclair and Mr. Alexander are waiting for you."

To Rachel's credit, she didn't give Mr. Alexander one of her simpering smiles. She just stepped out of the way to let the people behind her walk in.

Halfway to getting to her feet, while Mr. Alexander rudely remained seated beside her, Camille froze when she saw who was walking through the door.

Freddy.

Blue eyes widened, and his gait only faltered for a moment before he moved to the side, holding out his hand for the woman behind him to take it like the gentleman he was. With his blond hair perfectly styled, he was wearing a salmon pink suit that fit him perfectly. Next to her, Mr. Alexander made a derogatory noise even before his wife walked into the room, and she realized it was at the sight of Freddy in pink.

Mr. Alexander was an asshole bigot among other things, and

when he saw another man in pink, his toxic masculinity couldn't take it.

Which was likely deliberate on Freddy's part.

Finally standing straight, Camille's gaze dropped to the woman who was clutching Freddy's hand while doing her best to pretend she wasn't. Petite with auburn hair, wide hazel eyes, and stick thin other than her breasts, she looked like she was about to have a panic attack or flee the room. When Mr. Alexander made another derogatory noise, she flinched.

No, she was definitely not the snobbish bitch Camille had been hoping for, unless she was also an incredible actress. She looked exactly like what Camille had hoped she wasn't—a woman who had been beaten down by years of marriage to a self-involved, extremely entitled, abusive dickhead.

I am on the wrong side of the table.

The worst part was looking across and seeing Freddy on the right side, wondering what he thought of her.

They were both just doing their jobs, but... The way he looked at her with his carefully neutral expression... it made her chest ache. She wanted to scream that she wasn't *this* person.

But she couldn't, because she was.

"Mrs. Alexander, Mr. Johan." She managed not to choke on the words, gathering up the little pieces of herself and going into her carefully rehearsed speech. "Thank you for coming to meet us today."

Freddy opened his mouth, then closed it and gave her a short nod before pulling out a chair for Mrs. Alexander. The woman sat down, placing her purse on her lap and clutching it tightly now that she no longer had Freddy's hand for support. Her gaze came to rest on the middle of the table while beside Camille, Mr. Alexander glared across it.

"Can I get you anything to drink?" Rachel asked. "Tea, coffee, water?"

"A water for each of us would be great, thank you," Freddy said after a moment, giving her a smile. Rachel beamed back at him. Mrs.

Alexander kept staring at the center of the table. Mr. Alexander glared.

It was excruciatingly awkward as Rachel retrieved two water bottles from the mini fridge in complete silence. As Rachel left, Camille cleared her throat and lifted her chin, readying herself for the opening sally, but it was already too late. As soon as Mrs. Alexander reached for her water bottle, her husband struck.

"Really, Brittany? *He's* the best you can do?" Mr. Alexander sneered, looking between Mrs. Alexander and Freddy. "I thought you must have spread your legs to get a lawyer, but he clearly—"

Camille slammed her hand down on the table with a loud crack that made Mrs. Alexander jump, and even Mr. Alexander pulled back, surprise clear in his expression. Turning to him, she glared. The man shriveled.

"Mr. Alexander, you will keep quiet until you are spoken to. You will not insult your wife. You will not insult her counsel. This is a mediation." She spoke in a low voice, but her words were crisp and clear, and Mrs. Alexander and Freddy would both be able to easily hear her since the room was otherwise dead silent, no matter how quietly she talked. "If you do not want to ruin the mediation, you will be civil."

Despite his initial reaction, Mr. Alexander's face began to turn red as she spoke. She glared harder.

"It doesn't matter, anyway," Freddy said from across the table. His voice was nothing like it had been the other night. *This* Freddy spoke in a clipped, stern tone that wouldn't have been out of place from a Dominant. "It's too late. I told Mrs. Alexander that the moment Mr. Alexander turned hostile, we would no longer be negotiating."

"But—" Camille started to say, turning back to him as panic began to rise. Her instincts were screaming at her that they were about to get hit with something awful.

A file folder slapped down in the center of the table as Freddy got back to his feet. Glossy photos spilled out over the polished wooden surface.

Oh, fuck me sideways.

She didn't need to look closely at the tangle of limbs and naked flesh to know what she was seeing.

"Mrs. Alexander wanted to have a civil discussion. Since Mr. Alexander is incapable, we'll get straight to the point. Here is the proof of his infidelity over the past year. If this goes to court, so will these photos." Freddy looked at Mr. Alexander from across the table. "The prenup agreement is clear. You cheated, you are the cause of the divorce, you have to pay. Now, if you'll excuse us."

With his hand on the back of Mrs. Alexander's arm, Freddy got her up and moving. They were already halfway out the door when Mr. Alexander came back to himself.

"Now, wait just a minute!" He jumped to his feet, but Freddy ignored him.

"Sit down, Mr. Alexander!" The last thing Camille needed was for the hot-headed idiot to chase after Freddy and his wife in the middle of a law firm. As much as he'd deserved it, he wasn't the type to take any kind of insult well.

And if he tried to physically hurt Freddy or Mrs. Alexander, Camille would take him down herself, then she'd probably be out of a job. She was pretty sure she was going to be blamed for this, even though it was all her client's fault. Closing her eyes for a moment, Camille counted to ten.

When she opened them, Mr. Alexander was still staring at the door angrily, his fists and jaw clenched, but at least he hadn't gone running after them.

"I take it these are all legitimate?" she asked coolly, scooping up the photos and stuffing them back into the file folder. Mr. Alexander gave himself a shake, as though he was just coming back to himself, and glared up at her.

"What the hell was that? You work for me! You're supposed to be helping me keep my money from that bitch! You don't—"

"Mr. Alexander." Camille snapped out the words. She was starting to not care what the partners of her firm thought. The lowering thought was that she cared more now because she cared about what Freddy thought of her, but she knew that was only partly true. It was more like the last straw on a long, long pile-up of bullshit that had been poured onto her back. She didn't have it in her to placate this asshole, who was making her job a lot harder than it had to be. "I am supposed to be your lawyer, your representation, which includes keeping you from making massive mistakes like the one you were about to."

Getting to his feet, apparently feeling at a disadvantage with her standing over him, Mr. Alexander glared at her.

"What massive mistakes?" he asked sarcastically as if he didn't believe she actually had anything she could point to. His complete lack of self-awareness was no surprise, but it didn't help the situation at all.

"I already told you, but I will repeat myself. Mr. Johan's firm is highly respected. They have a reputation for taking on the cases of women whose husbands owe them alimony, and oftentimes, going to court means you will end up paying more than you might have otherwise. He will dig into every last bit of your finances. He will find every account you have and every resource available to you, and that is what the percentage will be based on." She glared back at him. "That is what he would do *without* provocation. If you cannot keep a civil tongue in your head about your wife, there will be no more meetings with them where you are present because all you'll do is hurt your case."

Huffing, Mr. Alexander looked like a puffed-up banty hen with all his feathers aquiver. Camille's grandmother would have laughed her ass off seeing him like this. She wished she could find it more amusing, but she already knew what was going to happen next, even though she was one hundred percent in the right.

"Well. Well... I'm going to have a talk with Jared about this and about your attitude!"

Yup, saw that coming.

Shaking her head, she watched as he stormed out of the room and down the hall. At least she had the pictures because she had a feeling, she was going to need evidence for the partners. Though, since they didn't want to deal with Mr. Alexander, there was a pretty decent chance she would still be the one working with him, no matter what he said to them.

But they'd expect her to placate him.

Sitting down heavily, she stared at the carefully crafted notes she'd spent the past twenty-four hours working on.

I would have been better off spending the day in bed with Freddy.

She was pretty sure she wouldn't be getting the chance again any time soon. The way he'd looked at her, as if she was guarding the villain, whereas he'd been a knight in salmon pink armor for Mrs. Alexander. He'd looked damn good doing it, too.

Taking a deep breath, Camille gathered up her things and got back to her feet. There was only one thing to do right now—keep on moving.

8

———————

Freddy

Normally, being behind the front desk of Marquis soothed Freddy as he let go of the week's trials and tribulations, but not tonight. Now, he couldn't be here without thinking about Mistress Camille, also known as Ms. Sinclair, representing Nicholas Alexander III, asshole extraordinaire.

On the one hand, he knew not every lawyer could choose their clients. On the other hand, Donaldson Law Group had a reputation, and in his opinion, it wasn't a great one. He was sure her client would beg to differ. Freddy hadn't expected to see her there any more than she'd expected to see him.

He'd seen the way she'd frozen.

He'd also seen the shame in her eyes.

He was having a really hard time reconciling the woman he'd made her out to be in his mind with the woman he'd met today. Which wasn't necessarily fair, but he wasn't feeling very fair right now. He was still pissed off on Brittany's behalf and more determined than ever to get her everything she deserved and more. At least Camille hadn't let her client's mouth run for too long. It could have been worse.

As it was, Brittany had been shaking for a good half an hour after the meeting while Freddy took her out for coffee and soothed her. She'd been determined, though, to keep moving forward with getting her fair share from her husband, despite how frightened she'd been.

"Hey. Are you okay? You are a lot less chipper than you were at lunch." Morgan bumped her hip into Freddy's. Since it was Friday night and there was a show—a fire play demonstration by Master Will and his sub Gina—they were extra busy, so he was helping out until the show started. After that, Morgan should be able to handle anything that came up on her own, though he'd be around. He almost always was on the weekends.

"Yeah, I'm sure I am." He rubbed his forehead. There was a lull between seating people. For some reason, even though they had plenty of time to stagger in, people tended to arrive in clumps. "I saw Mistress Camille this afternoon. She's a lawyer, and she's representing an absolute asshat."

"Oh, wow. How did she handle it?" Morgan asked, her eyes widening.

He started to say something, then stopped.

How had she handled it?

"Well, she was surprised to see me," he said slowly. "I don't think she realized… I didn't realize. I mean, Camille isn't that uncommon of a name. Her client started in on mine, and she stopped him in his tracks." She'd verbally slapped him down hard and fast.

"Okaaaaaay." Morgan drew out the word, obviously waiting for him to continue.

"That was it, really. I dropped a bunch of evidence of his cheating on the table, which means that he's not going to be able to get out of the prenup, and basically threatened him with bad press, then got my client out of there." Leaving Camille to deal with the aftermath.

He was sure Mr. Asshat hadn't been happy when they'd left, but at that moment, he'd felt like she deserved to have to deal with him since she worked for him.

He was starting to feel a little worse about how he'd reacted to who she worked for. Especially since she'd immediately jumped in when the blowhard started talking out of his ass. It wasn't as if she'd let him keep going or even attempted to act as though his behavior was acceptable.

Just because she worked for Donaldson didn't automatically mean anything about her as a person. Sometimes, people couldn't choose where they worked. It didn't mean she liked it, and from what he'd seen today, even if she was representing Mr. Alexander, it didn't mean she thought very highly of him.

"I think I was surprised to see her there because… well, the firm she works for doesn't have a good reputation, especially when it comes to the kinds of clients they take on."

"So, you thought she'd be better than that?" Morgan raised her eyebrows.

"Pretty much."

"But you don't know how she got the job or why she chose to work there."

"Yes, I get it." He gave her a mock-stern look, and she giggled before quickly changing her expression as a couple came up the stairs from the first floor of Marquis. While Morgan seated them, it gave Freddy a few minutes on his own to think.

He came back to attention as a large figure appeared at the top of the stairs, then relaxed when he saw it was Master Connor. Newer to the club, Master Connor was already getting a reputation as an indulgent Dom with a soft hand and a penchant for cuddling and aftercare. The subs adored him, even those who thought he was too much of a pushover.

"Hey, Freddy. I was supposed to meet Law here, but he's not downstairs. I figured I'd check up here."

"He's in a meeting with Mistresses Olivia and Julie," Freddy replied, smiling brightly at the big man. "They should be finishing up soon." He was pretty sure they were talking about the next class of newbies and possibly some more advanced classes. There would probably be a lot more requests for fire play instruction after tonight's show.

"Ah, gotcha. Let him know I'm downstairs when he comes out?"

Nodding, Freddy waved as the big man turned around and went back downstairs. A moment later, Morgan returned to the desk.

"I think you should text her," Morgan said forthrightly as she took her place beside him. "It can't hurt, right?"

Freddy wasn't sure, but he was surprised at how strong the impulse was to take her suggestion.

<u>CAMILLE</u>

If there was ever a night for comfort food, it was tonight. Camille refused to feel bad about ordering her dinner in. She didn't have the energy to cook after being chewed out by Donaldson Senior that afternoon.

The giant asshat.

Their job wasn't to make clients happy, it was to win their cases for them, which she couldn't do with her hands tied behind her back trying to make Mr. Alexander happy. She was pretty sure nothing would make him happy. Nothing ethical anyway. The idiot signed a prenup that left far too many things unclear, but the proof of cheating cleared up most of them. If he'd had any brains, he would have kept the cheating under cover better. She shouldn't have been surprised. He wasn't the type to be discreet.

Some of the photos had been of him and a woman having sex in a backyard. Whose backyard, she had no idea, but it hardly mattered. He'd completely fucked himself over with that. Well, not completely, there were still a few things they could quibble over, but none of it would be worthwhile monetarily, not really. He would pay more in legal fees to fight it than he would to just pay her.

She probably shouldn't feel happy about that, but he was a giant dick getting his just desserts, and it wasn't easy for her to feel sad about it, either. Mostly she felt sad for herself because Donaldson Sr. wanted her to do the impossible. Again.

She wanted to call someone and talk things out so badly, but she didn't know who. It was a sad realization that her job had not only sucked out her soul, but it had sucked all her friends away as well. Not that she'd ever had a ton of them.

Introvert, party of one.

She used to have a few really good friends. Her people. Over the years, she'd slowly stopped seeing them. Stopped talking to them. Sure, they might be there if she called now, but they'd also be full of 'I told you so's,' which was not what she needed.

There was really only one person she could call.

Sighing, she picked up the phone while she waited for her food.

"Hello? Camille?" Julie's warm greeting washed over her like a balm. Julie wouldn't say 'I told you so.' Not about the job, although she'd be perfectly happy to about Camille's love life.

"Hey, Julie. Sorry to bother you." Camille hesitated because she didn't know how to jump to what she wanted to say.

I had an amazing scene with Freddy the other night, and now he probably thinks I'm evil.

Ugh.

"No worries. If you're calling about your membership application, I can tell you that you got in," Julie replied. "I'm with Law and Olivia right now, and we're discussing whether you'd need to take the class. I'm happy to keep standing in as your sponsor if you'd rather jump right back in."

"Definitely." The introduction classes were good things, but Camille didn't need them. She wasn't sure she'd be able to show her face at the club anytime soon, not after this afternoon. The classes were at Marquis where Freddy worked. He'd be a lot harder to avoid there. "Thank you."

"No problem. We don't do the sponsorships too often, but since I knew you from before and I know you have plenty of experience, it's just about getting you back in the saddle. I want to hear all about the other night when you have the time, but I've got to get back to this meeting."

"Of course... when you're done, can you give me a call back?" Camille hated the plaintive note that entered her voice, but she couldn't keep it out entirely. Her emotions were all jumbled.

Yes, she wanted to be a member, and she wanted to get back into kink.

However, she wasn't sure she could face Freddy again.

If she could erase his knowledge of who she worked for, she'd want to scene with him again, but there was no putting that cat back in the bag.

"Sure, do you need to talk now?"

"No, it can wait if you're in a meeting."

"I'll call you as soon as I'm out— Oh, hey, what's this?" Julie's voice changed, filling with confusion, which made Camille sit up. She couldn't see whatever Julie was seeing, but she wanted to know, too.

"Flower delivery for Julie Kim." The reply was harder to hear but still audible, and whoever was talking was obviously amused. "Arrived downstairs just a few minutes ago."

"Who the hell even knew you were here?"

"Calm down, Law. I'm sure plenty of people do."

"You can't tell me this isn't a little creepy."

"It's a little weird that whoever keeps sending these things knows when I'm here, but it's not that creepy. There are a lot of people who work here. It's not like I'm invisible when I go in and out. It'd be a lot creepier if things started showing up at my home address."

Ah, yes. Camille relaxed back against the couch. She'd heard about Julie's secret admirer. Julie occasionally got a delivery at Marquis, usually food or flowers, and a note that contained a compliment but no signature. It sounded sweet, but she could also see why Master Law, who taught classes at Marquis with Julie, thought it was creepy.

She remembered lots of kids and teenagers being into secret admirer stuff when she was younger, but most of them had left that behind when they hit adulthood. Now, it seemed more like a stalker thing, but Julie was right when she pointed out that everything was coming to her at Marquis, *not* at home, which might have felt like an invasion of privacy.

The masculine voice muttered something she couldn't quite hear.

"Camille? Sorry, got a flower delivery." There was a little note in

Julie's voice that made Camille think her friend was happy to get another delivery, and that made Camille happy for her. She remembered Julie as having a reputation as a hard nut to crack when it came to relationships. Whoever was wooing her was doing a damn fine job so far. "I'll call you when we're done with the meeting?"

Camille's doorbell rang.

"That sounds good. My food just arrived, so it's perfect timing."

"Great, I'll talk to you in a bit!"

That would give Camille more time to figure out exactly what to say. She wasn't great with being vulnerable, and right now, she felt more vulnerable than she had in a long, long time.

FREDDY

"I think you should text her."

Morgan was just full of opinions this evening. He wanted to encourage her voicing her opinions, he just wished she was having opinions about something else.

"Text her and tell her what?"

"That you wished you'd seen her under different circumstances, but it was still nice seeing her today?"

Had it been nice seeing her today? He wasn't sure. His first reaction had been excitement until his brain had caught up and reminded him of why he was there.

While he was mulling that over, another duo came up the stairs. Morgan squealed with happiness, waving at her friends, Carolyn and Marissa, obviously having a night out with each other. Freddy pasted his smile onto his face.

"Hey, guys! Where's Amy?" Morgan asked, her brow wrinkling in concern. "I thought she was coming tonight."

"She's at the gym." Carolyn waved her hand. "Still having trouble keeping the weight off."

"Not for lack of trying. She told me she has a doctor's appointment next week," Marissa said. Something in her tone indicated she wasn't happy with Carolyn's attitude, which was a first. Usually, it was the two of them teaming up and Amy's opinion either being ignored or beaten down.

"Oh, well, I hope everything's okay. Here I'll show you to your booth." Thankfully, Morgan was on top of things, so Freddy didn't have to interact with the Diva Duo. He really didn't know how Morgan and Amy managed to be friends with them, but to each their own.

Morgan had gotten him thinking, though.

Was he really going to let where Camille worked get in the way of the spark they'd felt?

Would she be comfortable being the one to reach out after the way things had gone down today?

Maybe he should text her.

Getting out his phone, he rested it on the desk in front of him. For all that he was supposed to be good with words, he was struggling to come up with a good opening line.

Just start with the truth.

Glancing up to make sure no one was coming up the stairs, Freddy unlocked his screen and opened his texting app.

Freddy: *Hello, I just wanted to say that I'm sorry about how today went down.*

Staring at it, he deleted the message. That wasn't the truth. He wasn't sorry about how things had gone with the Alexanders. He was just sorry she was the one representing Brittany's husband.

Freddy: *Hello, I just wanted to check in with you and see how you are after today.*

Okay, that was better.

A moment later, another group was coming up to the top of the stairs. Morgan wasn't back yet, so he got them seated before returning to check on his phone. Nothing back so far. Maybe she hadn't seen it.

Or maybe she didn't want to talk to him after today.

The disappointment that filled him at that thought let him know that he wasn't ready to be done with her yet. No matter where she worked.

9

—————

Staring at Freddy's message, Camille didn't know what to say. She honestly hadn't expected him to reach out after this afternoon and didn't know how to answer. There were too many variables up in the air. She didn't know what she wanted from him or what she was even allowed to want from him.

Everything felt like a complete mess and comfort food could only help so much.

Thankfully, before she could get too much into her head, Julie called her.

"Hello?"

"Hey, Camille. So, what's going on?"

Trust Julie to get straight to the point. For all that she seemed to be enjoying her secret admirer, she wasn't one to play games normally. Camille sighed, then spilled her guts. She might have hesitated a bit more before Freddy texted her, but now the pressure to have someone to talk to about all of this had built up to a breaking point, and she couldn't hold it in any longer.

When she finally reached the end of her word vomit, with Freddy's text, she felt a little lighter. A little empty, too, but at least didn't feel like she was going to explode anymore. Right now, she would take what she could get.

"Wow. Okay. Well, that's unexpected," Julie said after a moment.

"You're telling me. How is my luck this bad?" Camille leaned back against her sofa, letting her head fall back and putting her hand over her eyes to block out some of the light. She didn't have a headache yet, but she was pretty sure if she didn't find a way to relax, she would get one soon. Tension headaches were pretty common for her during the past few years.

"It could be good luck. You and Freddy hooked up before knowing you had rival clients, so he knows there's another side to you. Pretty sure if we'd introduced you after today, both of you would have balked."

"Yeah, I don't think that's good luck, considering that I am extremely attracted to the attorney I'm working against."

"Lucky for your love life if you two can get past this. Which, in my opinion, you should try. It's not like the Alexanders are going to be your clients forever. That's the best part about your job. Once you're done with them, you're done."

"As opposed to your job, where they keep coming back for more," Camille teased. Julie was a kink-friendly couples' therapist. She was pretty much a vault about her clients, but Camille knew she had some long-running ones. It was the nature of the job.

"Sure, but if they're assholes, I can choose not to see them again. The beauty of owning my own practice."

The truth of that statement sent jealousy shooting through Camille. She would have loved to have her own practice, but she'd never felt secure enough to make the jump. She couldn't, not while her mom's care relied on her.

"You do have a point," Camille mused. With the awfulness of the present, she hadn't thought ahead to the future.

Nicholas Alexander III wouldn't always be her client. She was stuck with him for now, but once the divorce proceedings were over —and with the file Freddy had presented them today, that would likely be sooner rather than later, despite what Mr. Alexander thought—she and Freddy wouldn't be on opposite sides of the table anymore.

Of course, there was no guarantee it wouldn't happen again in the future. She'd been working for Donaldson for five years now. Freddy was clearly an experienced lawyer, and the other night was the first time they'd met. Their firms both serviced large areas with a lot of people.

Theoretically, it could be another five years before they saw each other across a mediation table again. The idea of still being at Donaldson in five years made her want to shrivel up, but it was still a good point.

"How much do you want to sacrifice yourself to your job? I'm not saying you two should hook up again now that you're at cross courses, but there's nothing to say you can't get to know each other a little better until you're done with these clients. You can still be friendly. Plenty of lawyers do it." She snorted. "Heck, I happen to know a top defense attorney who Tops a state prosecutor. If they can make it work without it being a conflict of interest, why not you?"

Why not me?

A little rush of hope went through Camille. Julie tended to be… well, not a Debbie Downer exactly, but she was ruthlessly practical. If she didn't see this as an insurmountable problem, why should Camille?

I used to be a positive person.

It felt like a distant memory. On the other hand, she was reclaiming other sides of herself. Why not reclaim that part, too? She and Freddy could probably work something out. Maybe even scene together if they agreed to keep that part of their lives completely separate from their work.

If he was on board, that was. That, right there, was the root of her fear. Rejection. Her assumption that he would reject her was so strong, she wasn't even giving him the chance to, despite that he'd texted her first.

"You're right. You're right."

"Of course, I'm right. Now, get off the phone with me and get on the phone with him."

Camille laughed as Julie hung up on her. She was right, though.

Shaking her head, she pulled up Freddy's text message. She was already feeling better about... well, everything. Even if Freddy didn't want to see her again, she could handle that. She'd go to the club and meet someone else. Today was not the end of the world.

Camille: *I've had better days. I'm really sorry about my client. Are you available for a call?*

Normally, she hated talking on the phone but some of what she wanted to say, the explanations she wanted to give, were way too much to type out. Anxiety rippled through her, but to her relief, it only took a few moments for her phone to buzz with a response.

Freddy: *Sure, can I call you in five minutes?*

Camille: *Yes, I'm totally free this evening.*

That was an understatement. She mindlessly scrolled through the streaming options without finding anything she wanted to watch, which was what usually happened. How could there be so many options yet none of them feel right? Half the time she ended up watching a bunch of trailers and adding them to her watch list but not actually watching anything.

It was a relief when her phone rang, not just because she was feeling anxious about talking to him and wanted to get it over with but because she needed something to tear herself away from the television, she wasn't even watching.

"Hello?"

"Hello... uh, I'm not sure what to call you." The little stumble made him laugh and Camille smiled.

"Camille is fine outside the club and work."

"Yes, ma'am." He cleared his throat. "I'm at Marquis tonight. I just took a break from the front desk, so my wires are feeling a bit crossed."

She could understand that. It was probably the same way they'd both felt earlier today when their professional and personal worlds had collided for the first time.

"My wires have felt crossed all day." She sighed. "I just wanted to apologize, personally, for my client's behavior. I wish I could say I'll be able to better control him in the future, but I can't give you that guarantee. As much as I wish today had been the end of things, I seriously doubt he's going to give in that easily."

"He's an ass."

"Off the record? He's the worst. Not even the partners want anything to do with him, other than when they're playing golf. That's how I got saddled with him in the first place. I don't really want to talk about work, though, other than as it relates to us… if today didn't totally turn you off." Might as well put it all out there on the table.

The two glasses of wine she'd had while she was eating helped with the blunt honesty.

"It was a shock, but I'll get over it."

She winced. Apparently, she wasn't the only one going for blunt honesty.

"Trust me, I'd much rather be working somewhere like Addison, O'Shane, and Smith, but they weren't hiring when I was looking. Donaldson was, and they offered the right amount of money." Her voice lowered. "My mom is in a memory care unit, and it's expensive."

There was a short pause.

"I'm sorry to hear that. I'm glad you got her into a care unit. That can make a huge difference. I know it did for my grandmother." The sympathy in his voice was like a balm to her frayed nerves.

He'd judged her for where she worked. She didn't blame him because she judged herself, but she did have her reasons. As much as she didn't want to care what he thought, his opinion already had weight with her.

Talking about falling in deep, fast.

Part of her didn't know why she was already telling him all of this. Was she really this desperate for human connection? Or was it specific to him?

"Thank you. It's been… rough. While I might not always love what I have to do, it pays the bills."

"I can understand that."

FREDDY

Talking to Camille was making him feel better about today. Morgan had been right. He'd been judging her too harshly, and part of that was because of how protective he felt about Brittany. Since Camille was representing Brittany's husband, who was a colossal douche, it could have been easy to paint her as someone who didn't care about how her job affected people, but it was clear she did.

The fixer in him wanted to run straight to the partners of his firm to see if they had any openings for her or knew of any other firms that might have an opening, but he doubted she would appreciate the efforts. More likely, she'd take it as an insult. Not only that, but he didn't think the partners would be very impressed either, considering he knew very little about her.

The urge to help was still there.

"So... does that mean you'd be willing to scene with me again?"

"Yes." This time he didn't need to hesitate or stop to think. There was a connection between them. She felt it, too. They'd fit together on New Year's Eve, and before this afternoon, she'd been haunting his thoughts.

Well, even after this afternoon. She'd just been haunting them in a different way, but it hadn't stopped him from wanting to see her. He just hadn't felt very good about that desire until after talking to Morgan.

"Oh. Good." She made a relieved noise. "I want to see you, too, but I would understand if you didn't want to after today or if it was too much of a conflict of interest..."

"We should probably keep things friendly until the Alexanders are no longer our clients, and we're not working against each other, but yes, I would like to see you more in the future."

She chuckled.

"Well, that's one way to motivate a quick divorce."

Freddy had to laugh. She wasn't wrong. He wanted to get it over with quickly for Brittany's sake, but having a personal stake in when it ended definitely added another sense of urgency.

"It should be quick, anyway," he pointed out. "Mr. Alexander is the one dragging his heels." He managed to keep his voice neutral, though he was sure that didn't entirely hide his feelings on the matter.

"Yes, well." Camille paused. "Between you and me, I think he knows he's not going to get what he wants. He just wants to see Mrs. Alexander and make her as miserable as possible throughout the process. He can't stand the fact that she's leaving him. Not because he loves her or cares about her, but because he sees it as a personal insult that she wouldn't want to be with him." She snorted.

"I'm sure we can figure something out," Freddy said, his mind turning over. The fact that she was cooperative instead of hostile would help. "Maybe I can get Brittany to insist that all communications be handled through me, no more mediation. She's feeling guilty about leaving him, which is why she agreed to meet today in the first place, but I'm working on that."

"Good, because she shouldn't feel guilty at all. I don't know how she stayed with him for as long as she did. I can barely manage to spend a few hours with him. More than that and I'd probably need a lawyer myself."

Laughing, Freddy's mood lifted even further.

"I have to get back upstairs, but I'm glad we got a chance to talk tonight."

"Me too. Thank you for calling."

"Of course. Have a good night, Mistress Camille." Even though he didn't need to say it, he enjoyed doing so and enjoyed hearing her quick intake of breath even more.

"Good night, Freddy."

10

———————

An email pinged in Freddy's inbox at the same time as a text message from Camille.

He opened the text message first.

Camille: *I'm so sorry. I've explained to him multiple times that the pictures you provided are the nail in the coffin as far as he's concerned, but he's insisting on fighting anything we can, and there are still a few sections left that are unclear and are unaffected by the fact that he cheated.*

Freddy sighed. He knew that, too. Of course, she was a thorough enough lawyer to have caught those weaknesses in the prenup. The asshole didn't deserve her.

The email she had sent was a purely professional request for another mediation session. Truthfully, Freddy was relieved to see it. He knew Mr. Alexander had been calling Brittany, and he'd been worried the man would show up at her sister's house soon. No telling where that would end up. Brittany's sister, Ashley, was not at all happy with him and extremely protective of her sister. Ashley's husband was all too happy to be the one to 'take out the trash,' as he'd put it.

It might be why Mr. Alexander had decided to go through the

lawyers rather than trying to handle things on his own. Maybe he realized he'd be risking his own skin to approach her by himself. At least the man had some survival instincts, if nothing else.

Freddy quickly shot back an email to make an appointment. He also emailed Brittany and told her Mr. Alexander had requested another session and encouraged her to let him handle it on his own. The sooner Mr. Alexander realized he wouldn't have access, the faster they may be able to get this over with. Freddy would have a much easier time playing hardball without her present.

When she was there, he had to walk a delicate line between what he *wanted* to say and upsetting her. The second to last thing he wanted to do was cause her more distress, though he would to get her everything she deserved from her ex.

Picking up his phone, he texted Camille to give her a heads up.

Freddy: *We'll meet again, but I'm going to try to convince Brittany to stay home. Don't suppose you could do the same?*

Camille: *I wish, but if she's not there, it might keep him from insisting on another attempt. I wish I could have talked him out of this one, but one of the partners came in to argue for it as well.*

Wincing, Freddy shook his head. He and Camille had been texting back and forth for close to a week now. She didn't talk much about her job, but the impression he got was it was slowly crushing her soul. Or maybe not so slowly at this point. Julie had paused to talk to him over the weekend and hinted as much. She'd seemed thrilled when he told her he and Camille were still talking.

A knock on his open door made him look up. Zoey Addison, one of the firms founding partners, was standing there, and she raised her eyebrows at Freddy.

"Everything okay?"

"Yeah, just..." He hesitated, then decided to go for it. Zoey was the kind of woman who made people quake in their boots, but she also had a heart of gold and a huge dose of empathy, especially for women in bad situations, which was how the firm had gotten started. "The other lawyer on the Alexander case... she wants to work with me and make things go smoothly, but her client is..."

"A complete and total jackass?" Zoey laughed at the expression on Freddy's face. He didn't think he'd ever heard her curse before. A slight sneer lifted her lip. "I'm familiar with Nicholas Alexander III. And his father. And the Donaldsons. That's part of why I decided to give Mrs. Alexander to you instead of taking her on myself."

"So, you can watch from afar as I take him apart?" he asked with amusement. Zoey's dark eyes glinted, and she raised her hand to run it along her perfectly styled hair. With her Chanel suit, Jimmy Choo shoes, and two perfect strands of pearls around her neck, she looked exactly like what she was—a powerhouse.

"Perhaps. You are very good at what you do." She smiled broadly. "I also had a feeling your personal aesthetic would offend his sensibilities."

Freddy laughed.

"I noticed that. I'll be wearing my best pink suit to the next meeting." The one he normally reserved for friends' events rather than work, but if Zoey was going to encourage him…

She snickered and nodded her head with approval.

"Perfect." Her smile dimmed. "How is the lawyer working on his case? I heard through the grapevine that Donaldson chose her to make Alexander look better in the courtroom. Apparently, they think he'll come off looking better if he's using a black woman to represent him."

"That doesn't surprise me. She's very good, but she also has ethics and is doing her best to keep him happy, while also keeping him in check."

"Now that's a heck of a balancing act." Zoey looked at him contemplatively. "Would you recommend hiring her?"

"In a heartbeat," he answered before he could think about it, but it was the truth. From everything he'd seen from the opposing side, Camille was conscientious, detail-oriented, and didn't let her personal feelings get in the way of doing her job. She also had a staunch moral code she adhered to, no matter how her client pushed her to break it. He was sure Donaldson had probably pushed her to break it too. She bent, but she hadn't snapped. Yet.

The urge to help her get out of that job had grown stronger with every day that passed, even though their relationship so far consisted entirely of texts.

"Interesting. We don't have any openings," Zoey replied, answering the question in his eyes. "But I was asked by a friend to keep my ear to the ground for promising, experienced lawyers who might want to make a change."

"I'll see if I can find a way to work it into the conversation."

Giving him a piercing look, Zoey nodded thoughtfully and moved away from his doorway, leaving him with the uncomfortable feeling she'd gotten more out of what he hadn't said than he had.

CAMILLE

Julie: *Want to come to Marquis with me this Friday night? Olivia and Luke are putting on a show.*

Now that was tempting.

The door to her office opened, and she dropped the phone flat on her desk, feeling as if she'd been caught out doing something wrong as Donaldson Sr. strode into her office. Not that there was anything wrong with checking her phone. There wasn't. Even if she wasn't looking at work right now. She'd been working nonstop all morning. Yet she still felt guilty that her boss had walked in the exact moment that she wasn't.

He eyed her as though he knew she'd been slacking, looking down his long nose at her.

"Good morning, Mr. Donaldson." Camille got to her feet, smoothing down the plain black dress she was wearing. It hadn't taken long to realize the firm preferred if everyone dressed as though they were on their way to a funeral. His eyes raked over her, as if trying to find fault with her attire, though she told herself she was reading too much into things. "What can do I for you?"

"Camille. How is everything going with Nicholas?"

She gritted her teeth against the dismissive way he said her name, which was completely at odds with the friendlier way he used Nicholas' first name. If she tried to call him "Wes," she knew she would be immediately slapped down for the familiarity, but that didn't stop *him* from using *her* first name. There was no point in calling attention to the hypocrisy. It wouldn't matter to him.

"I reached out to Mrs. Alexander's lawyer and scheduled another meeting. However, I'm not sure it will matter, considering the evidence they have of his infidelity. Truthfully, I think it would be best for him to move forward with the divorce and accept the terms of the prenup rather than contesting it. At this point, there's nothing to be gained by further meetings, especially as his hostile behavior isn't likely to convince her to negotiate."

"Well, it's his money to spend," Donaldson Sr. said with a wave of his hand that made Camille want to shake her head.

She didn't understand any of the partners. Supposedly, they were friends with Mr. Alexander, or golf buddies at least, yet they had no problem letting him rack up billable hours on a useless quest. Definitely not how she'd want any of her friends to treat her.

"Just keep him quiet during the meeting and make him happy."

Before she could protest or ask how he thought she was going to manage babysitting the manchild *and* keeping him happy, the man was gone. At least he closed the door behind him so no one could see her banging her head on her desk.

Sitting up, she took a deep breath. Her tolerance for the bullshit here was getting smaller, not necessarily a bad thing, but she still needed to keep her temper. She still needed this job.

What I need is to look for a new job.

She hadn't the first few years, even though she'd wanted to, because she hadn't wanted to look flighty, disloyal, or as if she was jumping from job to job. However, she'd put in five years here. That was more than some. Why hadn't she started looking for a position at another company?

Had she forgotten or had she just gotten too beaten down? Too tired.

Well, that ended today.

First things first. She texted Julie back.

Camille: *I'll be there!*

Julie: *Great! Ladies' night out!*

Sounded good to her. A night out with a friend *and* a good show, especially since it was going to be Olivia and Luke. It would be good to watch another Dominatrix work. Get her head back in the game. She might even see Freddy while she was there.

Ignoring the urge to text him, she got back on her computer to get back to work... and update her resume. It was time for her to take control of all aspects of her life again. Feeling invigorated, it didn't take her long to get through her paperwork. Pulling out her phone again, she started looking at job listings and emailed some of her old friends who were still in the area, asking if they knew of any openings.

It felt really, really good.

For the first time since she could remember, she walked out of work, feeling happy.

***

<u>*FREDDY*</u>

"Where's Brittany?" Mr. Alexander glared at Freddy before averting his eyes, as if the bright pink suit Freddy was wearing was too offensive to look at. In contrast, Camille was grinning and looking at him like he was a pink Starburst she wanted to unwrap. Freddy had to avert his eyes from her because he didn't want Mr. Alexander to notice anything between them.

"She won't be joining us today," Freddy said smoothly, setting down his briefcase and pulling out his chair. "I've been authorized by her to handle all the negotiations. If there is something that requires her input, I'll contact her, and we can handle it later."

"You can't do that."

"Yes, he can." Camille's firm tone made the man sit back and cross his arms over his chest like a pouty child. "Honestly, we're lucky to have even that much concession, considering how the last meeting went." The look she shot Mr. Alexander had him looking away from both of them.

"My client is willing to negotiate, however her main concern is that Mr. Alexander leave her alone."

"Like I'd want to be around that bi—"

"Mr. Alexander." Camille didn't raise her voice, didn't even look at the man. He shrank back into his seat, shoulders hunching over protectively.

It was one of the hottest things Freddy had ever seen. He had to shift in his seat to make his pants a little more comfortable. He loved this suit, but the pants were a little tighter than some of his other options.

Camille's gaze met Freddy's. "That sounds like something my client might be interested in. What are the terms?"

Brittany was willing to give away her rights to just about everything that was left in exchange for her husband leaving her be after their divorce, her fear that he might not let her go so easily overriding everything else, but that's why Freddy was here. He understood her fear and her priority, but he was going to make sure she got what she deserved. If giving up some of the material items she was entitled to meant giving her peace of mind, he would do that, but he'd also impressed upon her that he couldn't write a contract that kept Mr. Alexander from contacting her.

He was also doing his best to make sure she got most of what she was entitled to, pointing out that she could use the extra money to move or hire security.

"She's not getting *any* of my money," Alexander finally snapped out when Camille prodded him again. "Not unless I get to see her again. If she wants my money, she can beg for it."

"Or we can see you in court where she'll likely get all of it," Freddy said coldly. "Although the terms of these sections were not affected by your infidelity, in court, it would likely be taken into consideration."

"May I have a moment with my client?" Camille asked politely, her tone as cold as Freddy's.

He knew it wasn't directed at him. Nodding, he stepped outside for a few moments. The door was thick, but he could still hear Mr. Alexander making demands of Camille.

For some reason, he hadn't gotten it through his head that he couldn't do whatever he liked. He'd gotten a prenup before the wedding, and because of it, Brittany was already getting less than she likely deserved for putting up with his selfish ass for so long, but that still wasn't enough for him. He didn't want to have to give Brittany anything at all, even though he was the one who insisted she not work and be completely reliant on him. That she was still leaving him obviously pricked his pride.

Sighing inwardly, Freddy did his best to wait patiently until Camille opened the door again.

"Sorry about this," she said, and her dark eyes were filled with sincere apology. "I think we're going to have to adjourn for today while Mr. Alexander and I talk through some things."

"I see," Freddy said, giving her a wry smile to offset his tone. Then he stepped around her, his face falling into a more serious expression for Mr. Alexander, and picked up his briefcase. "That is no problem as long as Mr. Alexander understands if he contacts Mrs. Alexander, by any means, she will immediately end any attempts at negotiation, and we will see you in court. I'm sure the public spectacle would be quite interesting."

At least he could keep the asshole from contacting Brittany for a bit and hopefully give her a reprieve.

Mr. Alexander glared at him, jaw clenching.

Hopefully, Freddy hadn't just made things harder for Camille, but in this case, his first priority had to be his client. Still, he shot her an apologetic look as he left.

11

Camille

Another hard talk with Mr. Alexander, another visit from Donaldson Sr., and Camille was ready to take the first job offer that came her way if it paid the same. The desire to jump ship was overwhelming. Calling her mom at the home and getting to talk to her for a bit helped get Camille back on an even keel. She couldn't just up and go without a replacement job. She didn't have the savings for herself, much less to take care of her mom, for any real length of time.

At least she'd gotten the process started. She'd even gotten an email back from a firm in Baltimore, requesting an interview. Not that she wanted to move back across the state, but she was starting to think the commute would be worth it.

Putting together a list of the things she and Mr. Alexander had talked about, she shot it off to Freddy. Granted, he wasn't willing to bend on much, but after Freddy had dropped his threat, the man had seemed slightly less combative. She'd learned that, underneath his pricked pride, he also didn't want her to have any shares in his company, and that *was* something they could push for, especially if he was willing to give on some of the other sections.

While she had a feeling Freddy was right about what would happen if they went to court, the fact Mrs. Alexander was still open to negotiating meant Camille might be able to make Mr. Alexander less unhappy. She didn't have a lot of hope he'd actually be happy with her efforts.

She couldn't do anything about him sulking because Mrs. Alexander hadn't shown up and was clearly happy to do everything by proxy. It was a good move on Freddy's part. Though Mr. Alexander seemed determined to drag things out, without Mrs. Alexander there to torment, he seemed to have lost most of his energy for it.

As soon as she was home, she called Freddy.

"Hello, beautiful. How was your day?"

Just hearing his voice made her smile, though that greeting didn't hurt either.

"I thought we were keeping things professional," she teased.

"Don't you call all your co-workers beautiful?" The mock innocence in his voice got an outright laugh from her.

"You are trouble." She sighed. "Sorry about today, but I think we got some real work done. Did you get my email?"

"About the shares? Yes. I think Brittany's main concern will be getting him to leave her alone. She doesn't want anything to do with the company or him, so that shouldn't be an issue if you can get him to agree to it."

"I'll do my best. If you can put up a big show of reluctance and make every concession begrudgingly, that will help."

"Oh, believe me, every concession *will* be begrudging on my part," Freddy replied dryly. "Normally, I wouldn't show it because I get great satisfaction out of denying assholes what they want, but I'll make an exception in this case since I think both you and Brittany would prefer it that way."

Knowing she was part of the equation made her feel warm inside.

"I do love watching you take him apart," she said. "It's hot."

He chuckled.

"I feel the exact same way about you."

"I don't take him apart,"—Camille wrinkled her nose—"though I want to sometimes."

"I don't think you realize the effect you have on him. Trust me, he feels taken apart."

Hm. Well, that was something to think about. She had definitely been firmer with him the past week than she had originally and knew part of that was because Freddy was there watching, but it felt good. It felt right. Like she was alive again.

That night at Marquis had kicked off so much more than she'd realized.

"I'll have to take your word for it. I feel like I'm holding back so much, maybe it's hard for me to see what I am doing."

"That makes sense. Hopefully, you won't have to hold back much longer." A sultry note changed in his voice, and she knew he was thinking about their agreement that they would scene again after they were no longer working at cross purposes with the Alexanders.

"I got the acceptance for my membership to Marquis and Stronghold." She'd be occasionally serving as Dungeon Monitor to get a discount on her fees, but it would be worth it. "And Julie and I are going to the show at Marquis on Friday."

"Ah, so you're her guest. We were all taking bets on whether she was going to bring someone to try to prod her secret admirer into speaking up."

"No, just me." Camille laughed. "She's busy pushing me, but once she's done with me, I wouldn't be surprised if she puts her mind to figuring out her admirer."

"I'll be glad when she does. I've tried to figure out who it could be, but we don't have that many single submissive men at the club, and we all know Julie is hetero. The mystery is killing me."

The fact Freddy didn't even have a guess was interesting. She would have thought he'd have at least a suspicion. From what Julie and Olivia said, he had a firm finger on the pulse of the club's submissives and always knew what was going on with everyone.

"Are you going to be watching the show?" she asked, not knowing which way to hope. As much as she wanted to see him outside of work, doing so would be tempting fate. Not to mention tempting herself.

"I'll be seating people, just like last Friday. I usually help out during the rush, then I'm off for the rest of the evening unless I feel like hanging around. So, I'll see you there."

"Good. I'm looking forward to it."

"Me, too."

They chatted for a few more minutes, then he had to go. Camille sighed as she laid on the sofa. Her apartment suddenly felt very lonely. At least she had Friday to look forward to.

———

FREDDY

It had been a long time since he'd been nervous at Marquis, but tonight, he was a bundle of anxious butterflies. Every time someone reached the top of the stairs, he let out a sigh of disappointment when it wasn't Mistresses Camille and Julie. Morgan said it was like working next to an anxious frog.

He couldn't help himself.

He'd dressed up a little, wearing grey slacks with a bright blue shirt and a grey corset vest with black laces that made him look damn good. Usually, he went for comfort when he was working, but knowing Mistress Camille was coming in made him want to look his very best.

The more he'd gotten to know her, the more he liked her. Even though they'd been keeping everything mostly within professional boundaries, who she was as a person had shown through.

Some kind of sixth sense sizzled in the air, lifting the hairs along the back of his neck, and he jerked his gaze to the top of the stairs. Somehow, he'd known that *this* time, it was her arriving. And he was right. She and Mistress Julie reached the top of the stairs at the same time, two stunning opposites.

Despite her heels, Mistress Julie only came up to Mistress Camille's chin. Mistress Julie was dressed in all black, while Mistress

Camille was wearing bright red, making them stand out even more next to each other. The tight red corset wrapped around Mistress Camille's curves pushed her breasts up to an incredible height, nipped in her waist, and showed off her hips. Her pants were a matching red but made of stretchy material that hugged her thighs before flaring out at the knees, like bell bottoms. Her hair was pulled into little twists that were decorated with shiny red beads. She looked stunning and dangerous at the same time.

The kind of woman he could spend hours worshiping. Preferably with his tongue.

"Mistresses," he greeted them with a smile, though he knew his gaze lingered longer on Mistress Camille. Her dark eyes met his, and it felt as if the room was filled with electricity. But he was supposed to be working. "Welcome. May I take your coats?"

They handed over the coats they were carrying, Mistress Camille shooting him a special smile. Freddy beamed back at her before hanging them up.

"Thank you, Freddy," Mistress Camille said, and the note of approval in her voice made him want to preen.

Seeing her at the club was a completely different experience than seeing her in the office. It was as though all the pent-up sexual tension was leaking out now that they didn't have to suppress it.

"Let me show you to your table." As much as he wanted to indulge in small talk, something, he was tongue tied. Not his normal state.

Grabbing up the night's menus, he led them to their table, putting a little saunter in his step. He knew the pants he was wearing made his ass look fantastic. Some men might discount how much a woman enjoyed looking at a pair of well-fitted pants, but Freddy knew better. Women appreciated a fine ass as much as men did.

"Here you go," he said when they got there, stepping back so the two women could slide into the booth. Mistress Camille brushed by him on the side he was standing, perhaps a little closer than necessary. He might have wondered if it was intentional if she hadn't peeked up at him when she sat down and shot him a flirtatious wink.

His whole body was buzzing.

Unfortunately, he had to walk away, but that little wink made him feel like he was floating the whole way back to the lobby. When he got back there, Morgan raised her eyebrows at him.

"Back so soon?"

"I couldn't exactly stand there and flirt."

The look she gave him was of pure exasperation.

"Why not? I have this covered." She gestured at the front desk, and he realized part of her objection was because she thought *he* thought she couldn't handle it on her own. Even though it was a Friday night, she would certainly be okay for five or ten minutes.

"It wouldn't be professional. We agreed to keep things professional until we're not representing opposing parties." As much as that sucked.

"Oh..." Morgan blinked. "So, it's just going to be lots of longing glances and heartfelt sighs until your clients get divorced?"

"Well, until they figure out how they're going to settle things, at least." Once they'd signed off on the papers, Freddy would consider himself free of any obligation to *not* fuck opposing counsel.

"It's kind of Romeo & Juliet but with opposing legal firms." Morgan giggled. "It sucks, though, having to wait."

"It does, but we're still talking and texting a little. Taking things slow isn't the worst thing." It had been a while since he'd had any kind of real relationship, and in the past, he'd had the habit of jumping in too far too fast. He really wouldn't mind being able to jump into things with Mistress Camille faster, but he was good at trying to convince himself.

Something Morgan picked up on. She snorted.

"Are you trying to convince me or yourself?" she asked, echoing his thoughts.

"Sometimes, you're too smart for your own good," he joked, nudging her with his hip and making her giggle.

The time flew by. Just knowing Mistress Camille was in the next room, having dinner, made him antsy. He already knew he would be hanging around tonight instead of leaving before the show ended, hoping to catch a glimpse of her on the way out. Maybe she'd be interested in having a completely professional drink at the bar.

What he wasn't expecting was for Mistress Julie to come out of the main room five minutes before the show started and pin him with a look.

"Freddy, I have to go. My cousin is having some kind of issue she needs help with. Can you go keep Mistress Camille company through the show, so I haven't totally abandoned her?"

If anyone other than Mistress Julie was doing the asking, he would have suspected a setup, but she wasn't that kind of person and was anxiously shifting from foot to foot like she wanted to run out of there. Whatever issue her cousin was having, it was enough to make her worried.

"I..." He wanted to say yes. Of course, he wanted to say yes. But should he say yes? It would be one thing to run into each other at a bar, it was something else entirely to watch a kink show with her. How the hell was he supposed to do that and remain professional? It would be pure torture and not the fun kind.

"Say yes," Morgan hissed at him. "Stop overthinking it and go!"

That would be her advice. It was also what he wanted to do.

"She would love to have your company, but she'll stay on her own if she has to," Mistress Julie said.

Well, that decided it.

"I would be honored." He nodded at her. "I hope everything is okay with your cousin."

Something flashed in Mistress Julie's eyes.

"Don't worry," she said grimly. "It will be. Have a good rest of the evening."

Morgan handed Mistress Julie her coat, shooing Freddy toward the door at the same time. Heart in his throat, he gave her a wave as he entered the room.

This evening was either going to be amazing or the worst case of blue balls he'd ever had.

12

———————

Camille

This was awkward. She was stuck waiting on pins and needles to find out if Freddy was going to join her, or if she was going to end up watching the show on her own. Both of which were potentially embarrassing in their own way. She had put herself on the line a little, telling Julie to ask if Freddy could come join her.

If he said no... awkward.

If he said yes... possibly awkward.

Part of her had wanted to leave when Julie got the call that her cousin needed help—from the sounds of it, she'd caught her boyfriend cheating on her and wanted out of their house asap—but Julie had insisted she stay and enjoy the show. Then she'd suggested that she send Freddy in to take her place and staying suddenly sounded a lot better.

As long as he said yes and didn't feel obligated to do anything or take it the wrong way or...

Before she could think of any other worst-case scenario, the door to the lobby opened, and there he was. The vest he was wearing made him look even leaner and hotter than ever, giving him a quintessential male V-shape and making him stand completely straight. Camille had seen the vests on social media but never in person.

He looked just as good in it as any of the guys online.

Because of where her booth was and Julie leaving the curtains open, Freddy was able to meet her gaze from across the room. Her breath caught. The energy between them was electric, an attraction she couldn't deny. She felt a surge of relief that he'd come in.

This didn't feel awkward at all.

Dropping his head in acknowledgement, Freddy crossed the room, moving with an elegant stride that almost made it look like he was dancing as he rounded the circular stage in the center. With the way the booths were set up, she couldn't see anyone else, but she could hear the murmurs of appreciation as he moved, and possessiveness spiked through her.

She wanted to claim him as her own but didn't have the right to. Not yet.

Her pulse raced as he stepped up to the table, stopping right in front of it and putting his arms behind his back. She didn't have to see them to know that he'd crossed them, holding his elbows in his hands.

"Mistress, would you like some company?"

"Yes, please, Freddy. Sit down." The last two words came out as the order they were, and she smiled when he immediately slid into the booth. The dishes from her and Julie's dinner had already been cleared, leaving the table's surface empty. "Thank you for joining me."

A smile curved his lips, and he lifted his head to meet her gaze.

"Believe me, Mistress, the pleasure is all mine." Then his expression shifted to a more serious look. "Though… should we talk about expectations?"

Putting her hand on the table, palm up, she reached towards him in offering and he took it, his hand lying easily atop hers.

"This is an unexpected situation," she replied gently. "We can watch the show together as friends. Or we can play, and tomorrow, everything goes back to our original agreement."

He mused on that for a moment.

"Do you have a preference, Mistress?"

She'd had time to think while she waited for him. Time to prod her emotions and figure out what she really wanted.

"I would love to play, if you're amenable. I already know I want to scene with you again, and if I have to wait, I will, but I'm even happier if I don't." That was the full truth. Holding back her own desires was like trying to repair a broken dam, but she would do it for him.

He stared at her for a long moment, and her heart sank. Then he said the last thing she expected.

"There's a room open tonight, Mistress. The foot and shoe room."

Camille blinked, her mind racing. She had *not* come prepared to spend the night. On the other hand, it wasn't like they had to spend the whole night. They could scene, then go home. It would extend their time together beyond the show, something she hadn't even hoped for because she wouldn't have thought it possible.

It opened up a whole new world of possibilities, but was it smart?

If we're going to break our rules tonight, might as well break them all the way.

"Can you still reserve it for us?"

"Yes, Mistress. I'll be right back." Freddy's eyes lit up and unlike before, he moved *fast*. Still elegant, but much more quickly. The lights were already dimming when he returned, the show about to start. He managed to slide back into the booth just before it went completely dark. "The room is all ours."

"Good boy." Reaching out, she found his thigh with her hand in the darkness and heard his quick breath, felt his muscles tense and relax under her palm. She squeezed lightly, digging her fingers into his inner thigh, and he moaned softly, making her own arousal jump with interest. She could feel her nipples budding, rubbing against the stiff fabric of her corset as her pussy plumped and dampened.

The lights came up on stage to show a set of chains hanging in the middle and a small cart laden with various floggers. Camille hummed with approval, as did Freddy. Julie had said Olivia and Luke were going for a more sensual scene tonight, exactly what Camille was in the mood for.

The pair walked out onto the stage. Olivia was wearing a black corset with red laces and black leather pants that had red ribbon lacing up the back from the ankles to just underneath the curve of her ass. Her red ankle boots with a very high heel that made her nearly Luke's height but didn't cover up any of the pretty decoration on the back of her pants.

Camille made a mental note to ask Olivia where she got them because she wanted a pair if they came in her size.

Luke, of course, was buck naked, his cock already half-hard and bobbing in front of him. He walked with supreme confidence, the swagger of a man who knew he looked damn good naked. They were a beautiful couple.

Walking to the center of the circular stage, Luke came to a halt under the chains and reached up, putting his forearms through the loop and holding onto them with his wrists crossed. The chains would give him a place to brace and help hold himself up, showing off the long, lean muscles of his body, so Olivia could circle around him and flog him wherever she wished.

Shifting closer to Freddy, Camille could feel the heat from his body against her side. Moving her hand on his thigh, it slid down toward his knee, then back up again. They were close enough, she could feel his shiver. He was sitting bolt upright in the booth, as was she, thanks to the corsets they were wearing.

As Camille watched Olivia pick up the first flogger, her mind was half on the show and half on trying to figure out what she could do with Freddy while they watched.

Stepping up to Luke, Olivia put her hand on his back and said something low in his ear. The flogger she held in her hand was fairly lightweight with many long strands that fluttered against her leg. He said something back, and she smiled, patting his muscular shoulder before stepping away and lifting the flogger.

Freddy sighed as they began, Olivia expertly wielding the flogger and flicking it over Luke's shoulders and buttocks, avoiding his lower back where his kidneys were. Camille slid her hand farther up Freddy's thigh, feeling the bulge of his erection beneath his pants as it brushed against the side of her hand. On stage, Luke's erection was growing as well, and he shuddered, muscles flexing, as the many leather strands fell again and again.

FREDDY

It was pure, delicious torture as Mistress Camille's hand moved closer and closer to his cock. She hadn't told him what to do, hadn't told him to do anything, so Freddy didn't dare move. His hands were on the table, and he turned them so he could lay his palms flat against the wood to keep himself from moving them.

As much as he wanted to touch her, he hadn't been given permission. He didn't know what she had in mind for while they were watching the show, wasn't sure she *did* have anything in mind, but he knew better than to try to push his own agenda.

He wanted to be a good boy for her.

With her hand on his thigh, waiting to see what she would do next, it wasn't easy to concentrate on Mistress Olivia and Luke. He did his best because he loved watching a good flogging as much as anyone else. He loved seeing the connection between the couple. A long time ago, he'd had a crush on Mistress Olivia—who hadn't—but they never would have worked together. He was happy she'd found the partner she needed, and whenever he watched them all he could think was, *I want that.*

Not that he wanted Mistress Olivia, but that was the kind of connection he wanted, the kind of trust and intimacy, the kind of relationship. They worked together, and their chemistry was off the charts.

Right now, he and Mistress Camille definitely had the chemistry. He was hopeful the rest would come.

This is for tonight only.

For right now.

A taste of what was possible.

Tonight only... until they were done with the Alexanders. Then they could have a lot more nights like tonight.

Mistress Camille's hand moved, her palm covering the bulge at the front of his pants. Freddy groaned louder, his hips trying to rock forward despite his seated position, his hands pressing flat against the table in an effort not to move them. If it wasn't for the corset vest, he would have slumped in the booth, trying to get more contact. His whole body ached with the need for more.

She laughed softly as Mistress Olivia finished with the light flogger and moved to the table, picking up a cock ring to sheathe Luke's dick before she chose a new flogger with thicker strands and knots at the end. Heavier, thuddier, and more painful, though Luke's skin would be nicely warmed up from the lighter one.

No wonder Freddy's body was aching with envy. It was all too easy to imagine himself in Luke's place with Mistress Camille being the one circling around him. Tormenting him. Pleasuring him.

The way she was right now with her hand atop his cock but not actually gripping it, the fabric of his pants was a barrier between them.

"Lean back," she murmured.

Freddy did as he was told, moaning with relief when she undid the front of his pants and allowed his cock to spring free... not that he thought he was going to be allowed to climax any time soon. This wasn't the blue balls situation he'd predicted at the beginning of the night, but he had no doubt that was what was about to happen. Unless Mistress Camille was feeling extremely generous... Even if she was, there was an inner part of him that rebelled at the idea of coming before her.

He'd rather endure the teasing and erotic torture so he could satisfy her first and only then reap his rewards.

With her hand wrapped around his cock, she pumped, gently... slowly... prolonging the torment and making him want to writhe in place. He gritted his teeth, his muscles tensing as he kept the rest of his body still. Another pump, and he shuddered with the effort.

On stage, Mistress Olivia circled Luke, flogging his thighs, along with the rest of his body, getting dangerously near his erection with the heavy flogger strands. And still he hung there. No safeword. No flinching. Nothing but utter trust in his Mistress.

Sitting next to Mistress Camille, Freddy was determined to do no less.

13

Body throbbing with need, Freddy followed Mistress Camille down the hallway to the shoe room. The cancellation from earlier today had been a godsend, allowing them to continue their evening after the show was over. And it had been quite a show. By the time Mistress Olivia had worked her way through all the floggers, both Luke and Freddy had been quivering messes.

While Luke had ended up bent over a table while Mistress Olivia pegged him from behind, Freddy's erotic torture was still ongoing. She hadn't let him cum. Worse, she hadn't let him touch her.

Watching the sway of her ass as she walked, he hoped all of that was going to change soon.

When they walked into the room, she paused to look around. The shoes decorating the walls were the majority of decoration other than the mirrors also on the walls. There were several chairs as well, which could serve different functions, including a Queening Throne. Freddy gave that particular piece of furniture a hopeful look.

He'd enjoyed the last chair she'd sat in, but there was something particularly hot about having a gorgeous woman sit on his face.

Turning to face him, Mistress Camille's expression didn't give anything away.

"The same limits and safe words as last time?" she asked.

"Yes, Mistress."

"Very good. Come here, Freddy. I need help getting my corset off."

He eagerly leapt to obey. It felt a little odd to be undressing her while he was still fully dressed, but he wasn't going to argue with the order she wanted to do things in. Though she only took off the corset and not her pants, he realized she was making herself more comfortable.

He, on the other hand, was still tightly constricted by his vest, something she seemed to enjoy as she circled him, her heavy breasts swaying, dark brown nipples pebbled and hard.

"This is very nice," she murmured, running her hands over the stiff fabric of the vest. It was thick enough that feeling her touch through the fabric was rather difficult, but that didn't stop his quick intake of breath.

"Thank you, Mistress. I wore it for you."

She paused in her perusal, eyebrows lifting as she met his gaze.

"Because I was coming tonight?"

"Yes, Mistress."

"Even though you didn't know we were going to play?"

"Yes, Mistress." He batted his eyes, grinning at her. "I wanted to be pretty for you."

Laughing softly, Mistress Camille wrapped one hand around his neck, tugging him down slightly for a kiss.

"You are *very* pretty, Freddy. You are also a bit of a brat, hm?" She didn't wait for an answer.

Their lips met, and he let her control the kiss, meeting her movements eagerly, his tongue sweeping against hers as the kiss deepened. Keeping his hands at his side rather than reaching out to touch her was an act of willpower that made his muscles strain. Then her lips pulled away just enough for her to speak, moving against his as she did so.

"You may touch me."

With a groan, he wrapped his arms around her, feeling her soft, warm curves fill his hands as he moved them up and down her sides. Her breasts flattened against his vest as she slid one hand into his hair, tugging hard enough to make him moan again while they kissed.

And kissed.

And kissed.

His cock rubbed against her through the fabric of their pants, and she panted slightly as she broke from the kiss again.

"My breasts," she murmured, and that was all she had to say.

Freddy was more than happy to fill his hands with the plush mounds, running his fingers over her nipples, before using his mouth and sucking each taut bud between his lips. She kept her grip in his hair, her other hand running over the short hairs of his neck.

"Good boy. Just like that."

Freddy worshiped her breasts, lavishing attention on them, using his mouth, tongue, and fingers to stroke the soft mounds and hard nipples. He was so involved, at first, he almost didn't notice when she tugged his hair. She had to tug a second time, pulling him away from his homage.

"Pants."

No need to tell him twice. He dropped to his knees and helped her roll off the tight pants. They came away easily once they reached her knees since the lower half of the legs were so loose. She wasn't wearing any underwear, and Freddy's mouth watered. He was at exactly the right height to press his mouth to her gorgeous pussy since they'd left her heels on.

Glancing up at her, he tried to convey his wishes with his eyes.

***

CAMILLE

Lord, she loved a man who loved to eat pussy, and Freddy was definitely one of them. Considering the attention he'd already lavished on her breasts, making them swollen and achy in the best way, she'd be a fool not to accept the invitation in his gaze.

And there was a Queening Throne.

"Go lie down at the throne." The order came out as a seductive purr, a voice she barely recognized because it had been so long since she'd used that tone. Fuck, it felt good. Freddy scampered to obey, still fully dressed.

Hm. That wasn't going to do at all.

"Wait."

He froze, just as he had been about to get down on the padded area in front of the throne.

"Pants off."

Without hesitation, without turning, Freddy undid his pants and let them drop, not questioning why she wanted him to keep his top on. The vest was too delicious to take it off yet, though she'd have to make sure he was breathing the way he was supposed to. With the pants off, his cock and ass played peekaboo with the bottom of his shirt, giving her a little peep show as he got into position. The front sides of his shirt fell open as he laid on his back, framing his erection as though it was a present for her.

A nice, big, thick present.

Stepping over him with one leg, she sat down on the throne. The whole setup was meant to be comfortable for him, with a headrest that should put him at a good height to pleasure her. It was even adjustable, she realized after a moment, though his current position was just about perfect, so she didn't mess around with the possibilities.

Sitting on her throne, she stretched out one leg to run her heel along the length of his cock as his tongue pressed into her pussy. His hips and dick jerked at the touch, and she felt the vibrations of his moan against her sensitive lips. The sensation was exquisite.

Letting herself fully relax on the throne, Camille used her heels to tease him a little, but mostly she enjoyed having her pussy worshiped by a fervent devotee to the craft. Long, slow licks. Fast, sweeping curves. He did it all, driving her arousal, her need, higher and higher until she was gripping the armrests and crying out with ecstasy... and even then, he didn't stop.

Camille rode his face, his tongue, letting go of her worries and cares, letting her passion soar. Sucking her clit into his mouth, the tiny nub vibrated between his lips, and she ground down on the chair, shuddering with the sensations swelling through her.

"Fuck!" Wave after wave of ecstasy crashed over her until she was practically insensible. She leaned forward, slapping her hand down on his vest. "Stop!"

Immediately he stopped, his hot breath panting against her pussy, and she shuddered as she drew herself back together. It felt as if she'd splintered apart into a million pieces, leaving her shaky and breathless. There was a long moment of silence before he broke it.

"Mistress?" The concern in his voice helped her regain her footing. She needed to make sure he knew he hadn't done anything wrong. If anything, he'd done everything too right. So right, she hadn't been able to handle the glut of pleasure.

"Very good boy, Freddy," she said, leaning down to pat his rigid cock. It bounced beneath her hand, and she stroked her nail against the thick vein on the bottom, making him jerk. She felt, as much as heard, his moan as more heat wafted over her pussy lips on his exhale. "You deserve a reward."

Pushing herself to her feet, she was pleased to see him looking up at her, his lips glazed with her passion, his eyes hot with desire. He wouldn't have stopped if she hadn't stopped him. Something to keep in mind for later. Freddy was *very* eager to please.

"Let's go to the bedroom. And I want to get you undressed."

"Yes, Mistress."

FREDDY

With his hands cuffed to the bed, he couldn't touch Mistress Camille the way he wanted to, but he wasn't going to complain, not with the way she was looking at him. Straddling his thighs, she slid a condom over the length of his dick. Once she'd gotten his vest and shirt off, she'd wanted him tied to the bed, and he had been happy to oblige.

His body was humming happily with pent-up arousal, though he was a little worried he might not be able to last as long as Mistress Camille would like him to.

"You have a very nice cock," she murmured, gripping the base with one hand while the other tugged on his balls, hard enough to make him gasp with pain, even as pleasure curled through him. "I'm going to enjoy riding it."

Freddy's only response was a whimper as she squeezed his balls hard enough to bring tears to his eyes. Despite the pain, he knew she was being careful, gentle, none of it going beyond what he could handle. Cock-and-ball torture could be agonizing, which was not his thing, but it could also be a counterpoint of erotic pain to erotic bliss, and that was something he *did* enjoy when done right.

She was doing it *very right*.

His cock bobbed, the sheathed length tapping against his body as she tugged and twisted, just hard enough to make him writhe and cry out without pushing him over the edge, and he'd need to say his safe word. The entire time, he could feel her gaze on him. Watching him. Gauging his level of pain and pleasure. All of her attention focused on him as she tormented him.

Which turned him on even more.

That focus, that attention to him, was what he needed. What he craved. Especially because it was *her*.

"Does that hurt, Freddy?" Her voice was a soothing croon, as if she was asking him if it felt good instead of the other way around.

"Yes, Mistress. *Fuck*." She'd pressed a hard finger right into his perineum. Freddy writhed again, caught somewhere between heaven and hell, where pain melded with pleasure until he couldn't tell which was which.

"You're going to take the pain for me, aren't you?"

"Yes, Mistress." His back arched as her finger relented, rubbed, then pressed in hard again, rocking against his body while she tormented his delicate sack. Rolling his balls between her fingers, she squeezed hard, closing her fist and crushing them just enough to make him pant for breath as hot pain wound through his throbbing arousal.

"Such a good boy."

She squeezed again, another pulse of pain amid the pleasure of her praise. Freddy gasped for breath as she neared his breaking point. Releasing him, her finger moved away from the delicate area between his balls and his anus, her grip releasing the tight squeeze on his balls… then she straddled him.

Fuck, yes please.

Thighs braced on either side of his body, her breasts hung in front of her as she positioned herself over his cock. Her wet heat touching the tip, she sighed with pleasure as she pressed down, her body opening for his rock-hard dick. They both moaned as she lowered herself onto him, his hips thrusting upward of their own accord to impale her.

Bound as he was, there was nothing he could do as she took her time with him. She was riding him for *her* pleasure, lifting herself up, sliding back down his shaft, grinding her pussy against his body with abandon. Her soft moans and sighs of pleasure rippled through him as he grit his teeth against his own impulses, letting her take him as she pleased. Giving her everything she wanted. Trying to make it last.

Her hands moved up his body, reaching his nipples and pinching them. Freddy arched beneath her with a cry, his hips jerking upward, cock thrusting into her.

"Oh, yes…" She breathed out the words, pinching his tender nipples again, making him writhe for her. "Harder, Freddy. I want you to come for me."

That was all the permission he needed. Freddy surged beneath her, his hands gripping the chains binding the restraints around his wrists, making the headboard creak as he moved beneath her. She rode him, and he thrust upward, meeting her body every time she fell atop him.

Her breasts bounced and swayed with the motion as they moved together, their moans and panting breaths joining in a hot symphony. He could feel her getting closer, and despite her command, he was determined to wait until she had found her bliss again before reaching his own climax.

Thankfully, he didn't have to wait long.

Mistress Camille shuddered, coming down hard and rubbing her pussy against him, eyes half-lidded as her muscles clenched around him. Freddy thrust again, though he didn't have much room to move, then groaned as she cried out, her movements becoming jerkier as her pleasure took over.

His tortured balls tightened, tingling. He cried out her name, his cock pulsing with every spurt of pleasure that emptied into the condom. The sheer ecstatic bliss left him trembling and limp beneath her.

Leaning forward, she pressed her face into the curve of his neck, snuggling with his bound body, her soft breasts flattened against his chest, and made a happy humming noise. Smile curving his lips, Freddy rested his cheek against her forehead, closing his eyes to enjoy the moment.

She'd ridden him to completion and was now using him like a teddy bear, though his cock was still embedded inside her and slowly softening.

It was a perfect moment. He wished it could last forever.

14

———————

Maybe it was a little weird to come in on the weekend and do more work at his second place of work, but sometimes, Freddy needed to get out of his apartment and be around people. Not necessarily interact with them but just be around them. It didn't hurt that free food was provided, along with drinks when he was done if he so desired.

That made the bar at Marquis one of his favorite places to be on a Saturday morning. Sunday was usually too busy, but Saturdays had a nice busy hum of activity without becoming frenetic.

Today, it felt especially nice because it made him feel closer to Mistress Camille. As much as he would have liked to have slept over with her, they'd reluctantly parted ways and gone home after their scene.

Logically, he knew it was better that way.

Emotionally, he didn't give a fuck. He had wanted to spend the night cuddled up next to her again.

Which was probably why he was so focused on the Alexander case this morning, going through the prenup with a fine-toothed comb *again*. He wanted to make sure he didn't bend on anything Brittany really needed just to get things over with faster. The fact he would be working with her wishes to get things moving along made him feel less guilty, but he wanted to make sure he didn't let her give away the farm just so he and Camille were no longer adversaries.

"Want another coke?" Shane, one of Marquis' main bartenders, sidled up to Freddy on the other side of the bar. Of medium height with broad shoulders, he had a salt-and-pepper beard, but since he shaved his head, no one knew whether his hair would match. Freddy was pretty sure the man and his wife were both in the scene, though they weren't members of either Stronghold or Marquis.

Some people preferred to keep things private, which was fine. Freddy just got total Dom vibes from him. Some of the subs treated him almost as a Daddy figure.

"Yes, please." The caffeine was necessary, and he didn't like coffee, almost sacrilege for a lawyer. Sure, he'd drink it if that was the only way to get the caffeine he needed, but he preferred just about any other drink.

"So, you and Mistress Camille?" Shane flashed him a grin when Freddy laughed.

The bartender always had his finger firmly on the pulse of club gossip since a lot of the members liked to frequent the bar. Some of them outright talked to him about what was going on and others just forgot to speak quietly enough to keep their business to themselves. It didn't surprise Freddy that Shane knew what was going on.

"Sort of. We're working opposite each other in a rather contentious divorce, but as soon as that's over..." He let his voice trail off suggestively.

"That's great." Shane's smile brightened. "I'm really happy for you man."

Simple words, but they made Freddy preen. There was just something about the way Shane said them that reeked of those Dom vibes Freddy sensed. It was also acknowledgement that Shane thought they'd be good together, and he valued the other man's opinion.

"Thanks. I'll be really happy for me, too, once it can actually happen."

That made Shane chuckle. Then he looked up, past Freddy, and his expression flickered. Freddy twisted in his seat to see what—or who—he was looking at.

Zach, another member of Stronghold and Marquis, was stomping toward the bar with a scowl. His dark eyes lifted to meet Freddy's gaze, and he faltered, some of the storm in his expression clearing and leaving behind what looked like sadness.

Uh oh.

That didn't look good, and Freddy had a suspicion about why. Zach was one of the more complicated members of the club. He came to the Stronghold Doms class with a friend, now very much an ex-friend, who hadn't known much about kink to begin with. While he'd been trained as a Dom, identified as a Dom, and also identified as straight, the relationship he'd ended up falling into was with Kincaid—another Dom and a man.

They were a really great couple, but there were some cracks in the relationship. For one, Zach was a sadist and had a need to top, neither need being something that Kincaid could help him fulfill. So, sometimes Zach scened platonically with submissives. Kincaid sometimes joined him for those and met his needs that way. The difficulty with that was his favorite partner seemed to be a woman named Amy, who was engaged to someone else. Theoretically that would make her the perfect platonic partner, but from some of the looks Freddy had seen Zach give her, he wasn't sure Zach's feelings were entirely platonic.

Add to the fact that Zach wasn't 'out' outside of the club, and things got even more difficult. Kincaid had stayed in Maryland for the holidays while Zach went to visit his family on his own. They didn't know he had a boyfriend, even though he and Kincaid had been together since the prior Christmas—though they'd been very new at that point and the separate holiday hadn't been an issue.

"Oh, hey," Zach said, giving Freddy a wan smile. He didn't look like himself today. Rather than being neatly shaved and combed, his facial hair was looking scraggly and rough, and when he unzipped his coat, Freddy could see a stain on the shirt he was wearing.

He'd never seen Zach anything less than perfectly turned out.

"Hey, how ya doing?" Freddy asked cautiously. He and Zach weren't particularly close, though they did talk sometimes. Zach had come to him a few times for advice about bottoming, specifically about being a bottom to another man.

"I've had better days." Zach sighed heavily and took the barstool next to Freddy, scanning the bottles behind the bar before he focused on the beer taps. "Something on tap, please, Shane."

Nodding, Shane moved to grab a glass.

"Everything okay with you and Kincaid?"

"Not really." Zach sighed, scrubbing his hand across his face and through his dark hair. He glanced down at his shirt and made a face. Presumably, he'd just noticed the stain but seemed to shake it off rather than get upset, which meant he had other things more important to be upset about. "He's not issuing any ultimatums, but I feel like they're coming. He's tired of being in the closet with me, and I can't blame him, but I'm not sure I'm ready to come out yet."

Wow, okay, so they were getting right into it. Freddy made an encouraging noise, not sure what to say. It seemed as if Zach needed to vent more than a real immediate response.

"He's been patient. He's been more than patient, but... fuck. I don't know. We've been together for a year, but I'm still not sure this is what I want for the rest of my life, you know? And why throw my family into turmoil when next year I might be in a regular relationship with a woman?"

Freddy winced.

"Did you tell Kincaid that you feel like your relationship isn't regular?"

"What? No, fuck... I didn't mean it like that..." Zach groaned and banged his head on the bar in front of him, not lifting it until Shane silently slid his beer glass to him. "Except I guess I kind of did or else I wouldn't have said it, right?"

"It's okay to struggle. Society has convinced us that heterosexuality is 'regular.' White people are 'regular.' Men in charge is 'regular.' That's how we're conditioned."

"Yeah, but I like to think of myself as evolved." Making a face, he picked up the beer and took a sip rather than chugging it like Freddy had half-expected. "I guess I haven't evolved as much as I like to think."

"We're all works in progress." Freddy patted his shoulder sympathetically. "As long as you're doing the best you can and recognizing where you can improve, that's all you can do."

"Well, that makes me feel a little better." Zach's smile was half-hearted. "But seriously, if that's how my brain is wired, how is there any hope for Kincaid and me? And do I want to spend the rest of my life getting some of my needs met by scening with people I'm not in a relationship with? He says it's fine, but I feel like I'm cheating."

Poor Zach. He didn't say it outright, but it was clear he'd been raised with certain ideas of how his life was supposed to go, what it was supposed to look like, and right now, he was struggling with reality versus the dream. Freddy understood. He'd been raised much the same way, though his parents had been one hundred percent accepting when he'd come out as bisexual. That made things a lot easier, even if they'd been a little confused about what it entailed and had asked a lot of uncomfortable questions.

"So, your family wouldn't be supportive if you brought Kincaid home?" he asked. "If you feel comfortable talking about this. You don't have to."

Zach gave him a wry smile.

"That's awfully nice of you to say after I just word vomited all my issues all over you," he joked, taking another sip of his beer. Across from them, Shane started wiping down the gleaming surface of the bar, which made Freddy smirk. "I don't know. I know my sister wouldn't care. My mom would try, but I have no idea how my dad would react. I'm pretty sure my grandparents on my dad's side would take it really badly, but we hardly see them because they're pretty awful to everyone."

"That's hard. My parents were always pretty outspoken about their beliefs, so I was pretty sure it would be fine, but I still had the fear maybe I was wrong. Like, maybe they were only accepting of *other* people's kids being part of the rainbow alphabet, but they wouldn't be of me."

"Yeah, that's how I feel about my mom. My dad has never talked about it much, and I think he's more of the 'don't ask, don't tell' variety, but I don't want to bring Kincaid home to meet them, then have to act like we're just friends because it'll make my dad uncomfortable... but I also don't want to make my dad uncomfortable, especially in his own home."

"Invite them out here?" Shane suggested.

"Maybe if I hadn't just had yet another fight with Kincaid about it." Zach's shoulders slumped. "It's like a vicious circle. I don't tell my parents about him because I'm afraid the relationship will fall apart, and I'll have told them for nothing, but my relationship is falling apart because I won't tell my parents about him."

"Sounds like the easiest solution might be to tell your parents about him," Freddy said gently. "Telling them about part of yourself doesn't equate to 'nothing,' even if the relationship doesn't last."

"It might for me. I can't see myself with another guy. My interest in men begins and ends with Kincaid. Besides, if it does go badly, he'll feel like it's his fault for pushing me. I might even resent him. But if it goes well, he might resent me because we've been fighting about it for so long. There's no way for me to win here." The words were filled with bitterness.

Freddy's heart hurt because he thought the two of them were a good, if complicated, couple. He was rooting for them, but this wasn't going to be something easy to get past.

"I guess it comes down to what you really want. If you want to keep your relationship with Kincaid, you'll have to tell your parents, eventually," Freddy said gently, rubbing Zach's shoulders.

"I know." Unfortunately, Zach sounded more miserable than determined. "But what if I tell them and I lose him, anyway?"

Yeah. Freddy didn't have a good answer for that one. He looked across the bar at Shane, but the bartender seemed to be at a bit of a loss as well.

Sometimes, there were no easy solutions.

15

———————

Camille

"So, how was last night?" Julie's smile matched that of the Cheshire Cat, smug and completely pleased with herself.

"Oh, are *you* who Freddy was with last night?" Olivia asked before Camille could respond, her eyebrows rising on her forehead with interest as she opened her napkin and settled it on her lap. "I was wondering when I saw that he'd reserved a room at the last minute."

Julie's eyes lit up, and she sat up straighter.

"You two got a room?!" Sheer delight colored her voice, and Camille sighed. Julie was going to be a pain in the butt to deal with, taking all the credit for matching Camille with Freddy.

"Yes, one of the rooms had a cancellation, so I had Freddy reserve it for us." She gave Julie a look. "Since we agreed that last night would be a onetime thing, for now, we wanted to make the most of it. No, we did not stay overnight."

Although she had considered it, but in the end, the need to keep some boundaries—and the lack of clothing for her to change into the next morning—had won out. She knew it had been the right decision, even if she'd regretted it almost the second she got home and had to get into her lonely, empty bed. But it had been the right choice.

At least Julie had messaged her this morning to distract her from her regrets, asking if she wanted to meet her and Olivia for lunch at Murphy's Meals to make up for being ditched the night before. Even if being ditched had come with some very nice benefits, thanks to Freddy being on hand to keep her company. If she hadn't heard Julie's distress when her cousin called, she would have suspected it being a setup.

"Well, I hope it was a good night," Julie replied smugly in a tone, indicating she was completely sure it had been. Camille wasn't about to malign Freddy by lying and saying it hadn't been.

Still.

"It would have been better if we didn't still have our clients hanging over our heads," she said with a sigh. At Olivia's confused look, she explained that she and Freddy were representing two opposing sides in a contested divorce, though she didn't give names or go into details. Still, Olivia was astute enough to pick up on the fact that Camille's client was a jerk, the same way Julie had. That or maybe she just assumed due to knowing Freddy and his firm's reputation that he was on the side of the good and the righteous.

"So, basically, as soon as you're done with your douchebag client, you can date Freddy?"

Julie choked on her drink at Olivia's blunt summation.

"As soon as the divorce has been resolved, I can date Freddy," Camille replied smoothly. "But I wouldn't want anyone to think that I'm not giving my client my best services because of who I'm dating."

"Are you worried you might end up on opposite sides again?" Olivia asked, leaning forward on one of her elbows while she stirred her drink with the straw. It looked like her brain was whirring with possible hazards for Camille and Freddy, something Camille had already thought about a lot.

"No, because if we start seeing each other and end up across from each other again, I can let the partners know it's a conflict of interest, and they'll be able to make a decision based on an established relationship. That's a little different from dating or starting a relationship while we're working at cross purposes." A bit of guilt trickled through her. Last night was not something she should have done.

On the other hand, it made her more determined to do her job to the best of her ability. Possibly even better than she would have otherwise since her personal dislike of Mr. Alexander made it very hard to want to give him her best. So, really, he might be better off this way.

"Yeah, I can see that," Olivia said thoughtfully.

Camille had the oddest feeling she'd just passed some sort of test. Well, maybe she had. Julie had mentioned Olivia was very protective of all the submissives in the club.

Which was why she didn't let the little shot of jealousy that trickled through her affect her too much. As much as she wanted to say another Domme didn't need to worry about her Freddy, the truth was he wasn't her Freddy yet. In some ways, Olivia had an even better claim to watch out for him than Camille did. That might grind her gears right now, but she was glad he had a good friend looking out for him. Mostly. She would just have to look forward to the day when she was the one with the right to look out for him.

"Well, I knew you two would hit it off." Julie's smugness continued unabated. "Though I didn't expect the rival clients wrinkle, but at least it's a temporary situation."

"Yeah, it could be worse. By the way, how did things go with your cousin last night?" Camille didn't want to talk about her and Freddy. Talking more about what they *weren't* doing would only depress her. Although the topic of conversation she'd chosen wasn't really an upper either, but she was curious.

Julie's face darkened with anger.

"We got her stuff moved out, but I thought I was going to have to beat her boyfriend's ass before Connor stepped in. Misogynistic asshole... her ex, not Connor... didn't have the intellect to realize I could have killed him where he stood, but he sees a big man and suddenly, he's making himself scarce."

"What was Connor doing there?" Olivia seemed as confused as Camille felt.

"Oh, he and Sandra work together," Julie replied. "Sandra's not kinky, but she knows I am and knows about Marquis and Stronghold. Somehow, kink came up at work one day, then she told him about the clubs, and that's how he ended up here."

Olivia blinked. "I had no idea."

Camille got the feeling the Domme wasn't usually in the position of not knowing.

Their food arrived, derailing the conversation, and when it picked back up, it was about some of the behind-the-scenes stuff at Marquis and Stronghold. Julie and Olivia were invested, and Camille was interested. With the holidays over, the next big event would be Valentine's Day. Not something Camille had celebrated in a long time, but she couldn't help but think about Freddy now…

She could only hope all the papers would be signed before then, and she could have a Valentine for the first time in years. Not that she'd particularly cared the years she hadn't had one, but right now, she wanted any excuse to spend time with Freddy.

"Oh, look at her, getting all day dreamy about Valentine's Day," Julie smirked.

"Hey, do you think your secret admirer will reveal themselves on Valentine's Day?" Camille asked, deflecting the best way she knew how. Besides, it was a legitimate question.

To her surprise, Julie made a face.

"I'm not sure I want to know."

"How can you not want to know?" Olivia stared at her, which almost made Camille laugh. She might not know Olivia well yet, but she wasn't surprised she hated the idea of not knowing something.

"Knowing might ruin it." Julie shrugged. "Right now, it's a fun mystery, but part of it is not knowing who it is. What happens if it's someone I'm not attracted to or not interested in? Then I'll have to feel bad. I know it's coming eventually, and while best-case scenario it's someone I might have chemistry with, I honestly can't think of a submissive at the club whom I would *hope* it is. So, I'd rather not know."

Camille blinked. Okay, she could see that since Julie did know all the submissives at the clubs.

"Do you think your mind might change about some of them if you knew they were your admirer?" she asked.

Julie shrugged. "It's possible."

"I was thinking it might be Mark," Olivia said, watching Julie closely. "You scene with him on a fairly regular basis."

"It's definitely not Mark," Julie said, shaking her head. "He has a crush on a woman at his gym, but he's too shy to approach her and too worried she might not want anything to do with a submissive like him. I'm working on helping him with his confidence. He's a delightful sub, but there's no spark." She said it rather wistfully.

Camille felt bad that she'd been so caught up with her own life and with Freddy, she hadn't noticed her friend was yearning for a little romance, too.

"Well, maybe there'll be a spark when you find out who they are. If not... there are new members coming in soon, and you'll get to meet all the single ones first," Olivia pointed out with a small laugh.

"There is that." The hint of wistfulness was gone, and Julie was back to her usual, brisk self. "In the meantime, I enjoy having a little romance without having to actually do anything about it. Hopefully, my admirer understands there's no obligation on my part to reciprocate, but I'll cross that bridge when I come to it."

"I'm going to hold out hope for you that when they do reveal themselves, there's a spark," Camille announced, laughing when Julie shot her a wry look.

"You do that. You know, it's nice to see you being more yourself."

"It's nice feeling more like myself."

"How's the job hunt going?"

"I've gotten a few phone interviews scheduled, so we'll see how those go." Camille shrugged. "I'm hopeful, and I'm sure as hell not giving up. If I don't find a new firm... maybe I'll strike out on my own."

That was an absolutely terrifying thought and not what she actually wanted to do, but she was starting to feel as though there was no way she could stay at Donaldson, not for any amount of money. Even if it meant having to move her mom to a different home. Her mom would want her to be happy.

She wasn't sure how she'd deal with the guilt if it came to that, but she knew her mom would be mad at her for sacrificing her own needs. She might not be able to say so right now or be able to participate in the decision-making process, but Camille knew if her mom was capable, she would have already told Camille to get out of Donaldson and to move her. That it wasn't worth it.

"I bet you'd do great. Have you asked Freddy about openings at his firm?"

"No, and I'm not going to."

Julie gave her a look as if she thought Camille was cutting off her nose to spite her face, but Camille ignored her. Beginning a romantic relationship and starting to work at the same firm sounded like a recipe for disaster. Workplace romances were hard enough to navigate when it was between long-time workers.

She didn't want to get a new job only to find herself at the center of relationship drama and possibly out of both at the same time. Maybe she was playing it safe, but there was nothing wrong with that.

"So, I think I'm going to propose to Luke on Valentine's Day," Olivia said, successfully dropping a conversational bomb and diverting all attention to her.

Camille wasn't sure if she'd done it to help Camille out or just because she'd been dying to share the news, but either way, she was grateful.

16

———————

Camille

"Mr. Alexander." Camille glared at the man from across her desk. "You are not listening to me. No, I cannot force your wife to show up for meetings. She has handed all control over to her lawyer. The fact that he is willing to meet with us at all is a major concession."

"But I don't want to meet with him. I need to see *her*." Nicholas Alexander III was looking more like a sulky boy, pouting at her from his chair. "You're my lawyer. You're supposed to get me what I want."

"I'm your lawyer. I'm supposed to help you through your contention of the divorce and to clarify the sections in the prenup that are unclear," she snapped back. "That does not mean you'll get everything you want."

She was down to her last nerve with him. Blinking at her as if shocked she would dare speak to him in such a manner, he stared like he was seeing something different than before.

"So, you can't get her in for a meeting?"

"No."

"Well, then, I don't want to give her *anything*. If she wants me to agree to splitting the assets I earned after we got married, then she's going to have to come here and say that to my face." His face was getting very red, and Camille doubted seeing it would do anything but convince his ex that she was making the right move.

"I don't think she's going to agree with that. We can move things along much faster—"

"I don't want to move things along faster. If she's going to leave me, she's going to have to fight for it." He slammed his fist down on the chair, and Camille throttled the urge to reach across the desk and slap some sense into him. "She doesn't get to be free of me that easily!"

"Then we will end up in court, where you will lose everything she's currently willing to concede. She will still leave you, and she might even do so with some of your company's shares. I'm not going to be a party to dragging this out just to massage your ego or whatever it is that's causing you such distress. Either we meet with Mr. Johan again and figure out an agreement that benefits you, or I'm going to tell him we're prepared to go to court, where you can potentially lose everything."

Mr. Alexander gaped like a fish, which would have been funny if she wasn't so damn frustrated with him. She couldn't enjoy his comical expression when all she wanted to do was throw him out the window.

"We'll see about that," he huffed, getting to his feet, glaring at her. "I am paying you to get me what I want."

"What you want isn't possible," she replied coldly.

"We'll see about that," he repeated, as if saying so would make it true. Turning on his heel, he stormed out of her office and slammed the door behind him. Camille sighed and rubbed her temples.

She had no doubt he was heading straight to the partners to complain, but she'd told him the truth. If he wasn't going to be cooperative, there was nothing she could do for him, and complaining to the partners wasn't going to change that.

However, she did send off an email to Freddy requesting another meeting and noting Mrs. Alexander's presence was requested as well. That way, she'd done her due diligence, and when he told her fuck no, she could pass that along. Which she was very glad for an hour later when Donaldson Junior appeared in her doorway, glaring at her.

He liked her even less than Donaldson Senior did, or at least wasn't as good at hiding his condescension.

"What's this I hear about you not giving Nicholas your best efforts?"

The accusatory note in his voice put her back up immediately. Rather than answering him immediately, she finished typing out the sentence in the brief she was working on before looking up and folding her hands in front of her on her desk.

"I don't know," she said evenly, meeting his gaze with every evidence of calm serenity. It always pissed him off more when she remained calm, no matter how he acted, and she was petty enough to keep her emotions under control for that reason alone. "I have no idea what Mr. Alexander told you, though I can tell you that I don't appreciate being presumed in the wrong when you haven't asked me anything about my discussion with him."

Junior glared at her before covering his expression and sauntering in, looking down his long nose at her. Rather than sitting down, he stood just behind the chairs on the other side of her desk, looming instead of putting himself on an equal level with her.

"Well, Camille, Mr. Alexander is very upset with the service he's receiving from you. Please, tell me how your discussion with him went, from your side." Derision dripped from his voice, making it clear he didn't think she had a single defense.

Little prick.

"Mr. Alexander wants meetings that include his wife, which is not something I am capable of providing him when she has no interest in attending any meetings with him. Her lawyer has been very clear that she will *not* be present and that he's been authorized to handle all the negotiations. The fact she's still willing to negotiate, when she has proof of him cheating, is a miracle and frankly, one that Mr. Alexander needs to appreciate more. However, I don't think his interest is in saving himself money. It's in torturing his wife by dragging the proceedings out." She raised an eyebrow at Junior, pretty sure he was aware of this.

He flushed, his gaze darting away. Yup. Guilty.

Clearing his throat, he reached up to adjust his tie.

"Be that as it may, it's our job to procure satisfactory results for our clients—" he started to say, but Camille cut him off.

"It's our job to procure satisfactory divorces," she corrected him. "As I said, Mr. Alexander is lucky his wife is willing to have her lawyer talk to us at all. She could easily insist on going straight to court, and she'd probably get everything, or almost everything, that's on the table. However, if you think I'm doing a poor job, I'm happy to hand over the negotiations to you. Despite the benefit of Mr. Alexander's billable hours, I'm not a miracle worker, and if he's not satisfied with my work, perhaps he would be happier if you handled things."

As she expected, Junior started to bluster. He knew it was a losing proposition as well as she did, and he didn't want to touch it with a ten-foot pole. Asshole.

"Just, do your best to make him happy," he finally said after what seemed like a whole minute of sputtering. Lifting his chin, he turned on his heel and hurried out the door, though he didn't slam it behind him the way Mr. Alexander had.

Whatever. At least they were both out of her hair now. Camille considered that a win.

Freddy

"You know there's no way Brittany is coming to any of the meetings, right?" Freddy asked. He hadn't been able to keep himself from calling Camille after he'd gotten home from work—officially off the clock—under the pretext of talking about the Alexanders.

Really, he just wanted to hear her voice, but it was a good excuse. And it gave him something to do while he heated up his dinner. Frozen chicken noodle soup. Yum. He had a tendency to make things in large batches to heat up later. Cooking for one was rather tedious.

Camille snorted.

"That was my cover-my-ass email, thanks to Mr. Alexander making a complete ass out of himself today. It's not that he doesn't care about the money, he does, but he cares way more that she's leaving him. I get the feeling if he'd been the one to initiate the proceedings, he wouldn't be bothering with any of this."

The sheer exasperation in her voice set off all his subbie instincts. This conversation would be so much better in person, preferably on the couch with her feet on his lap so he could massage them. If only.

"All Brittany wants is for him to leave her alone." Freddy shook his head. "I'm pretty sure she's planning on moving as soon as she can to make sure she never runs into him again."

"That's probably smart. Her being the one to leave him has been a hit to his pride or his ego or whatever, and that's never good with an entitled jerk."

She sounded incredibly tired, and Freddy's fingers itched. He wanted to be able to help.

"I tried to offload him on one of the partners today when he came in to chew me out for not keeping Mr. Alexander happy, but no go. It was worth a shot. I seriously need a new job."

Freddy facepalmed.

"Actually, I forgot to tell you—"

"Not at your firm," she interrupted him. If her voice had been anything but teasing, that might have hurt, but as it was, he could tell there was no malice in her words. "I don't want to mix a new relationship with a new job. But if you hear of any openings anywhere else..."

His heart was buoyed that she'd referred to them as a 'new relationship.' He was incredibly pleased to be able to give her a lead.

"Actually, one of my firm's partners mentioned to me that she has a friend who asked her to keep an ear out for promising, experienced lawyers who might be interested in making a change. I'm not sure what firm her friend works at, but I can find out."

"Please do," Camille said fervently, sounding pleased. "That would be great. My patience with Donaldson is at an all-time low. I honestly don't know how I've been working there this long. It's like I've been in a fugue state or something."

"I bet it wasn't as bad when you first started," Freddy replied. He'd seen it happen a lot, not just in abusive relationships, but in toxic workplaces. "Things tend to get worse as you get used to it, and inertia can make it hard to get out, and the next thing you know, you turned around and you're the frog in boiling water."

"The what?"

He laughed at her scandalized question.

"You haven't heard that before? If you put a frog directly in a pot of boiling water, it jumps out immediately. But if you put it in cold water and slowly turn up the heat, it adjusts and doesn't realize it's in danger because it's a slow process."

There was a long moment of silence. Hopefully, he hadn't grossed her out, but it was a true fact and a good metaphor for a lot of situations.

"You know, I think that's exactly it," she said thoughtfully. "Because it wasn't this bad at first. They were never the best employers, but they've gotten steadily worse, month by month, and they sure as hell didn't treat me this way when I first started working there. I got used to more and more bullshit from them, and it was so normal, it's as though I didn't notice it anymore."

"I'll talk to Zoey tomorrow and get her friend's firm's name," he promised.

"Thank you." He couldn't see her smile, but he could feel it.

"Of course." He chuckled. "Maybe you'll have a new job before the Alexanders are done, and you can pass them off."

She laughed.

"One can only hope. The way Mr. Alexander is dragging this out, there might be more truth to that than I would wish. I'm so done with his bullshit, though, so I'm going to push for him to wrap things up. And not just because of… us." She said the last sentence a little hesitantly.

"Trust me, I don't blame you, and I would never think that you would undermine a client professionally because of a personal relationship," he reassured her. "You're too ethical and too good a lawyer for that. There really isn't much you can do for him, and honestly, I'm going to be pushing to move things along faster. At this point, I think it'll be easier to hash things out in court than dealing with him directly, though I hate to do that to you."

"Do what you need to do. I'm going to try to get him to sign, though. Then if we go to court to fight about it, we go to court. If he annoys the judge as much as he annoys me, there's a chance they'll close things out even faster."

Wasn't that the truth?

"That would be nice." He cleared his throat, making a completely awkward segue, but they'd exhausted this topic, which wasn't much fun to talk about, and he wasn't ready to get off the phone with her yet. "How's your mom doing?"

"She's good, thank you." Camille's voice warmed, changing to a completely different tone with the new topic. "I'm going to see her tomorrow."

They ended up talking for an hour, not about the Alexanders or work, but about their lives. He was perfectly happy to sit and listen to her talk about her mom and some of her childhood, and he shared some of his stories as well.

Hearing about how she'd decided to become a lawyer resonated with him. She wanted to help people, which he could definitely see as part of her personality. Working for Donaldson must be killing her. First thing tomorrow, he was going to talk to Zoey and get things started for Camille—any firm would be lucky to have her.

It was infuriating that the partners at Donaldson either didn't recognize her worth or, worse, realized what she was worth and handed her a bunch of crap, anyway. By the time Freddy went to bed, his mind was swirling with the possibilities.

Did he want to be Mistress Camille's white knight in shining armor, coming to her rescue?

Yes. Yes, he did.

17

Mr. Alexander finally got his wish—Mrs. Alexander showed up to sign the agreement that Camille and Freddy had hashed out with input from Mr. Alexander. As Freddy had told her, Mrs. Alexander had been perfectly happy to relinquish rights to Mr. Alexander's company. She wanted nothing to do with it or him. She just wanted out.

He'd finally agreed to things as long as they both signed in person together, so he could watch her do it.

At some point in the time since they'd been separated, Mrs. Alexander had gotten her backbone. She met his gaze evenly, perfectly serene, no matter how hard he glared at her. If he wasn't Camille's client, she would have been amused. Thankfully, he kept things civil without her having to come down on him. It was as if he'd finally realized he'd lost.

When everything was done, Mrs. Alexander and Freddy got to their feet. Mr. Alexander sat next to Camille, still pouting, as she got to her feet as well. She pushed away the urge to kick him. If his momma never taught him manners, it wasn't her job to take up the slack.

For a moment, it looked like Mrs. Alexander was going to say something, then she shook her head and turned her back. Maybe it was Camille's imagination, but it looked like the woman's steps were lighter and her head higher than when she'd come in.

"Thank you very much," Freddy said, giving Camille a head nod. He didn't offer the same courtesy to Mr. Alexander, not that it mattered. The man was sitting with his arms crossed, glaring at the wall as if it had personally offended him. "Have a good rest of the day."

"Thank you, you, too." She couldn't help watching as he left, sighing inwardly. It felt like any lightness in the room was sucked out the door with him, leaving her with a pouty manchild.

"I shouldn't have signed that," Mr. Alexander grumbled, shaking his head. "I can't believe I let you talk me into signing."

"I 'talked you into it' because it was the best possible option," Camille replied, not bothering to sit down as she gathered her papers. "You get to keep your company's shares, as you wanted, and you're only paying half of what you might have had to out of your current assets, which was a major concession. If you'd dragged it out further, we would have ended up in front of a judge, and you could have lost on both the shares and the payments."

He huffed, but apparently didn't have anything further to say. Thank goodness.

"Okay then, I'll be in touch. It's been nice working with you, Mr. Alexander. If you have any further questions, you can email or call me, as always." She pasted a smile on her face as she lied through her teeth. He huffed again, and she retreated.

Chances were, as soon as he'd had a few minutes to think, he was going to be off to complain to the partners. However, there was nothing to be done unless they flat-out lied to him about what they might be able to do for him... in which case she was going to hand over everything to them and wash her hands of it. No matter what they said. Even if she had to quit.

She'd already had a promising phone interview with Everly Murdoch from Murdoch Family Solutions, and she was meeting with her next week for an in-person interview. While she couldn't be sure she would get the job, she had another phone interview with a different firm tomorrow and two others that had emailed her back. All of them had flat-out told her they didn't need references from her current firm. They were aware of her and her work and didn't trust what any of the Donaldson partners might say about her. She could have cried with relief.

So, that was one small upside to Donaldson's reputation. She hadn't realized they were well-known for taking promising lawyers and either grinding them into dust or turning them into the same kind of 'gives a bad name to lawyers' practitioners as the senior partners.

She hadn't been back at her desk for ten minutes before her phone rang.

"Hello?"

"Camille, what's this about you forcing Nicholas to sign an agreement he didn't want?" Donaldson Senior sounded upset but not accusatory, thankfully. Unlike his son, he knew how unlikely it was Mr. Alexander's accusations were untrue. Still, she had to roll her eyes.

Since Junior hadn't gotten him what he wanted the last time, Mr. Alexander had decided to go running to Daddy.

Straightening, Camille pushed her shoulders back. It was time to end this.

***

F̲R̲E̲D̲D̲Y̲

"How does it feel to be a free woman?"

"Like I could walk on air." Brittany grinned, then threw her arms around Freddy, causing several passersby to give them odd glances. "I can't thank you enough. I would have conceded on everything to him if it hadn't been for you, but I'm so glad I didn't."

Despite the biting cold of the winter air, Freddy felt warm from the inside out. This was exactly why he did what he did.

"You deserved everything you got and more, just for putting up with him for so long," he said baldly.

"You're right," she admitted, one of the first times she'd done so instead of prevaricating. She looked up at the big office building looming over them. "I feel kind of bad for his lawyer, though. She seemed nice."

"She's doing her job, and sometimes, asshole clients are part of the job. You, however, have been a delight."

"You have been, too." She tightened her hold on him again before releasing him and stepping back. "I really can't thank you enough."

"You can thank me by following through with your plan—move to New York to be closer to your parents and find happiness," he said gently. "That's all I want for you."

"You're a great guy, Freddy. I hope you find some happiness too."

"Oh, I will." He didn't think about the effect of his words before they slipped out.

"Oh?" Brittany's eyes lit up with interest. "Have you met someone?"

Freddy tended to be friendly with his clients, though he did his best to maintain necessary boundaries, but he had told Brittany he was single when he'd first started working on her case, when they were getting to know each other. She'd been at a loss, making conversation and bemoaning how hard it was to be single at her age. Since she was only a few years older than him, he'd sympathized and told her he was in the same boat.

"Yes, I have, though nothing official yet," he admitted.

"Oh, I'm so happy for you... That gives me hope."

"Good. You should have hope because you, Brittany Adams, are a catch." He deliberately used her maiden name, which she'd told him she planned to go back to.

"God, it feels good to hear myself called that again." Happy tears sparked in her eyes. Impulsively, she reached out and grabbed him for another hug, which he was happy to reciprocate. She'd really come into her own once the asshole had stopped harassing her, and he was so proud of the way she'd handled herself today. "Knowing I never have to see him again. I'm leaving this weekend for New York, and I'm not coming back except to visit my sister."

"Good for you. Though I hope you'll occasionally send me an email to let me know how you're doing." Freddy always said that to his clients. Some of them did, some of them didn't, but he loved hearing the good updates.

"Of course, I will. Thank you again." She released him for a second time, and he could tell this was the final time. "Have a good one."

"You, too." He waved, watching her get into her car and head off before walking to the corner to grab a taxi and head back to work.

It had been a good morning. Even better now that Camille would be free to see him... he hoped. There was always the chance Mr. Alexander might change his mind about today. He couldn't see her tolerating that, but on the other hand, she might not have a choice.

Restraining the impulse to call her and find out how she was doing, Freddy sent a text. After a few minutes of waiting for a response, he tucked his phone into his pocket with a sigh. She'd get back to him when she could.

CAMILLE

"If Mr. Alexander tries to claim that he was coerced or otherwise pressured, I will not only have to recuse myself from taking his case. I will stand in court and testify that he signed of his own free will." She'd even enjoy it. Though, of course, she didn't say that part out loud.

She was so sick of Alexander Assholery. It was a damn good deal. He'd gotten more than he'd deserved. Then the second he signed it over, he started having second thoughts, maligning her in the process.

"Now, Camille—"

"No." She shook her head. "I will not support his claim, not in any way. He and I had multiple long discussions about what he was and wasn't willing to concede. He ended up with quite a bit more than he would have if we'd had to take it to court for a judge to decide. Mrs. Alexander wanted to be done with him. All he wants to do is drag it out because he's upset that she dared to initiate the divorce. I am not going to perjure myself because of his pride. If he wants to fight it, you'll need to find someone else at the firm to represent him because I got him the best deal possible."

There was a long moment of silence, and Donaldson Senior seemed to be at a bit of a loss. He'd come in expecting her to bow down to whatever he said. Camille knew she would have never lied for Mr. Alexander, but she also knew that a year ago, heck even two months ago, she would have been much more circumspect in *how* she was speaking to Donaldson Sr. Not anymore. She didn't care enough to keep herself in line.

Behold my field of fucks, for it is barren.

"Well, I'll have to talk to Nicholas." Donaldson Sr. sighed. "If you say he made the decision on his own, then I have to believe you. He's been known to go back and forth on decisions. I know he can be a lot to handle, but he's a good guy."

"I'm sure he is."

Sure, he was, but she didn't contradict Donaldson Senior. People like him were always full of excuses for their friends, no matter how badly behaved. It didn't seem to occur to them that making those excuses only enabled the bad behavior.

Not my circus, not my monkeys.

She was very hopeful to never have to deal with Nicholas Alexander III again other than if he visited the partners here at the firm. He'd never done so before, so she couldn't see why that would change now.

"Okay, well. I'll go let him know that we won't be pursuing the matter further." Donaldson Senior paused as if waiting for her to refute him, then let out another sigh when she didn't. He hung up the phone without saying goodbye.

"Thank you for all your hard work, Camille," she muttered, setting the phone down on its cradle. "Thank you for putting up with my asshole friend, Camille, and doing your best for him, despite him being a complete asshole."

The urge to leave this job was growing stronger with every passing hour. At least it was almost the weekend. Sighing, she checked her cell phone on impulse, anything to distract her from her actual job, and was startled to see a text from Freddy.

Freddy: *Is the Alexander case considered over enough for us to go to Happy Hour? Or maybe dinner?*

Her sheer relief and sense of anticipation told her what her answer had to be.

Camille: *Absolutely. Let's do Happy Hour. Marquis at five?*

After dealing with Nicholas Alexander III and Jared Donaldson Sr, she deserved a Happy Hour drink. Besides, she'd cleared her afternoon in case things went sideways with the Alexanders, which meant she didn't have anything left to do.

Freddy: *See you there.*

It would be like a little celebration. Suddenly, feeling much better, Camille unlocked her computer. Since she'd cleared her afternoon, she now had a chance to get ahead on some of her caseload. Despite Donaldson's reputation for the kind of clientele they took on, they also had completely normal people who came without the entitlement, who were going through one of the hardest things in their lives and needed help.

Camille didn't mind helping them. Having the Alexanders finished was like having a massive weight lifted off her shoulders. Now she and Freddy were free to see each other socially. If the issue came up again, she could let the partners know, and they would decide whether she would continue representing that client.

Too bad she couldn't arrange that he'd be on the other side of the table every time she got a client like Mr. Alexander. That would be like a Get Out of Jail Free card, and she would use it so fast...

If wishes were fishes.

18

Freddy

Back at Marquis. It was a good thing he loved this place since in some ways it had become a home away from home. Heck, sometimes, it felt more like home than his apartment did. Freddy loved being around people, and his apartment didn't come with that. None of his neighbors were overly friendly or interested in doing more than the typical wave or nod as they passed each other in the hall. Friendly, but not friends.

Whereas at Marquis, he felt like he was constantly surrounded by friends.

Great until they kept interrupting his date with Mistress Camille. Shane had taken to glaring at people who saw Freddy and lit up, coming over to say hi. Thankfully, she didn't seem bothered by the interruptions.

"You sure are popular," she teased, taking a sip of her red wine. They'd gotten drinks and appetizers. He hadn't told her they probably weren't going to be charged for any of it, since it was Shane on duty. Freddy had seen Olivia pass through and whisper something to the bartender. He was surrounded by matchmakers and interruptions.

"I have a lot of friends, and the subs know I'm always here to talk with if they need someone." He shrugged. It didn't really mean he was popular, more that he was in demand, which was fine. He liked being there for them and making sure they were taken care of.

"What about when you need someone?" she asked, tilting her head at him curiously.

Freddy opened his mouth to answer... then closed it as something a little painful tightened in his chest. It wasn't that he didn't have a lot of friends. He did. Of course, he did. He always had. But who did he call when he needed someone?

"Lexie," he said after a moment. "She's a good friend." But not his best friend because he didn't have one—or, at least, she might be his best friend, but he wasn't hers, which was fine. He'd learned a long time ago to be happy with what he got. He hadn't had a best friend in high school or college, but he'd always had a lot of good friends. If he was in serious trouble, he always had someone he could call.

It wasn't quite the same as having a best friend but more than some people had, and he'd made up his mind to be grateful. Camille's question still pricked that old wound.

"Freddy's one of those people who gives and gives and has trouble asking for anything for himself," Shane said, sliding a plate of burrata Caprese salad in front of them. Freddy gave him a dark look, Shane easily ignored. "Any given weekend, you'll find him in here, listening to someone else's problems."

"I'm not always listening to someone's problems," he argued.

"No, but you're almost always here in case someone is having one."

"I just like working here. It's less lonely." Shane's words were striking a chord. There were other places he could go work where he would be less likely to be interrupted. But he liked being here, where his people were... where someone could find him if they needed him.

Crap.

Shane might be on to something.

"I see." Camille smiled sympathetically at him as she moved some of the burrata and tomato to her plate. The finely chopped basil decorating it stuck easily to the food. "I'm more of an introvert myself."

"I am definitely an extrovert." He smiled at her, noticing that Shane was making himself scarce now that he'd said what he felt he needed to say. Meddling bartender.

Meddling Dom is more like it.

That was exactly what it felt like... a well-meaning Dom telling on him to his Dominant—annoying and yet heart-warming. It felt odd to have someone looking after him. The Dominants around the clubs tended to assume he had his shit together and often treated him similar to one of their own outside of scenes. It also felt really nice, especially since Shane was putting Mistress Camille in the position of being Freddy's Dominant.

It might be a little presumptive, but that was also why they were here. That's what Freddy wanted her to be and, hopefully, what she planned to be for him.

"How often do you come here on the weekends?" she asked.

"Most Saturdays," he admitted. "If I don't have other plans."

She raised her eyebrow at him.

"How often do you make plans for Saturday mornings?"

Sheepishly, he shrugged his shoulder. "Ah, not often."

It didn't take her long to pry more information out of him, information he was reluctant to give because the more he talked, the more he realized Shane was right. Not only that, the more he had to start looking at some of the choices he made and examining the reasons behind them.

Was he actually happy not having a best friend? Or did he just keep people at a distance because he was afraid of being rejected? Or of ending up having someone he considered a best friend but who only considered him a friend... again? And how much did that play into his desire to be there for everyone else?

———

Camille

Although they'd hit it off with the chemistry and the sex, and she'd seen his professional side at work, this was an unexpected and seemingly vulnerable side of Freddy. She was glad Shane had said something. She wasn't sure she would have noticed Freddy's quirk of personality on her own, though she liked to think she would have picked up on it, eventually.

He'd described himself to her as a service submissive, but it was sounding like he didn't hold himself to that just for his Dominant but for everyone in his life. The more they talked about it, the more uncomfortable he became, a bit of distress showing in his expression, and Camille decided it might be best to change the topic to something lighter.

"So, other than Marquis, what's your favorite thing to do in D.C.?"

Freddy's eyes lit up, both with happiness and relief, and she was glad she'd changed the subject. They'd come back to it, eventually, especially if they started a relationship. She wouldn't let any sub of hers wear themselves out—the way she wore herself out, if she was being perfectly honest—but it wasn't something that was going to be fixed with one conversation. He needed a break.

"The cherry blossoms. I love the festival but also just walking around."

"Oh, man, I haven't been to see them since before I lived here," she said wistfully. More than once, she'd driven from Baltimore to walk around the pink-lined Tidal Basin or through the street festival. One year she'd even run in the 5k, but it had been literal years. Once she'd moved to D.C., it had gotten harder to get herself together enough to go.

Before, it had been a fun trip to take with friends, whereas now she would have been going on her own, and she hadn't had the energy. Especially when no one was relying on her to go with them.

"Well, if you'd like an escort to them this year…" He winked.

"I would like that." Maybe it was foolhardy to make plans for several months in the future, but they weren't *real* plans. They were more like plans to make plans. If something happened, and it didn't work out between her and Freddy, no harm no foul. She just wouldn't go see the cherry blossoms. Or she'd go on her own. Or maybe see if Julie wanted to go with her. Olivia, too.

She had options, which was more than she could say for herself a year ago, but she really hoped things would still be going well with Freddy then.

"What about you?" he asked.

"I don't know," she answered honestly. "I feel like I haven't been to half of the things I want to go to. Even though I've lived in Maryland pretty much my whole life, I spent most of my time on the other side of the state, and when I got here... well, I meant to get out a lot more, but somehow, it didn't happen." She hadn't had the energy or motivation. "I really liked the Museum of Natural History and made the effort to go to the African American Museum, but that's about it."

He chuckled.

"If it makes you feel any better, I haven't been everywhere, either," he admitted. "I've lived right outside D.C. my whole life, and I still haven't been in the Washington Monument. Although that's not entirely my fault because it was closed for repairs a lot by the time I was interested in it. Maybe we could do that together sometime."

"That could be fun." Her tone was noncommittal. Heights weren't her favorite thing, and she wasn't sure there was much else going on with the monument. "Do you have a favorite museum?"

"The Air and Space Museum," he said immediately, grinning widely. "Especially the IMAX theater. And, of course, I have to get some dehydrated ice cream from the gift shop on my way out."

Shaking her head, Camille shrugged.

"If you say so. I don't think I've ever had dehydrated ice cream."

"It's more about the nostalgia than the taste or texture, so I can't promise you'd enjoy it, but you should absolutely try some. You never know. It might be your new favorite thing."

Laughing, Camille shook her head, but she already knew she would end up trying it. They talked about all the things Camille had wanted to do around the area but hadn't gotten the chance to do. She could practically see Freddy taking mental notes, which warmed her, but she was understanding even more about what Shane had said.

They were going over all the things she might want to do.

What about the things Freddy wanted?

<u>*Freddy*</u>

Tonight was one of the best times he'd had in a long time, because this was more than a scene, this was a date. And talking to Camille was even better than he'd imagined. The conversation carried easily, though some of her probing questions made him inwardly squirm. He hadn't realized how often he got people talking about themselves rather than sharing anything about himself until he realized how uncomfortable he was with the way she'd turn questions around on him.

It felt like stretching a muscle that didn't get used very often.

They stayed long after Happy Hour was over, eating their way through almost every appetizer on the menu and eventually getting dessert, until they finally, reluctantly, gave up their seats, and Freddy walked her to her car.

"I had a wonderful time tonight." The time had passed way too quickly as far as he was concerned. "Maybe... we could do something this weekend? Go see one of the museums you're interested in?"

"How about you show me around the Air and Space Museum?" She grinned at him, though her shoulders hunched in as the bitter chill of winter wind blew past them. Some of the streets in D.C. basically turned into wind tunnels, and she'd parked on one of them.

As much as he wanted to keep talking, he didn't want her to literally get cold feet because he was keeping her on the street.

"I would love to," he said honestly. As much as he wanted to scene with her again, showing her around one of his favorite places sounded as good as hot sex. A real date. A planned one, not impromptu like tonight. "We could get lunch, too, though the best food is at the Native American museum."

She laughed.

"I've heard that. Maybe we could do both? The Native American museum in the morning, have lunch, then the Air and Space Museum in the afternoon? Or is that too much?"

He wasn't sure if she was asking whether there were too many things in the museums for them to have time to do it all or if she was asking if that was too much of her, but either way, the answer was the same.

"That's perfect. Just make sure you wear comfortable shoes." He grinned, then his smile broadened when she reached out and pulled him against her.

"As much as I don't want tonight to end, I'm freezing and getting in my car. I can't wait for this weekend." She didn't wait for him to answer before planting a hot kiss on his lips. He angled his head to deepen it. They kissed for a long, wonderful moment before she pulled away, leaving his lips warm and tingling in the cold air. "Good night, Freddy."

"Good night, ma'am."

With a sweet smile, she got into her car and started it.

Stepping back, Freddy watched her drive away before he headed down the street to the garage where he'd parked.

19

"Oh my God, this is so good," Camille moaned around the mouthful of food she'd just spooned into her mouth. "The flavors are amazing."

"Here, try this," Freddy said, lifting a fork full of the seasoned meat from his plate. Watching her eat was its own form of pleasure. He passed the fork over and nearly sighed with her as she took a bite.

The whole morning had been wonderful. They'd headed to the top floor of the museum so they could work their way down until they reached the food. He hadn't been in a while, so the visiting exhibit was new to him, and the artwork was fantastic. They'd walked through the whole thing holding hands, stopping to point out things that caught their attention and chit chatting in general.

The only thing they didn't talk about was work.

"I've never had museum food like this," she said after swallowing. "I feel like it's usually fried food."

"A lot of the museums around here have gotten a lot better, but yeah, there used to be a lot more chicken tenders and soggy over-cooked cafeteria hamburgers and stuff like that. Now there's more variety in all the museums. The Museum of Natural History has great salad bowls."

Camille shook her head in amazement.

"I am kicking myself for not getting out more," she admitted, her lips turning downward. "I needed this. I don't care what happens with work. I'm going to make it a point to get out of the house more often and go exploring."

"If you want company, I'd be happy to help." He didn't want to be pushy, but he was really enjoying himself today and was pretty sure she was, too.

"Oh, I'm counting on you to know all the best spots," she teased. "It would be like having my own personal tour guide."

Freddy laughed. That didn't sound bad to him at all. Maybe they could even do some actual tours. She'd probably enjoy that. There were some really great ones downtown. He'd heard good things about a comedy tour and had always wanted to do one of the Segway tours if he could talk her into it. He didn't know why, because the people always looked ridiculous, but he'd always thought it would be fun to go on one.

"Eventually, I'm going to get you up to the top of the Monument if you leave it up to me." He winked, and Camille shook her fork at him.

"Don't be naughty," she replied, her voice turning a little huskier with the implied threat. It wasn't a real order, though, more like 'go ahead, so I have an excuse to punish you.' Freddy's favorite kind of order.

He grinned at her, unrepentant, and something sparked in her dark eyes. The air thickened around them, an erotic tension filling the space between them, before Camille blinked and shook it off. Still, the energy between them lingered.

"So, Air and Space is next. You said something about an IMAX theater? I won't lie. I wouldn't mind getting a break to sit down." She grinned. "Even though you warned me to wear sneakers, I'm not used to walking this much in one day."

Neither was Freddy, but he spent a lot of time on his feet behind the desk at Marquis, which helped. They finished lunch talking about all the things the Air and Space Museum had to offer and looking up movie times. Camille wanted to do it all, which sounded great to him.

Walking up the mall to the museum was freezing, so they were relieved when they stumbled into the warm museum entrance.

"Oh, wow," Camille said, unwrapping herself from her jacket and pulling off her gloves and earmuffs. The front of her hair lay flat against her head, held in place by some kind of band, leaving the back half of her curls free to fly. The wind had ruffled them a little but not much.

The plain green shirt she was wearing skimmed her curves, showing her shape without clinging to it. Her jeans did plenty of clinging. Draping her jacket over one arm, she reached out with the other hand and Freddy laced his fingers through hers.

"By the way, have I told you how good you look today?" he asked, making her laugh because it had literally been the first thing he'd said to her, and he'd repeated it more than once.

"If you're expecting me to get tired of hearing it, you're barking up the wrong tree." But her attention wasn't really on him. It was on all the things hanging above them and displayed around them. The main room of the museum had some pretty incredible, very large displays.

Watching her looking around, it was almost like seeing it for the first time again. He grinned, dropping quiet and letting her soak it all in. He couldn't wait to show her everything.

Camille

"I can't believe how much my feet hurt when I was wearing sneakers all day," Camille complained. Not just her feet. Her legs, in general. She was sore all over.

The massage Freddy was giving her feet and calves was definitely helping a lot. He grinned at her from his position at the other end of her couch, his strong fingers rubbing over the arch of her foot, pressing in and making her groan as pure relief slid through her.

"If you're not used to being on your feet for long periods of time, your feet are going to end up hurting, regardless of what shoes you're wearing. Heck, even if you *are* used to being on your feet."

"Do your feet hurt?" she asked, suddenly worried she'd become one of the people who took Freddy's help without thinking about what he might need. He shook his head, but she wasn't sure he was telling the truth.

"I'm good. The movies in the afternoon helped. If we did a second day of walking around like this, my feet would be hurting." He chuckled as she moaned again.

"There is no way I could do a second day in a row of this. One was enough. Next time, we're doing a half day until I build up more stamina," she said grumpily, though she'd had a great time. No regrets. They'd decided to continue the day by returning to her place and ordering in food. Now she was stuffed full of food from her favorite Greek place and getting a foot massage by an eager-to-please, very handsome, and extremely capable sub.

This is the life.

The life that she wanted, that she sometimes dreamed about. The life she'd been sacrificing to her job and to trying to take care of her mom... but what if she could have it all? There was a cynical part of her that immediately rejected that notion. Wasn't that what she'd heard over and over again her whole life? That she *couldn't* have it all? That she was always going to have to choose something?

Work or family.

Work or friends.

Work or vacation.

Work or children.

Always work, work, work, work or... But what did work give back to her other than money? Not that money wasn't important—it was, of course it was—but she knew her mom would approve of what was happening right now much more than she would approve of Camille bending over backward to the Donaldsons and Nicholas Alexander

IIIs of the world. Even if it meant the home she lived in wasn't as good as the one she was in now.

Camille let out a long, slow breath.

"Do you ever feel like you have to choose between work and everything else?" For the most part, they'd managed to avoid talking about their jobs today, but now she wanted to know. They had similar careers, both divorce lawyers, but Freddy managed to have a second job at Marquis *and* a large circle of friends he made time for, *and* now, he was taking her out.

Despite all that, he seemed perfectly at ease and happy with himself.

He took his time, thinking about her question, mulling it over, still rubbing at her feet before finally answering.

"Not really. At least, not in the sense I think you're asking. There are times when I miss something I wanted to go to because I have to work, but if there's something I *really* want to do, I find a way to do it. Sometimes, I have to make small sacrifices at work to be with my friends and small sacrifices with my friends to make sure I get all my work done, but I don't feel as if I'm choosing one over the other. If that makes sense."

It did.

It sounded like compromise. Rather than allowing one thing to run his life, he prioritized neither all the time and both some of the time. Unlike her, who had prioritized work completely, partly out of fear it would no longer be there if she didn't, and she needed the money.

Lately that was changing. She'd gone out New Year's Eve. She'd had lunch with Julie and Olivia. She'd gone out for the night with Julie even if she'd ended up spending most of it with Freddy. Now she and Freddy had gone on a date.

Nothing terrible had happened.

None of her work had been neglected.

If anything, she'd worked harder because she'd felt less stressed, less tired, and more energized. She felt better all around, even with sore feet. There was some satisfaction in having sore feet and legs, to be perfectly honest. Like she'd done something with her day instead of sitting at home, trying to recharge and still feeling exhausted at the end of it.

Now she felt exhausted but satisfied in a way she hadn't in a very long time.

"I think I've been stuck in an either/or mentality for a long time," she admitted. "Like I can only do one thing, and that one thing has been sucking me dry."

There was a long pause as Freddy thoughtfully rubbed up her calf, massaging the muscle and making her want to sink even deeper into the couch.

"Well, I'm glad you're getting away from that," he said finally.

It was exactly the right thing to say. He wasn't pitying her, which would have made her bristle, and he wasn't being patronizing. He was supportive and acknowledged the changes she was already making.

"Me, too." She grinned at him and shifted her legs slightly, bending her knees so her feet were braced against his inner thigh, the side of her foot against the front of his pants. Deliberately, she pressed her foot sideways to rub against the small bulge there. It responded by growing immediately, his cock twitching beneath the fabric and swelling against her foot. "Wanna help me get further away from that?"

Despite his quick intake of breath and his quickly growing erection pressing against her, he didn't jump at the suggestion.

"I don't know... is this our first date? I don't want you to think I'm too easy." He grinned widely as she laughed. "I'd hate to give the wrong impression."

"What if I like easy men?"

"Oh, well then I can be very easy." He groaned as her foot pressed more firmly against his cock, now a hard bulge at the front of his pants. "Happy to be of service."

There was still a teasing lilt to his voice, which had gotten lower and huskier when she shifted, using her feet to rub both his cock and his inner thigh. His magic fingers had stopped, now resting on her lower legs rather than massaging, and his jaw clenched as she pressed hard against his cock.

"I think what I would like is to have you tied to my bed, so I can do whatever I like with you," she said slowly, enjoying the minute changes to his expression.

Blue eyes opened, his gaze meeting hers, filled with heat, need, and anticipation—all the things she liked to see.

"As you wish, Mistress."

20

———————

Naked and bound to Mistress Camille's bed was not how he'd anticipated his night going. He hadn't wanted to assume this was what would happen, despite the date and despite her inviting him up to her place. He'd been happy to follow her lead on where the night took them, without presuming it would take them anywhere.

It was clear she hadn't been prepared, either, but she'd made it work. It had taken her a few minutes to find her cuffs, and she'd cursed under her breath when she couldn't find everything she'd wanted. He'd laughed and told her he was happy to do whatever she liked, including holding himself in place.

But she'd wanted him tied up.

So, now he had the cuffs around his wrists, a silk scarf looping through the D-rings to tie them to the bedpost, and same with his ankles. His arms were straight up above his head while his legs were spread, his erect cock bobbing over his body like an eager puppy ready to play.

The warm, inviting décor of the room, with its dark wood and sensual, red curtains on the windows and a matching comforter with cream accents on the bed, made him feel as though he was getting a secret glimpse at her inner self. The bedroom was definitely *her* private space, and it showed.

"You look delicious," she teased, running a finger down the center of his chest, all the way to his belly button, then lifting it rather than going lower.

"Thank you, Mistress." He winked at her. "I'm happy to be eaten..."

She laughed, exactly as he'd intended. Though some Dominants could be strict, he'd picked up on that she liked a bit of sass while they played. He had no doubt if he crossed the line he'd know it immediately, but she did want to *play*, not just scene.

"Not yet. I have a few things I want to get to first... even if I can't find my toys. Do you have any issues with blindfolds?"

"Only that it means I won't be able to look at your beauty."

Camille snorted, shaking her head. He didn't think she was denying she was beautiful. No, she was shaking her head at the schmaltz. He could live with that. It was fun to be schmaltzy, especially when it was appreciated, and despite her head shake, he could tell that she'd liked it. She didn't tell him to stop.

"You are going to be trouble." Leaning forward, she put the blindfold over his eyes. Bound and helpless in the middle of her bed, he couldn't see what was going to happen next. His dick was hard as a rock with anticipation, his nerves aquiver as he tried to hear her movements and guess what was happening. "I'll be right back."

Ah, fuck.

She was going to torture him with waiting.

The bed shifted as she got off, then his ears were straining as she left the room as he tried to hear what she was doing. Which was impossible. His heart rate kicked up, and he instinctively tugged on the restraints to test them. Not too hard because he didn't want to damage her bed, but his brain needed to know.

All the while, he kept listening for sounds... Was that the fridge opening? What room was she in?

What could she be getting?

The number of pervertables—household objects that could be perverted into sex toys—was endless. He trusted her to know which ones made *good* toys without being dangerous, but even once she came back in, he wouldn't know what she'd picked up.

Talk about erotic torture.

———

Camille

Returning to her bedroom, where Freddy waited for her, the sight of him in her bed, tied up and blindfolded, vulnerable and waiting for her like a good boy made her smile so wide, her face hurt. Not that he had a lot of opportunity to move, but she had secured the restraints with Velcro, heavy duty Velcro but still Velcro, and he could have gotten free if he really wanted to. Some subs might do it just to give their Dominant a reason to punish them, but while Freddy might be full of sass, he wasn't a brat.

"Good boy," she said, enjoying the sight of his cock flexing at the sound of her praise.

Walking to the edge of the bed, she laid out the items she'd found around the house. There wasn't as much as she would have liked. She wished she'd thought about ordering some new toys and implements now that she was getting back into the scene, but some part of her hadn't believed she'd really go through with it because every time she'd had the thought, she'd dismissed it. On the other hand, sometimes, it was fun to make do with what one had.

When the ice clinked against the sides of the bowl, Freddy's head turned toward the sound, trying to figure out what it was. Next to the bowl of ice, she put the long feather she'd found in one of her drawers, leftover from a hat she'd worn for a costume years ago. It had fallen out of the hat, and she'd kept meaning to repair it but never got around to it.

Sometimes, procrastination paid off. If it had been attached to the hat, she wouldn't have been able to use it for tonight.

The last thing she put down was a paintbrush. She wasn't entirely sure what she was going to use it for, but she'd grabbed it, sure she'd be able to figure something out.

Tomorrow, she would be ordering some new toys, regardless of how much fun it was to play with found objects.

Looking at her options, she picked up the feather. Brushing it lightly over Freddy's leg, she grinned when he didn't seem to feel it until it reached his thigh. He jumped, his head moving back and forth and tilting up, as if he was trying to peek under the blindfold.

"Naughty, no peeking," she said, giving the top of his thigh a short, sharp smack before moving the feather tendrils up to his stomach.

"Fuck!" He tightened his stomach muscles, flexing, and Camille grinned as she realized the problem—he was ticklish.

"Something wrong, Freddy?" she asked innocently, brushing it up to his chest, then back down again, holding back her sadistic giggles as he writhed and strained.

"No, Mistress." The words came out clipped, then he clenched his jaw, obviously trying to keep himself under control as she moved the feather. Brushing it up and down his torso, it wasn't too hard to find his most ticklish spots—right under his ribs, the outer sides of his stomach, and of course, his armpits.

He didn't want to laugh, which she took as a personal challenge. It also gave her an idea for the paint brush.

Freddy

"Fuck!" Freddy's toes curled. The ticklish sensation of something very lightly dancing over his skin had been exchanged for a firm but still ticklish stroke up his side and along the underside of his rib. He tried to twist away but couldn't.

Tickling was not one of his kinks. He'd never even thought about it as something to do, though he'd known it could be a kink for some people. Freddy had never particularly liked being tickled, and while the feathery strokes were both torturous and fun, it was enough, he almost called out his slowdown word. Before he could, Camille's hand wrapped around his cock, giving it a firm stroke as she ran what felt like some kind of small brush up his other side, causing him to writhe again.

With her thumb rubbing over the swollen head of his dick, the sensation felt different. Still ticklish. Still making him want to writhe and laugh. But now it was infused with the pleasure from her hand stroking him, the warmth of her palm heating his cock as she moved it up and down his shaft.

The conflicting sensations made him whimper.

Pain was something he was used to dealing with, but this? This was chaos for his senses, yet he wasn't sure he wanted her to stop.

The brush moved around his nipple, the stiff bristles moving over the tiny bud and making a little circle. Then her hand released his cock, and he moaned with reluctance, only to cry out as something icy cold replaced the brush, freezing his sensitive nub. Sensation play was not something he'd gotten to indulge much in at the club. Dominants wanted to whip, belt, flog, or spank when they were at the club. The opportunities for sensation play were much fewer and further between. He hadn't really felt like he was missing out since he loved impact play, but right now, he was feeling he may have been wrong about not being interested in sensation play.

Or maybe it was just because it was Mistress Camille.

The ice lifted, replaced by her warm, wet mouth. Freddy groaned, writhing again, only to gasp as the ice landed on his other nipple. Hot on one, freezing on the other, and unable to do anything about either. The ice was cold enough to hurt, but the heat warmed him from the inside out.

His skin quivered as she lifted her mouth and moved to the other nipple, but rather than moving the ice back to the first nipple, she slid the piece down his body. His stomach muscles quivered and contracted as cold water trickled over his skin as the ice melted. He shivered despite the warmth of her mouth on his nipple, her tongue teasing the sensitive bud.

"*Fuck!*" he screamed as she wrapped her hand around his dick again. This was no warm palm, the way it had been before. No, the piece of ice hadn't melted yet, and she was rubbing it up and down his cock, the rest of her hand cold from holding it, even if it wasn't freezing. His dick wanted to shrink away, but the friction felt too good, confusing his senses as she gave him the coldest hand job he'd ever experienced.

Icy water dripped down his shaft to his balls, making his whole body tremble as she tortured him with the hot and cold. It was heaven and hell, fire and ice, and so fucking sexy, he could barely breathe.

When her mouth lifted from his nipple, he felt her shifting on the bed. He heard the ice clink, but there was no sign of what was coming next until something dropped onto his abdomen, making his stomach muscles tighten again.

"Fuck, that's cold."

A low chuckle met his words, but she didn't say anything as she painted his body with the ice water. It tickled and was cold as hell, yet his erection was as thick and eager as ever. At this point, he wasn't sure anything would be able to make it deflate, he was so turned on. He groaned as she moved the brush over his body, occasionally pausing to gather more icy water on its bristles. She moved it over his most ticklish spots, making him gasp when she reached his armpits and suck in his stomach as she circled his belly button. When she moved it down over his groin, he shuddered, the bed creaking as his muscles tensed, and he pulled on the restraints.

Something hot and cold and so very wet engulfed his cock and Freddy cried out, thrusting up into her mouth as she swirled the ice around his shaft with her tongue. This time, he couldn't find the breath to utter a curse. She'd completely taken it away with the mix of sensations, the excruciating agony and ecstasy blending into a cacophony of erotic need that made his entire body rejoice.

She hummed her pleasure as he jerked upwards, the brush still moving against his skin, over his stomach, tickling him and teasing him as her mouth worked over him. He could barely think. The glut of sensations overwhelmed his senses, turning his brain into a pile of mush as logical and rational thought broke down, leaving behind pure desire.

21

Camille

With Freddy gasping and moaning, she smiled around his cock as she tormented him with an icy blow job. He thrust up into her mouth and cringed away in turn, as if he couldn't decide which he really wanted to do. The ice did nothing to cool her own desire as she hummed around his cock, enjoying tormenting him.

She rarely used her mouth other than as a special treat, but he *had* been a very good boy. Showing her around the city resulted in a very good day, and since she was using ice, she hadn't been able to resist. The results were delightful, and there was something very enjoyable about having a man's most delicate organ between her teeth. The trust involved made the act extremely intimate. Though some Dominants had a different opinion on the matter, that's how it felt for her. So, she wasn't against giving head, as long as it was well earned.

As the ice melted, her body was beginning to ache for satisfaction, tormenting Freddy arousing her desires. It was down to a tiny sliver when she pulled away, leaving him gasping. Shifting on the bed again, she took off the rest of her clothes, then straddled his waist before reaching up to slip the satin blindfold off his head. She wanted to see his face.

Blinking, Freddy stared up at her, his eyes coming back into focus after a long moment, then he stared at her appreciatively.

Running her hands over his chest, Camille smiled back at him.

"You're not going to cum until I tell you that you can," she said.

That was going to be difficult for him because he was highly aroused. She'd been sucking his cock, and now he was going to have to wait until she caught up with him.

"Yes, Mistress," he replied without hesitation, though she saw the flash of awareness in his eyes of the challenge.

Wriggling her hips, she got in position over his cock and sank down on him. Fuck, that felt good.

For him, too.

Groaning, his eyes closed, and his head tipped back as she impaled herself. The thick stalk of his cock stretched her open, her own slick arousal and the lubrication from the blow job making it easy for her to slide all the way down. Her muscles clenched as she moved, squeezing him tightly before releasing. By the time she settled on his body, rubbing her sensitive lips against his groin, he was panting for breath and so was she. Damn, that felt good. Leaning forward to get the best position against her clit, she shifted, then rose up again.

Lightly running her nails over his chest, she enjoyed watching his struggle as she moved atop him, bouncing up and down on his cock, taking her time and riding him for her own pleasure. It was like having her own living, breathing sex toy. Freddy's jaw worked, his muscles tightening and releasing as he fought against his need to cum.

"Good boy." She breathed out the words on a sigh as she rose up high and sank down low again, clenching around him as he filled her. Her swollen clit rubbed against his body as she rocked her hips back and forth, grinding down on him, and making him cry out as he surged upward from beneath her.

"Please..." The word was strained. Breathless. Music to her ears. "Please, Mistress."

A shudder of pleasure went through her body at his plea. She loved hearing him ask. Beg.

Leaning forward, she captured his lips, still rocking her hips, still rubbing against him. Squeezing his cock inside her, her own climax began to crest. She pulled away from the kiss long enough to give him permission.

"You may cum." Spoken in a husky whisper, the words were all Freddy needed.

He cried out, his hips thrusting upward while she pressed down atop him. Feeling his cock pulse inside her, the hot spurt of liquid triggering her own pleasure, she moved with abandon as waves of ecstasy rolled through her. Clenching around him, her pussy milked his cock of every last drop of cum before she collapsed atop him, resting her head in the crook of his neck.

"Good boy."

FREDDY

Waking up next to Camille in her bed, Freddy felt nothing but deep satisfaction. Every part of him felt good, from his head down to his toes. Looking at her, still fast asleep with her blue satin bonnet on her head, she looked like an angel. Part of him wanted to slip under the covers and wake her up with his mouth, but he wasn't sure how she'd feel about that. She hadn't given him permission to do any such thing, and they hadn't talked about boundaries while sleeping, but he made a mental note to ask later.

What he did feel comfortable doing was slipping out of bed to go to the bathroom, then heading to her kitchen. The impulse to take care of her was one he couldn't completely ignore.

Thankfully, she had several aprons hanging on a hook inside her pantry, and he snagged the top one. Cooking while naked was dangerous; he'd much rather be covered. Taking a swift perusal of what she had in her fridge, he decided on cinnamon French toast, eggs, and fresh fruit for breakfast. Humming happily under his breath, he got everything he needed out on the counter, then got the coffee pot started.

First thing was to chop the fruit. He wanted the other stuff warm when she woke up, so he'd get the cold food done first. Strawberries, melon, and bananas. While he was doing that, his phone buzzed on the counter, the vibrations making enough noise, it sounded like it was echoing. He snatched it up and waited, listening to hear if he heard any movement back in the bedroom.

Nothing.

Breathing out a sigh of relief that his surprise hadn't been ruined, he looked at the text.

Lexie: *What are you up to today? Want to do something?*

Freddy: *I don't know what my plans are for the day yet. I'm at Mistress Camille's right now, so I need to wait until she wakes up to find out if she wants to do something.*

Lexie: *I'm calling you.*

He didn't have a chance to respond and tell her no before his phone buzzed again, this time with a call. Sighing, because he knew it wouldn't do any good to ignore it, he answered the video call, and her scowling face greeted him.

"Don't yell at me. She's still sleeping, and I don't want her to wake up yet," he said quickly. "I'm making her breakfast."

Some of the scowl on Lexie's face cleared. Just a touch.

"Okay, that's really cute, but that's not going to get you off the hook. Did you spend the night? I didn't even know you had a date! What the hell, Freddy?!" Her righteous anger was delivered in a hiss rather than a shout, out of respect for his request, and Freddy felt a small pang of guilt.

This was what Shane had been talking about when he inferred that Freddy didn't let people in. He hadn't even thought to call Lexie and tell her that he had a date. Why hadn't he? Why had he kept it all to himself?

"I'm sorry." He didn't know what else to say since he didn't really have an explanation. "I guess... I don't know. I'm not used to having anything going on with me, so I'm not used to telling people when something is."

"Okay, well to be clear, as your friend, I expect regular updates when something exciting is happening in your life, whether it's work, a relationship, or whatever." She made a face. "You're not wrong that you don't usually have something new and different going on. I'm glad that's changing. So, she's not up yet?"

"No, and I'm trying to make her breakfast before she wakes up." He raised his eyebrow at Lexie. *Hint, hint.*

Lexie rolled her eyes.

"Okay fine, but I expect a call later. Or Happy Hour sometime this week. Something so you can catch me up on everything." She pointed her finger at the phone screen. "Got it?"

"Got it." He shook his head as they hung up, but the point had been made. He was really good at being there for his friends but less good at letting his friends be there for him or letting them into his life. Something to work on, especially if he wanted to be in a romantic relationship.

In the meantime, he had breakfast to make.

<u>Camille</u>

Waking up alone was not how Camille had expected to start her day. Frowning, she sat up. There was an indent in the pillow where he'd slept but not him. A noise outside the bedroom at least let her know he hadn't disappeared before she'd gotten up, not that she thought he would, but it was hard not to be a little paranoid when she woke up to an empty bed.

Yawning, she got out of bed, grabbed her robe, and realized she smelled coffee. And food.

Holy crap.

She didn't rush out to the kitchen, but she didn't *not* rush, either. She wanted to see what he was doing. The sight that met her eyes wasn't quite what she'd been picturing. Freddy was in the kitchen, preparing breakfast, but somehow, she'd missed that all of his clothes were still in her room. She was greeted by the sight of his very cute butt framed by a frilly white apron. A neatly tied bow right above his cheeks added to the cuteness factor, as did the ties hanging down to rest on the curve of his butt.

Turning to look over his shoulder, Freddy grinned at her, and Camille smiled back. Leaning against the doorway, she appreciated the attractiveness of a man who was so secure in his masculinity, he could wear literally whatever the hell he wanted and be perfectly at home.

It was hot.

"Good morning. Perfect timing, breakfast is almost ready." Seemingly at home in her kitchen, which was also pretty hot, Freddy pivoted to pour her a cup of coffee in a waiting mug. "Sugar? Cream?"

He was in full service submissive mode, and while part of her felt odd allowing someone else to be the 'host' in her home, he was clearly having such a good time, she didn't want to stop him. Besides, if he'd been without a Dominant for as long as he said he had, this was likely a need he'd been denied for far too long.

"I like the first cup black. Thank you," she said as he handed her the cup. "Everything smells amazing." It really did, no need to lie, thankfully. It looked delicious, too. Her stomach rumbled.

"Good. Go ahead and have a seat, and I'll get this plated for you," he said eagerly.

Bemused, Camille did as she was told without commenting on how bossy some service subs could be. She'd almost forgotten what it could be like. Power dynamics were always interesting, especially when it came to honoring a sub's needs. Freddy didn't even seem to realize how he'd spoken to her, and she could have called him on it, but she also didn't want to interrupt a nice morning or the nice gesture he was making.

Besides, she didn't want to be a twenty-four seven Dominant, and right now, they weren't in the bedroom, even if he was in submissive mode, so she would let it slide. It was certainly something to keep in mind for later if she was ever in the mood to deliver some funishment.

The happy little smile on his face as he brought over the gorgeously plated food—seriously, it looked like something from a restaurant—made her insides go all warm and fuzzy. This was what a satisfied submissive looked like, and she'd been the one to put that smile on his face. Her own sense of satisfaction swept through her, going far beyond the physical satiation she'd already felt.

Her in her robe, Freddy in her apron, they sat and ate breakfast, reminiscing about their favorite parts of the day before. It felt natural yet surreal, as if she was still dreaming because how could this be her life?

But she wanted it to be her life.

"What are your plans for the rest of the day?"

"Not sure," he replied, taking a sip of his coffee. "My friend Lexie wanted to get together, but I wasn't sure if you had anything you wanted to do. And I need to get some things done around my house. Laundry, grocery shopping, that kind of thing."

"The normal weekend activities," she quipped.

"Pretty much."

"I have an awful lot to get done, too," she admitted reluctantly. As much as she wanted to lounge about and spend all day doing nothing —preferably with him—she needed her Sundays. She also needed some 'her' time in order to get through the week. Despite how well he fit in her apartment, she was still feeling the urge to play hostess and entertain him.

As refreshed as she felt and as much as she'd needed the time with him and the outing yesterday, if she didn't get her downtime, she was going to be tired and cranky tomorrow at work.

"I'll get out of your hair after breakfast then," he said with a wink, as if wanting to show her he understood and was perfectly fine with having to leave. "I would love to see you again sometime very soon, though, if you're free."

"How about next Saturday for dinner?" As much as she wanted to spend every night with him, until the Alexanders' divorce was completely finalized, keeping things a little more casual—and to the weekends—was probably best. Yes, they'd signed off on the new terms for the prenup, but there was always a chance Mr. Alexander would decide to find something else to quibble about.

It would also give her more time to get used to being in a relationship again. She didn't fool herself into thinking this was casual or anything like that. The chemistry was too strong between them. Freddy was openly interested in having a relationship with her, and she felt the same way.

Thankfully, he also appeared to be on board with waiting until the weekend to see each other again. His wide smile was blinding.

"It's a date."

22

———

Camille

Walking out of Murdoch Family Law, Camille felt like she was walking on air, buoyed by hope. No official offer immediately on the table, but it had gone _very_ well. Everyone she'd met had been friendly, open, and interested in listening to what she had to say.

Not only that, but it was easy to see that they were happy with their jobs in a way people at Donaldson were _not_. There were lots of smiles on people's faces, even the people who looked tense had looked determined, not like they were about to burst into tears. Emily Murdoch had been confident without being arrogant. Camille had really liked her, though she put more stock in how satisfied all the 'worker bees' around the office appeared to be... and they all appeared to be in good spirits.

How management treated their employees said much more about a place than how they treated their clients or other management team members.

If she'd needed that reminder, walking back into her current office and feeling the aura of tension, worry, and unhappiness would have done it. People were _not_ happy here, not just her. The only people who seemed to be satisfied with themselves were the partners.

There were very few smiles, and all of them disappeared the moment a partner walked down the hall.

Yeah. She needed to get out of here.

She really hoped Murdoch decided they wanted her because that was where she wanted to work. She already knew it. That wouldn't stop her from going on interviews with other firms, but Murdoch was her top choice if she had any say in it.

As she walked through the hallway, a familiar voice made her spine stiffen, though thankfully, Mr. Alexander wasn't talking to her.

"I think it's really going to improve my swing—" His sentence cut off as he came around the corner with Junior, his lip lifting in a sneer the moment he saw her.

Camille met his gaze, staring back at him evenly without flinching.

"Mr. Alexander. Mr. Donaldson." She kept her voice neutral and slightly warm, giving away none of her real feelings about either of them. It was easier to do than usual after her interview, that little bit of hope keeping her uplifted.

"Camille." Junior nodded at her. Mr. Alexander didn't bother to answer, just made an odd noise in his throat as his gaze skittered away from hers, his smirk disappearing when he realized she wasn't intimidated by him.

They must be on their way to get lunch, then play some golf. At least he wouldn't be hanging around the office.

Her muscles slowly relaxed again as she went into her office and firmly shut the door behind her. Taking out her phone, she checked her messages. As soon as she'd left Murdoch, she'd texted Freddy to let him know she was out of her interview, and it had gone well. She wanted to see if he'd texted her back.

Of course, he had. She already knew it never took him long to respond unless he was in the middle of something, but she still grinned seeing it. Between him and the interview, she was feeling downright giddy.

Freddy: *I'm sure you blew their socks off! They'd be fools not to hire you. You've got this.*

His belief in her made her feel even better. Having a cheerleader in her corner, who was not only supportive but also knew her capabilities as a lawyer, was a huge boost to her ego. She knew he wasn't just saying it to be nice or out of ignorance. He knew what he was talking about and still believed in her.

Camille: *Thanks! It's going to be hard to wait another week for my next interview.*

Freddy: *Maybe I can help make the time pass faster. Do you want to do another museum this weekend before dinner?*

Camille: *I've heard good things about the Spy Museum…*

Freddy: *YES.*

She laughed at his answer, then winced when someone knocked on her door. Thankfully, it was just one of the paralegals with a question, but it was another nail hammering home how badly she needed to get out of there. Who worried about laughing at work?

People who worked at Donaldson, that was who.

It almost made her feel a little guilty about the people she'd be leaving behind, but she couldn't make the choice to leave for them. They had to make it for themselves, just like she had.

FREDDY

"I can't believe you didn't tell me any of this." Lexie threw her French fry at him. "How could you not tell me any of this?" There was some real hurt behind her joking, which made Freddy feel terrible.

He looked down at his plate. Part of him wanted to shrug off her question, to not give her a real answer because that was what he was used to doing, but he also knew that was how he kept people at a distance. She would know she was being shrugged off and would respond accordingly.

Worse, he now recognized it, and he'd be doing it on purpose, instead of without realizing it. Which meant he'd be hurting her feelings on purpose.

"It's come to my attention that I'm not a very good friend," he started hesitantly.

"Oh, please, you're an amazing friend. You're always there for all of us. You have a great listening ear and one of the best shoulders to cry on, and you're one of the few people who will protect me from Patrick." Lexie picked up another French fry but didn't throw this one, opting to eat it.

Freddy had to laugh. As if she needed protection from her hulking husband. Sure, Master Patrick was the owner of a kink club, and they were in a twenty-four seven total power exchange relationship, but he adored the ground Lexie walked on. She was a brat for the fun of it and had total trust that her master would never truly harm her. Though pain could be part of a scene, it would only be in the ways she'd agreed to at the beginning of their relationship and signed a contract for. A contract that could always be renegotiated if she changed her mind.

"Yes, the many times I've had to throw myself to your defense," he teased, the mood lightening for a moment before he sighed. "But, yes, I'm great at being there for other people. I am not so great at letting other people be there for me. And friendships are a two-way street."

Opening her mouth, Lexie frowned and closed it again, her bright blue eyes unfocusing as she thought about what he was saying. With her black hair and startlingly long lashes, her eyes were even more piercing than his own, and that was saying something. She was a force to be reckoned with, packed into a petite body, which sometimes made her seem like a chihuahua who was trying to play with the big dogs.

The thing about Lexie was that a lot of the time, the big dogs willingly followed her around.

"Okay, I can see that," she said after a moment. "So, that's why you didn't tell me about Mistress Camille."

"Partly. I'm not really used to talking about myself with people or making myself vulnerable in any way. If I told you about her, then things didn't work out, I'd have to tell you about that, too." He shrugged, more because he was trying to shrug away his own discomfort with the conversation, as though it wasn't that big a deal.

"Yeah, I can see the whole 'not being great at letting other people be there for you,'" she said sympathetically, her foot moving under the table to give him a light kick in the shin. "But you know that we want to be there for you, right? Everyone you've ever helped. You have a huge group of friends, all you have to do is beckon… especially since we've been trained to mind our own business unless invited in."

Freddy snorted.

"Yes, everyone at Stronghold and Marquis are infamous for minding their own business." The gossip train at the clubs was faster than Superman most days.

"Hey, we might talk, but we don't interfere without an explicit invitation," Lexie protested. She grinned. "Olivia would have our asses otherwise… and so would you, and you know it."

That was true. Freddy occasionally intervened without invitation, but it was very rare. Mostly he would step in to be someone to talk to, then ask if he could intervene if the person was struggling. Olivia, on the other hand, would step in on behalf of a submissive *if* she felt it was merited and urgent, but the Dominants had to specifically ask her for help.

"Okay, good point," he conceded. "But, yeah, it's hard to reach out sometimes."

"So, you're saying you'd prefer we just shove in when we see you need help?" Her tone was completely innocent.

"No, no, no, absolutely not." He pointed his fork at her. "Don't you dare, and don't you dare spread that around."

Lexie giggled wickedly.

"As long as you agree to start reaching out more, I won't have to," she said archly. "And I expect to be kept up to date on what's going on with you and Mistress Camille."

"I can do that. Right now, not a lot. We're keeping things to the weekends at the moment, but we talk on the phone every night during the week." Which was surprisingly easy to do, even though

Freddy had never considered himself much of a phone person. He preferred to text, but talking to Camille was easy.

They'd even had phone sex once during the week.

"Are you planning to do anything for Valentine's Day?"

The big day was barely a week away, and Freddy was at a bit of a loss.

"She hasn't said anything about it. I made a reservation at Marquis since those are filling up. She has a lot on her plate right now, so I don't know if she's up for planning everything. I figured I'd have that as a backup in case she wants to do something... but I don't know if she will."

"Maybe she's not a Valentine's Day person." Lexie shrugged and rolled her eyes. "You know Patrick isn't, which is why we have the party at Stronghold rather than going out on a date. A fancy date at an overly crowded restaurant is basically his worst nightmare."

"It wouldn't be my favorite way to celebrate, either, but I do like the idea of doing *something*. It's a good excuse to have some extra fun. Marquis' stage room can only hold so many people... or we could just spend the whole night in the hotel room."

"That does sound nice."

"But not something you want to do."

"Not something I want to do. I'd prefer to throw the party and run around all night, making Patrick chase me until he catches me, then has his wicked way with me."

Both of them laughed—and laughed even harder when their server swung by their table a moment later to check on them. He probably hadn't heard anything, but... no guarantees. Covering up her giggles, Lexie made a Herculean effort to get herself under control after the server left.

"Aaaaaaaanyway," she said once she'd stopped laughing. Freddy grinned, his mirth still barely restrained. "Did you hear the latest about Master Asad? Apparently, he's looking for someone to be his date to his brother's wedding and is having a bit of trouble."

"Really? I would figure most of the subs at the club would jump at that chance."

"Well, it's up in Pittsburgh, so they'd have to travel and spend the week with him. Even though he's looking for a fake date, he's a little wary of the submissives who are interested in going, seeing as it's a whole week. I don't think it helped that Tracey mentioned to him that fake-dating romances where the couple ends up realizing their true feelings for each other are a thing."

"Does he think commitment is catching or something?" Freddy didn't bother to hide his amusement.

"I think he's more worried about hurting anyone's feelings, but also about ulterior motives. He asked Patrick to help him pick, figuring Patrick knows best who would make a good fake girlfriend without getting attached. I have an idea, but I wanted to run it by you."

"If you try to play matchmaker, someone's probably going to get hurt," he said warningly. "Master Asad is definitely not interested in a relationship. I'm pretty sure he's allergic to them."

"Not wanting a relationship isn't the problem." Lexie took a deep breath. "I think he should take Morgan as his date. No, don't say no right away without hearing me out."

Since that was exactly what Freddy had been about to do, he clenched his jaw and nodded. He trusted Lexie. She knew Morgan's full backstory. They were two of the few submissives who did, though Morgan had gotten more comfortable talking with others about it. Freddy sometimes wondered if he really knew all of it. Occasionally, Morgan still seemed like she was holding back.

Sending her in as Master Asad's fake girlfriend sounded like a recipe for disaster.

"Alright. Convince me." He might not agree, but he'd hear her out, then tell her why she was wrong.

"Morgan needs to get away from Stronghold for a bit. Everyone wants to protect her, which is admirable, but she's getting better and starting to chafe at having everyone making her decisions for her." Lexie gave him a half smile. "She's not a twenty-four-seven submissive, even though she was forced to live like that for a while. She's starting to really come into her own, but I think she needs some time away from the club and away from all the Doms she looks up to."

"Okay, you're not wrong there." Freddy sighed. "I think a change of scenery could do Morgan some good, especially since I think you're right about her wanting to spread her wings. She won't say so because she doesn't want to hurt any of the Doms feelings when they've been so good about taking care of her... but the baby bird is getting closer to wanting to leave the nest. But why Asad's date to a wedding? Why not take her on a girl's trip or something?"

"Because Asad needs it. This isn't just someone deciding she should get out and spread her wings. He's someone with a need she can fulfill. Helping him out will do more for her self-confidence than a girls' trip would, and that's if she even wanted to go. Her group of friends and my group of friends don't really interact that much."

Good point.

"Fuck." Freddy ran his hand through his hair. "Okay, I can see it. That's why she moved in with Master Brian, because he had a real need. It wasn't just a whim."

"Morgan wants to give back. She wants to help, and she gets so few opportunities to do so. I think this would accomplish multiple things. She'd get to help out a Dom, she'd get away from Stronghold and Brian's house for a week, and she'd get to go where no one other than Asad knows her backstory. They'd be meeting her for the first time. She could be whoever she wants to be."

"Fuuuuck." He dragged out the word. "I hate how much sense you're making right now."

Lexie laughed.

"That's almost word for word what Patrick said. Then he said I should talk to you and get your opinion, since you're pretty close with her."

"I won't lie and say I'm not worried. If she started to develop feelings for Asad, that could go horribly wrong, but... it feels like there's a lot of good that could come from this for her."

"Hopefully, she knows better, but Patrick is still going to lay down the law with him. No sleeping with Morgan, no leading her on, keep the lines of communication open, and all that jazz."

"You think he'll agree to taking a date he can't fuck or scene with for a week? Especially when they've scened together in the past?"

"Hey, he's a big boy. He can keep his penis to himself for a week. Besides, we're going to point out that sex could confuse the issue since it *won't* be in the club. I'm pretty sure Asad will agree. Otherwise, he can find his own date."

Freddy tried to think of an objection, but he really couldn't. In this case, there wasn't a whole lot of risk, and the reward would be Morgan gaining even more confidence in herself as well as getting the chance to find out who she was away from Stronghold and her support system. The support system was great, but it could also be a little stifling.

He really hoped nothing happened that set her back, which was a very real risk, even if it was a seemingly low one.

Well, maybe she or Asad would say no, and Freddy wouldn't have to worry about it.

23

Camille

The Spy Museum had been as much fun as she'd imagined and even more interesting than she'd hoped for. They'd decided to just do one museum before heading over to Marquis for a drink and possibly dinner. The museum had been big enough, with enough activities, to take up the whole day.

Maybe it would be fun to try new restaurants, but Camille was more comfortable with the familiar, and after a day of doing something new, she wanted to go to a place where she knew exactly what she'd be getting. It was fun to sit in the downstairs dining room of Marquis and look around and wonder who knew what was happening on the second floor. Of course, being with Freddy meant she could just ask if someone was a member. A few of the answers surprised her.

They were midway through a thoroughly enjoyable meal when it happened.

"What the hell is this?" As if out of nowhere, Nicholas Alexander III made an extremely unwelcome reappearance in her life. Looming over them at the table, he glared at Freddy for a moment before turning his glare on her. "You're dating *him*? Is that why you forced me into that stupid agreement?" Completely flabbergasted, Camille's brain froze. She couldn't think of how to respond before the man turned. "Jared, are you seeing this?! She's dating my ex's lawyer! That's got to be a conflict of interest."

Freddy got to his feet. Despite the fact that Mr. Alexander was an inch taller, Freddy appeared even larger than life as his lawyer side took over, turning him from the happy sub to the fierce shark he could be for his clients. A few feet away, Jared Donaldson, Jr. was staring at her, his gaze going back and forth between her and Freddy, trying to figure out the truth. Both of them were dressed in slacks and dress shirts, contrasting to Freddy's jeans and sweater, but that didn't matter.

"First of all, your divorce has already been finalized. Which means there is no conflict," Freddy said, his voice colder than she'd ever heard it. "And it wasn't a stupid agreement. She made the best deal she could for you, and it was a better one than I would have liked. You got a lot more than you deserved, and it was because of her. If I'd had my way, we would have taken you to the cleaners, but your ex-wife just wanted to get it over with. Your lawyer was able to negotiate a great deal for you, so you benefited from both women, despite the fact you deserved neither of them."

Shaking off the panic and guilt that had frozen her, Camille lifted her chin. Freddy was right about everything. She'd done an exemplary job for Mr. Alexander, despite everything. She didn't bother to stand up. The man wasn't worth the effort, and neither was Junior.

"This is my personal time, Mr. Alexander. You are no longer my client. If you have a problem with the deal I made for you, perhaps you can ask yourself why none of your buddies at the firm wanted to take your case."

"Well, because I'm their friend. It would be a conflict-"

"No, it was because they knew you weren't going to be able to get everything you wanted and that I would get you the best deal possible. Which I did. Now, leave us alone." Behind Douchebag Number One, Douchebag Number Two had turned bright red and looked as if he was about to explode, but Camille didn't care. She was so tired of covering for the partners' inadequacies and the way they'd thrown her under the bus with this case.

"You—"

"Excuse me." Olivia's voice snapped out like a whip as she strode toward them, eyes flashing. It seemed everyone in the dining room had stopped to pay attention to the drama. "You are creating a disturbance. I am going to have to ask you to leave."

Both douchebags puffed up.

"We have a reservation—"

"You can't just—"

Olivia held up her hand, and miraculously, the gesture silenced both of them. They looked appalled but shut up. For the first time, Camille noticed the host standing off to the side, clutching a pair of menus. They must have been on their way to be seated when Mr. Alexander spotted her.

"You are in my house now, boys, and we have the right to refuse service to anyone." She glanced at Camille, raising her eyebrow as if asking what Camille wanted. Both assholes picked up on the look and turned back to stare at her, wondering what the connection between her and Olivia was.

"They can stay... as long as they sit down now and behave themselves," Camille said regally. She looked at Freddy and gave him a nod. He sat down and pulled his napkin back across his lap, then turned his back on the other two men and dismissed them with his actions as thoroughly as she had with her words.

Mr. Alexander appeared stunned as he realized he was only being allowed to eat on her sufferance.

The host seemed to have gathered her courage in Olivia's presence and stepped forward.

"If you would follow me, please, sirs, without any more interruptions."

Across the table from Camille, Freddy covered his laugh with a cough. His reaction made her think the young woman was likely a submissive, one who had a bit of a bratty side now that she'd regained her footing. Camille knew how she felt.

While Mr. Alexander toddled off after the host, Junior stopped for a moment to glare at her over Freddy's head.

"We'll talk on Monday."

"Yes, we will." She gave him a pointed stare. She was not going to be intimidated by him. As Olivia said, they were in *her* house. Marquis was hers. She could have them removed with the snap of a finger. And worry about her job didn't have the same kind of control over her that it had.

Besides, if he fired her for having a personal life, she could sue the pants off the firm, and she would.

Disturbed his threat hadn't had the effect he'd intended, Junior stared at her a moment longer. Olivia cleared her throat. Junior glanced over his shoulder at her, then scampered away, while the redhead shook her head. Olivia looked back at Camille, moving closer to the table, so she could talk without having to raise her voice.

"You should have let me kick them out." She sounded disappointed. Around them, conversation resumed since the show was over.

"Sorry for ruining your fun," Camille replied, a little smile lifting her lips. It would probably be less funny to her on Monday, but right now, she could joke about it, despite the little pit in her stomach that said she'd just messed up her life. She hadn't.

"Don't be. Now she can torture them all evening," Freddy said, turning his head to look up at Olivia. She smiled fondly at him.

"He's right. It's going to be a fun evening. Maybe I'll end up getting to kick them out, anyway. I'll certainly be keeping a very close eye on them." Sauntering away, Olivia followed to where the pair had been led. The table was on the other side of the dining room, thank goodness, but it meant she couldn't see what Olivia was doing to them.

Probably for the best since it would have been a little distracting.

"Well, that was... unexpected." She sighed, and Freddy looked at her with concern.

"Is it going to cause a problem for you at work?"

"Probably, but there's only so much they can do. I'm already looking for a new job, so if they give me even more reason to jump ship, oh well." She shrugged, even though she didn't feel quite as nonchalant as she was pretending to be. "I can power through until then. If Junior convinces the rest of the partners to fire me because we're dating, I'll have good reason to sue."

"What about your mom?"

The concern in his eyes made her want to reach across the table and kiss him. She loved that he immediately thought about what would be far more important to her than getting justice for herself.

"I can keep her where she is for a few months, which would hopefully give me enough time to find a job. Fingers crossed for Murdoch." She held up one hand with her fingers crossed.

Freddy reached across the table toward her, and she reached back to take his hand, their fingers twining together.

"Anything you need, I'm happy to give it to you," he said quietly, his gazed locked onto hers in a moment so achingly intimate, she could hardly bear it. Hearing him say that and knowing it was true, knowing he was there for her, that he wanted to help in whatever way she needed, made her feel painfully vulnerable.

"Thank you, but I hope you understand when I say I hope it doesn't come to that."

"Of course, I do." A smile tugged at his lips. "It's come to my attention that I'm not always very good about letting people help me, either. It's a struggle."

She had to laugh because he was right, and she believed he understood her problem on an intimate level. Squeezing his fingers, she filled her expression with all the gratitude she felt.

"Thank you."

Freddy

Convincing Camille to go to Stronghold after dinner wasn't difficult. He shot a message to Lexie to find out if any of the rooms were open for the evening. He nearly crowed with delight when he passed the answer on to Camille, and her eyes lit up.

Yes, the Office was exactly what she needed after the confrontation with her former client and one of her firm's partners.

One upside to being at Marquis over Stronghold was the amount of privacy it afforded, and there was no way to get a room at Marquis for tonight. They headed over to Stronghold as soon as they were finished with dinner. Camille hadn't actually been to Stronghold yet, and she wanted to look around. They would have some time to kill before dinner was ready, but Freddy had agreed, though he'd warned her they'd likely be ambushed by his friends. Alone time was much harder to arrange at Stronghold.

She said she didn't mind.

He really hoped she meant that.

The moment they walked through the door, Lexie lit up from where she was standing behind the front desk. Beside her, Angel beamed at him. It was all he could do not to facepalm. He knew damn well Angel wasn't on tonight. Though she occasionally volunteered to work the front desk when they didn't have anyone to cover it, Lexie was more than capable of handling it on her own. It wasn't like Marquis where she would have to lead people to their tables. All she had to do was get them checked in and take their coats and phones.

"Hello Mistress Camille," Lexie and Angel chorused together, beaming so hard, Camille actually stumbled. She recovered quickly, partly because she had her arm threaded through Freddy's, but clearly, she hadn't been expecting to be greeted by name, despite his warning.

Freddy sighed.

A deep chuckle came from Jared, who was standing next to the door between the lobby and the club.

"Fair warning, Freddy, the gang's all here tonight," he said when he looked over at him. "It's a packed crowd."

"Then how did we get a room?" he muttered, though he had noticed the parking lot seemed particularly full.

"Adam and I gave it up for you," Angel answered. Tonight, she was in full fetwear with one of her signature keyhole corsets that showcased her cleavage. The deep purple hue looked gorgeous next to her creamy skin and the brown curls that brushed her shoulders. "May you use it in good health."

"You didn't have to do that," he said, touched beyond belief. Angel and Adam's baby had just turned two, and he knew that getting out to the club could be hard for them. He'd even babysat baby Melody a time or two to make things easier on them. Angel's parents were usually on call, but when they weren't, Freddy had offered to be a go-to.

"I know we didn't, but we're very grateful for all the times you've given us a night off from parenting so we could do some coupling, and we wanted to give back to you." She grinned at him as Camille squeezed his hand and shot him a significant look.

Right. He was supposed to be getting better about letting people do things for him, especially his friends. Taking a deep breath, he nodded and did *not* argue with her.

"Thank you."

Lexie nudged Angel in the side, both of them beaming even brighter at Mistress Camille.

"See, I told you she was a good influence on him," she whispered.

Freddy didn't bother to point out that they could hear her. She knew and was doing it deliberately. He rolled his eyes while Mistress Camille laughed.

"You have me at a disadvantage," she said. "You know my name, but I don't know yours."

With a resigned sigh for extra dramatic effect, Freddy made the introductions. Then he introduced Mistress Camille to Master Jared on the way into the club. Once they were inside, it took them nearly half an hour to reach the bar so he could introduce her to Master Andrew and Kate, who were both working behind the bar.

Despite the crush of people and her preference for being an introvert, Mistress Camille handled herself with calm assurance. He still felt a little bad. He hadn't even realized how many friends he'd made, all who were thrilled to meet Mistress Camille because she was with him.

It made him feel warm and fuzzy and slightly embarrassed.

"Wow, you really have a lot of friends," she said when they finally made it through the crowd and managed to snag a bar table to themselves. Despite everyone being nosy, they were also understanding of him and Mistress Camille wanting some privacy. It didn't hurt that they stayed at the bar area where the Dominants tended to congregate, rather than in the Lounge, the area with a bunch of low chairs and loveseats and comfortable carpet, where the unattached submissives hung out.

"Sometimes, I forget how many," he admitted.

"What about that group over there? I noticed you waved, but they didn't come over." She tilted her head in the direction so as not to draw too much attention, and Freddy smiled, though it wasn't quite as genuine as before.

"That is a mixed group. I'm friends with about half of them and civil with the other half." Morgan was seated between Sam and Amy, chatting with Noelle, Caroline, and Marissa. He'd introduced Q, Sam's boyfriend, to Camille on their way through the bar area, but he was hanging out with his friends, including Master Law and Iris, and Iris and Noelle did not get along. "Are you sure you want to hear about the drama?"

Eyes alight with wickedness, Mistress Camille leaned forward, resting her forearms on the bar table. Her breasts pressed against her arms, deepening her cleavage.

"Absolutely. Spill the tea."

24

———

"So, Noelle and Iris were roommates until Noelle broke the lease without telling her. Then Noelle showed up at Marquis for the submissives class, claiming her and Iris' friendship ended because of kink. That she wants to learn about it and maybe renew their friendship."

"Right."

"And Iris is with Master Law, who is friends with Q, who is dating Sam, but Sam became friends with Noelle before she started dating Q."

"Yup."

"And now Sam and Noelle are hanging out with Marissa, who is the ex of the bouncer at the door."

"Who is now engaged to Angel's best friend, yes. And Angel used to live with Q."

"I feel like I need a map to understand the tea." Camille laughed, shaking her head. "It's like six kinky degrees of separation."

"It really is. Most of the time, there really isn't much drama, and when there is, it usually involves that group." He sighed. Both of them watched as Sam got up to join Q at the table where he was chatting with Master Law, Master Asad, and Master Connor. Iris was tucked under Master Law's arm, and when Sam slid into position next to Q, she and Sam both smiled and greeted each other.

None of them noticed the way Noelle glared daggers at them from across the room.

"Everything okay?" Mistress Camille asked gently as Noelle turned back to the others and said something that made Marissa and Caroline laugh. Morgan smiled, but she looked uncertain, while Amy appeared to be completely lost in thought and not paying attention to the conversation at all.

Freddy let out a slow breath, his muscles relaxing.

"Yeah, just... feeling defensive of my friends." He smiled at her. "And responsible for making sure none of the subs get out of hand."

So far, none of that little group had done anything that would get them kicked out. He kind of wished they would, but he didn't want Amy and Morgan getting mixed up in that. They both needed the club. Sometimes, he thought Marissa might, too. Why else would she keep coming back after Jared had moved on, knowing how many of his friends disliked her? Or maybe she only came because Caroline did.

Studying him thoughtfully, Mistress Camille nodded, and he wondered what she was thinking. She didn't say though.

"Any other tea?" she asked.

Freddy laughed.

"So much. See the man standing on the other side of Sam? That's Master Asad. Apparently, he needs a fake girlfriend."

Describing the many mini-dramas that took place around Stronghold with the members took a surprising amount of their waiting time, but not all of it. Eventually, they abandoned their table so Freddy could show her around the club. It wasn't long before their room reservation, so they went to the lower level first, where the Dungeon was. They'd be on the upper level where their reservation was when it was time instead of having to go up and down and back up again.

He kept a close eye on Mistress Camille's reactions to the various rooms and scenes. She seemed vaguely interested in the Medical room but not overly so. The many impact scenes at the spanking benches and St. Andrew's crosses seemed to be more her style, and she barely glanced into the Interrogation and Jail rooms.

They headed upstairs next, pausing to look in the windows of each of the rooms. Master Will was patrolling the hall as the upstairs Dungeon Master. He grinned at Freddy, giving him a discreet thumbs-up while Mistress Camille watched the throuple in the Locker Room. It was nice having someone who gave their approval quietly.

Tracey, one of the club subs, came out of the Office, cleaning supplies in hand, and brightened when she saw Freddy. She grinned at him.

"The Office is ready," she announced, eyes sparkling. Clearly, she was aware of exactly who was using the Office next.

"Thank you," Mistress Camille said, turning. Her eyes were lit up with excitement. She tilted her head at Tracey, who dropped her gaze to the floor. "Freddy, go on in and wait for me, I'll be right there."

Curiosity lit up inside him, but he obeyed, glancing over his shoulder to see Mistress Camille saying something to Tracey. His footsteps slowed as Tracey nodded, then Mistress Camille glanced at him, and his footsteps sped back up again. Entering the Office without any direction from her other than to go in, he came to a halt several steps inside, unsure what to do next.

Like most of the theme rooms, the Office was setup for roleplay, with a large wooden desk that had plenty of room for someone to crawl under it. Possibly two someones. It had been custom made for the purpose.

There was a large armoire and several filing cabinets, each containing all the toys and implements one might want to use. The drawers of the desk were also filled with goodies. The art on the walls was bland at first glance, but taking a moment longer to look would reveal there were some naughty scenes depicted.

There was one large chair behind the desk and two in front of it, a little smaller and a little lower on purpose. Freddy wasn't sure which

Mistress Camille would want him to take. He had a feeling she would want to be behind the desk, but sometimes, Dominants liked to switch things up, and he didn't want to make a presumption.

The door opened behind him before he could decide where to situate himself, and he turned to watch Mistress Camille come into the room. She took a moment to glance around, taking in the layout, then nodded at him.

"Thank you for coming in, Mr. Johan," she said, her voice brisk and professional—her work voice. He recognized it from when she was representing Mr. Alexander. It was also her 'in charge' voice. Clearly, she was going to be the boss for this scene.

If he hadn't gotten that message from her words, he would have figured it out a moment later when she went behind the desk to take the seat. Since they'd gone out for a date, rather than preparing to scene at a club, her clothes were a little more office appropriate than they might have been otherwise, though he doubted she'd ever worn a dress with such a plunging neckline to the office.

"Of course, Ms. Sinclair," he said, remaining standing where he was since he didn't know where she wanted him, even though she was sitting. "What can I do for you today?"

There was something about her tone of voice that made him think they were roleplaying that he was in trouble, which he did not object to. The not knowing increased his interest, and his arousal was already sky-rocketing, thanks to the quick way she'd taken control of the scene. Boss Lady Camille was really doing it for him.

She raised her eyebrow, giving him an imperious look, and confirming his suspicion he was in 'trouble.'

"You can explain yourself, Sir." Yup, definitely in trouble. "You lost this company a lot of money this quarter."

"I'm so sorry, ma'am," he replied quickly, sinking into the role, thankful she seemed the type to leave things in broad strokes. Roleplay could get bogged down in the details, but Mistress Camille was giving them both a lot of room to play with. "It won't happen again."

"I'm not sure your reassurances are enough, Mr. Johan, especially considering your overall performance this year. I think some real consequences might help motivate you since nothing else has."

"Whatever you think is appropriate, ma'am," he said earnestly. "I'll do whatever it takes to prove myself to you."

Raising her eyebrows, Mistress Camille leaned forward on the desk, giving him an intense look. His cock was already hard, but it jerked at that look. Fuck, she was hot when she was bossy.

"Whatever it takes?" she asked, her voice changing a touch, becoming sultrier.

"Yes, Ma'am." He could feel his heart pounding in his chest, wondering what she was going to ask of him. Something filthy, he hoped.

"Well, Mr. Johan, let me see what you have to offer. Strip."

Freddy put his hand to his chest, feigning shock.

"Ma'am? I'm not sure that's entirely professional." It was a bit of a risk, putting up some resistance, since not all Dominants liked that, but he was curious how she would react. Plus, it added a little more realism to the scene.

"I'm not looking for professional, Alfred." Oh, interesting. Hearing his full first name on her lips did things to his insides he hadn't been prepared for. "I'm looking for a man who will go the extra mile. The one who just said he was willing to do *anything* to prove himself. Now strip or turn around and walk out that door and don't come back."

Freddy stripped.

CAMILLE

Sitting behind the desk, watching Freddy strip off his clothes, Camille felt powerful, which was the whole point of this type of role-play. It was also making her feel a lot better after the confrontation with the two douchebags earlier. Some of the nerves in her stomach had already settled.

Maybe if nothing else worked out, she'd end up being her own boss. That would be fine, even if it wasn't what she'd wanted, but she was realizing more and more that her time at Donaldson was done.

Shoving away thoughts of her actual work, she took the time to admire Freddy's physique. His long, lean muscles. The way his hip bones had those cute little notches. The blond hair on his chest and neatly trimmed around the thick stalk of his cock, which was standing at attention.

"You seem to be enjoying how unprofessional we're being," she couldn't help pointing out.

To her delight, Freddy blushed and pretended to be bashful, covering his erection with his hand. Well, sort of covering it. The sneaky sub was using his 'embarrassment' to press his hand against his cock, giving himself some of the stimulation he was craving.

"You're a very attractive woman, ma'am," he replied shyly.

Camille smiled even wider. Naughty boy and a good actor, too, in a fun way. 'Shy' did not seem to be part of Freddy's make-up, but he was very cute doing it for roleplay.

"And you're a very attractive man. One I'd like to see all of. Move over to my desk and put your hands flat on top of it." She gave him a look to let him know she knew *exactly* what he'd been doing with his hands. Freddy grinned for a moment before slipping back into character, ducking his head as he moved into position.

The position required him to bend forward, spreading his legs outward, since he was quite a bit taller than the desk. His cock hung down beneath him, his back straight, as he peeked up at her, to see her reaction.

"Good boy," she purred. This close to his face, she could see the way his pupils dilated, his quick intake of breath, and his needy pleasure at the praise. "Now, stay right there while I figure out exactly what I'm going to do with you."

She glanced at the clock on the wall above the door. She had about ten minutes before the surprise she'd asked Tracey to arrange arrived, just enough time as long as she moved quickly.

Opening the drawer to her left, she pulled out the paddle. Freddy's head jerked up, and she saw his hot look of anticipation before he ducked down again, hiding his expression. Yes, paddle, and...

The other side of the desk held an assortment of plugs, probes, dildos, vibrators... and there were more in the armoire, according to Tracey. Thankfully, Camille didn't have to search. What she wanted was right there in the drawer—a remote controlled plug.

Since she needed new toys, she might as well add some of the ones she found at Stronghold to her collection, especially since she could use them right away instead of having to wait for them to be shipped.

Picking up one of the small bottles of lube and a few batteries, she put the paddle on the desk where Freddy's head was hanging down, so he would have to stare at it while she got everything else ready. While she unwrapped the plug from its packaging, got the batteries into the remote, and then lubed up the toy, she started lecturing him.

"This company has standards, Mr. Johan, and we need employees who are willing to take on any task, no matter how hard—"

"I'm fine with hard tasks," he quipped, making her lips quiver in amusement.

Clearing her throat, she went on.

"Who will bend over backward—"

"Or forward."

She reached out to give his ass a short, sharp smack. She'd been pretty sure he wouldn't be able to resist that one. Freddy gasped at the initial contact before moaning, his back muscles rippling, his ass lifting in response.

"And who are open to new challenges." She pressed the tip of the plug against his anus and began to push in, hard enough to make him groan. Smiling at the sound, she pulled the plug part way out before pushing in again, giving him time to adjust—but not much. "Do you think you are that man, Alfred?"

"Yes, Ma'am." The words came out on a gasp as he pushed back, taking more of the plug inside him, the little lines around his hole flattening out as it was stretched wide around the slick toy. Camille pushed it all the way in, enjoying the way he shuddered as the toy nestled inside him, his body closing around the stem between the bulb and the base.

That done, she reached around him to pick up the paddle.

"I'm so glad to hear that, Alfred," she crooned, running her free hand down the center of his back to his buttocks. "Of course, we need to punish you for not meeting our standards this last quarter."

"Yes, Ma'am," he replied eagerly, dropping his head down and pushing his hips back to thrust his ass higher in the air.

The black base of the plug between his cheeks peeked out at her. Smiling, Camille flipped the switch on the vibrator to the lowest setting.

"You're not allowed to cum until I tell you to."

Freddy groaned.

25

Freddy.

The low hum of vibrations in Freddy's ass were a complete tease. Groaning, he clenched around the plug, his body eager for more sensation. It felt good but not nearly good enough.

Mistress Camille brought the paddle down on his ass. The hard length of wood was long enough to catch both cheeks. He cried out, gasping at the hot sting, the dull, throbbing thud that went deeper into his flesh, and the way his cock pulsed in response. Pain enhanced pleasure, and he was feeling both.

"I'm sorry, Ma'am," he said, maintaining the role he'd been assigned. "I promise this next quarter will be better."

"Oh, I know it will, Alfred. If not, your ass will pay the price again."

The paddle smacked against him again, and Freddy dropped his head, his fingers curling against the desk as heat and need and pain washed over him in equal measure. One of the things he liked best about the paddle was the sensation seemed to go deeper than some of the lighter implements, giving him more of what he craved all at once.

It was a good thing this was just roleplay. Otherwise, 'Alfred' would be very tempted to turn in another quarter's lackluster performance if this was the kind of punishment he had to look forward to. On the other hand, he'd never want to disappoint his Mistress. That would be far worse than any physical punishment she could dole out.

"Yes, Ma'am." He shuddered as the paddle came down again, clenching and wanting to hum along with the vibrations that were teasing him.

Each swat burned hotter, and when the wooden edge caught a bit of the plug, jostling it inside him, his knees buckled. With a whimper, he managed to stand straight again. Mistress Camille's hand ran over his ass, nearly making him jump since he hadn't been expecting her to touch him.

"Nice and hot," she said approvingly. "Now... under the desk with you."

Although he was a little surprised, she was stopping the punishment so soon—he hadn't been keeping count, but it couldn't have been more than ten swats—Freddy obeyed with alacrity. If she wanted him under the desk, he was going under the desk. He was pretty sure he knew why.

The desk had been built with two specific purposes—making it easy for someone to be bound atop it and making it easy for someone to perform oral sex below it.

On his knees, the plug still buzzing gently, his buttocks hot and throbbing from the paddling, Freddy grinned as Mistress Camille pulled off her underwear before pulling up her skirt and sitting down. Her legs spread wide, butt on the edge of the seat, her lower body tilted in such a manner, it was easy for him to slide between her thighs and press his lips to her wet pussy. No need to order him to do anything.

He dove right in, relishing her moan of pleasure as his tongue parted her lower lips. Being under the desk was oddly quiet, but he still heard her sigh of pleasure, though it seemed farther away. With her chair pushed in all the way, the darkness under the desk made him feel like he was in a cocoon.

A sex cocoon.

Which was why the knock at the door made him jump.

Mistress Camille's fingers slid into his hair, gripping him tightly, and keeping his face firmly in place between her thighs.

"Come in."

What the...

It was part of the roleplay, he realized a moment later. He'd bet just about anything that this was what she'd prepared with Tracey.

But it wasn't Tracey's voice he heard, it was Morgan's.

"Hello, Ms. Sinclair, I have the reports you asked for."

"Thank you, Morgan, bring them over here please."

Oh, so that's how they were going to play it, were they?

Freddy was happy to meet the unspoken challenge. Mistress Camille was going to keep roleplaying, and Freddy was going to do his best to break her out of character.

With her hand still in his hair, he dove back into her pussy, ignoring whatever she and Morgan were talking about. Mistress Camille let go of his hair, probably feeling it looked a little odd above the desk and giving him free rein to do what he liked. Using his shoulders, he spread her thighs wider, his tongue dipping and swirling. Accidentally bumping his head on the desk caused a brief pause in the conversation happening above him, but it didn't slow him at all.

He was doing his best to bring Mistress Camille to orgasm while she was talking to Morgan, and a bump or two on the head was hardly a deterrent.

Suddenly, the vibrator in his ass kicked up a notch, going from barely there to a medium, pulsing buzz that sent hot spears of pleasure piercing through him. Freddy moaned into her pussy, his ass clenching as ecstasy gripped him. The urge to grip his dick growing stronger, he put that need into his oral efforts, doubling down on his intention to give her pleasure since he couldn't have his own until she said so.

<u>CAMILLE</u>

A hot flush heating her cheeks, Camille was struggling to concentrate on what Morgan was saying. The stunning redhead grinned at her. Camille had asked Tracey to have Morgan interrupt them at a set time. Camille knew Morgan and Freddy were close and figured it would be better to include someone she knew he was friends with rather than just any old body.

"Thank you for bringing this to my attention, Morgan," she said as Freddy sucked her clit into his mouth, simultaneously bumping his head on the underside of the desk again.

It was all she could do not to gasp, keeping everything normal from the waist up while everything from her waist down was buzzing and humming with pleasure. The most she'd been able to do in retaliation was make sure Freddy was buzzing inside too, which only seemed to have encouraged him even more.

"Of course, Ms. Sinclair. Have a great rest of the ev— I mean, day." Morgan grinned and skipped out of the room, apparently very pleased with having played a part in the scene.

Leaning back in the chair, Camille rolled it back just an inch, enough so she could see Freddy's blue eyes peering up at her, his mouth firmly pressed against her pussy as he continued to lick and suck. Now that their audience was gone, and she didn't have to pretend to be working anymore, she gave herself over to the physical sensations.

Gripping his head with both hands, she rubbed her pussy against his lips and tongue, moaning with abandon in pure pleasure.

"Use your fingers," she demanded, shuddering and clenching as his fingers pressed into her, his tongue still hard at work on her clit. He pumped his fingers back and forth, curving them in just the right spot to make her cry out as ecstasy flared. She leaned back even further, giving him full access to her pussy. Thrusting his fingers inside her, twisting and stroking, his tongue laved her most sensitive spots as she squirmed in the chair. "Oh fuck... fuck, Freddy!"

Throwing her head back, she cried out as passion surged, her body tightening and releasing a wave of erotic bliss that crashed over her senses. He kept licking, sucking, and moving his fingers inside of her, pushing her higher and higher until the waves finally ebbed, leaving her delightfully satisfied.

Now, it was his turn.

"Very good boy," she murmured, gentling her hold on his hair and stroking the damp strands as she scooted back. His fingers and mouth fell away from her, his lips and chin still glossy with the evidence of her orgasm.

It was highly enjoyable seeing him so disheveled, his hair askew, mouth wet with her juices, rather than the put-together professional he so often appeared. This was Freddy completely unbuttoned and undressed.

She held out her hand so he could take it and get to his feet.

"What would you like to do, Freddy? We still have the room for another forty minutes. Submissive's choice." Partly because she hadn't come into the night with a plan and partly because she wanted to know what he would choose. There were plenty of things she could do, she didn't *need* a plan to finish out the scene in a satisfying manner, but she wanted to know what he wanted.

His eyes lit up with delight, making her feel even happier about making the offer. Not all submissives wanted a say in what happened to them or even found it stressful, but some enjoyed being able to choose something for themselves now and then. It didn't surprise her that Freddy was one of the latter.

"I would like to be pegged, Mistress." He looked at her imploringly, as if worried she was going to turn down such a charming invitation.

Her smile widened. It looked like she would be getting more than one new toy tonight.

"Then get up on the desk, on your back." She gave his fingers a squeeze before letting go. "If you can tell me where I might find a strap-on in here..."

Freddy looked as if he was floating on air when he pointed to one of the filing cabinets. He got onto the desk while she was looking through the options, and she smiled when she glanced over to see him in position and waiting. Knowing what was coming, he'd put himself on the edge of the table, his legs spread wide, hands draped over the sides of the table and gripping them to help him keep position.

Holding it on his own wouldn't be very comfortable, but she'd be there in a moment to help.

Picking up a harness that looked like it would fit her, she selected a medium sized dildo to go on the front, along with a slightly larger attachment for herself. The dildo for Freddy was longer, but not thicker than the plug he currently had inserted.

Since she'd left him buzzing the entire time, she waited to turn off the remote until she had the strap-on in place, the dark brown cock jutting out in front of her while her pussy clenched around the one inside her. Sadly, no vibrations here, but she didn't really need them, and neither would Freddy.

He'd watched her while she got ready, and as she approached, his eyes flared with hot passion and need. It didn't change, even when she turned off the plug's vibrations.

"What's your safeword, Freddy?" she asked, moving to the side of the desk where his ass was nearly hanging off the edge.

"Red... but I'm not going to need it."

Pressing her lips together to keep from smiling, she didn't chastise him. He was being a little sassy, but he was also expressing his confidence in her. Picking up the little tube of lubricant, she spread the last of it over the dildo while he watched, his growing anticipation evident in his expression and the heat in his eyes.

"Ready?" she asked, taking hold of the base of the plug.

"Yes, Mistress." His gaze never left her face.

There was something achingly intimate about anal sex. Perhaps because it had been considered taboo for so long, perhaps because the potential for pain was so high, she'd always considered it an act that required a great deal of trust. Not something she took for granted.

Easing the plug from his body, she replaced it with the tip of the dildo.

The buzzing vibrations were gone, but this felt so much better. He stared up at Mistress Camille as she began to push into his ass. The dildo she'd chosen was thick enough, he still felt the slight burn of entrance but not so thick that she couldn't move quickly. Thank goodness. He wanted it quick.

Hard.

Dirty.

His whole body was aching with the need for release.

"Harder, please," he begged when she thrust in slowly. He didn't want slow. He wanted to *feel it.*

"As you wish," she murmured and pulled back. At the same time, her hand wrapped around his cock.

Freddy cried out, his back arching upward in sheer pleasure. The dildo moved, going in deep and hard, her hand moving on his cock in unison with the thrusts.

"Fuck!" His hands tightened their grip on the edges of the table as the pleasure ripped through his body. The slight sting as his ass was stretched again and again only served to enhance his pleasure, like adding salt to something sweet so it tasted even better.

He writhed for her as she moved, gasping and moving his hips to meet her thrusts. Her breathing was getting faster, her soft moans joining his louder ones as her passion grew again. Since she'd already had one orgasm, she would be even more sensitive, and he was sure she was nearing a second climax.

All he had to do was hold out so she could reach her pleasure again... hold out until she told him *he* could come.

Which was much easier said than done.

He felt each thrust as it stretched him, the tip of the dildo rubbing against his prostate and making his body spasm. The tightness of his balls was becoming painful, adding to the cacophony of sensations gripping him. Her hand moved harder and faster on his cock as she got closer to her orgasm, and resisting the sensations running through him was becoming more and more difficult.

"Please... fuck, please, Mistress... I need to cum..." He wouldn't be able to hold out much longer. If she didn't give him permission, he was going to end up cumming anyway, and he desperately didn't want to disappoint her.

"Good boy, Freddy... you may cum."

She thrust in again and he cried out, his cock pulsing in her hand as spurt after spurt of hot liquid splashed against his stomach. The thick streams of fluid coated his body as she pumped, her own soft cry joining his, her head thrown back as her body shivered with pleasure.

Closing his eyes, Freddy went limp as his body released all of its tension, fully satisfied and satiated.

Mistress Camille was the perfect woman. The perfect Mistress.

Was this what falling in love was like?

26

Stroking Freddy's hair, Camille turned her head slightly to press her cheek against the top of his head. Aftercare for Freddy was cuddling, which she rather enjoyed, even if they were squished onto the same sofa. At least it was a sofa that was big enough to handle being squished on to. Someone had obviously anticipated that people would want to be able to lie down at least mostly next to each other, instead of having to be on top of each other.

"That was amazing." It was the third time he'd said it, yet another burst of happiness flowed through her.

Sadly, it was accompanied by the tiniest bit of nervous tension. As much as she didn't want to let Donaldson ruin her weekend or her time with Freddy, now that she'd worked off some of her nervous energy and the scene was over, her brain was refocusing on her life problems instead of the scene.

"It was," she replied what she'd said the first two times he'd said it. Telling the truth was no hardship.

Watching Freddy writhe for her, having him at her mercy, giving him the pleasure he craved... No, fuck Donaldson. There was no way she was giving this up. They didn't get to control her life outside the office, and there was nothing wrong with her and Freddy having a relationship. The Alexanders' divorce was finalized, and she and Freddy weren't working on any other cases against each other, so there was no reason they couldn't date.

Yet her stomach wouldn't settle.

"Is everything okay?"

Dammit. Her submissive was far too observant at times.

"Just worrying about Monday and work, but that's really not what I want to think about."

He ran his hand down her side, offering a bit of reassuring comfort.

"Want to go hang out with my friends? I'm sure there are plenty of distractions happening downstairs."

Sure, she described herself as an introvert, but that offer sounded really appealing right now. Maybe because she wasn't ready for the night to end. Tomorrow, she was going to have to think a lot more about work and her problems. Being at Stronghold was like being in a little bubble outside of time, and unlike Marquis, the whole club was dedicated to kink and kinky people. There was no chance she'd run into anyone from her firm here.

Freddy would know if anyone was a member and would have given her a heads up.

Just like the second floor of Marquis, this was a place where she could relax and be herself. Unlike Marquis, she could do it while hanging out at the bar.

"Yeah, let's do that." She felt his jolt of surprise but saw his pleasure as they got themselves together and headed downstairs. More than pleasure—pride. He was enjoying being seen with her.

Which was just about the cutest thing in the world. She took pleasure in *his* pleasure at being with her. Now that they weren't so jazzed up and eager for their scene, she was feeling much calmer and much less overwhelmed by the many people he knew in the club.

"Uh oh," Freddy murmured a few moments after they walked onto the main floor. She looked at him, but he wasn't paying attention to her and didn't seem to realize he was speaking out loud. He was looking at the dance floor.

"What's wrong?" She squeezed Freddy's hand, and he jumped.

"Oh, ah... well, club drama. Of course. You remember Rae, from earlier?" he asked, tilting his head toward where a number of people were dancing.

Rae was the pretty black girl with the long braids, with a few green braids threaded throughout the dark brown. Camille nodded as she spotted Rae dancing with a handsome Asian man. The two of them were moving well together, then the man bent his head to kiss her, one hand sliding up the back of her neck to hold her in place.

Beside Camille, Freddy winced.

"Okay, well that's Master Damian."

"What's wrong with him?"

"Nothing, exactly, but he's a relationship kind of Dom, and Rae and Master Brian have been doing this kind of 'will they, won't they' dance around each other. If she's out on the dance floor with Master Damian..." Freddy's voice trailed off, and he looked around as if trying to spot Master Brian.

"If she has a thing for Master Brian, why would she be interested in a different Dom?" Camille turned her head. She had been introduced to Master Brian but wasn't sure she remembered which Dom he was.

"Because Master Brian is a Daddy Dom and Rae keeps insisting that's not what she wants. I figured being around each other would eventually wear her down... Ah, crap. Yeah, there he goes." Freddy sighed.

Following his gaze, Camille saw a dark-haired man leaving the club.

They were much too far away to go after him, but it looked like he had a friend right on his heels.

"Wow." Camille shook her head. Right into it with the club drama, apparently. Since she wasn't involved, she could feel some amusement, but it faded when she saw Freddy's expression. He was the kind of guy who felt deeply and was protective of his friends. All of them. And he was a helper. His inability to fix things for Brian and Rae was probably going to bug him. She squeezed his hand, pulling him in close to her.

"You can't make people's decisions for them, you know."

"I know, but the world would be so much easier if they let me."

That made her laugh, and he smiled.

"Come on, who else can we hang out with?"

"Depends. Do you want the dirt on whatever's going on with Rae and Damian?" His voice was hopeful.

Personally, Camille didn't care, but she could tell Freddy did. She was also nosy enough to be curious, even though she didn't know them. Distracting herself with other people's drama didn't sound like the worst thing in the world, and she wanted to see more of how Freddy maneuvered through his relationships in the club.

If she was going to have a relationship with him, it meant understanding how he operated in 'his' space. It came to how much he gave of himself and whether she'd ever need to step in. She was quickly coming to realize he not only felt responsible for the people in the clubs but that he struggled with not stepping in to fix things for them.

FREDDY

Though he wasn't sure it was the right decision, he was glad Mistress Camille was willing to spend some more time at Stronghold. With all the work he did at Marquis, he wasn't able to visit Stronghold quite as much as he would have liked. Now that he was here again, he realized how much he missed it. The atmosphere. The people. The energy.

Every part of his backside ached and throbbed with the remembrance of their scene. He could walk without a problem, but movement came with a reminder that he'd just gotten a paddling and a pegging.

Making his way to the table where Law and Iris were talking to Master Asad and Master Connor, he smiled when they saw him and

Mistress Camille coming and immediately made space. Since Master Kincaid had gone after Master Brian, and Master Mitch and Domi were nowhere to be seen, he figured Iris was probably the best source of information if he wanted to know about Rae and Master Damian.

"You two look like you had fun," Master Asad said when they reached them. Master Connor smiled while Master Law shook his head, and Iris giggled. Pretty much the expected reactions from all of them. For all that he was a huge bear of a man and a Dom, Master Connor was very quiet most of the time and was much more like a teddy bear than a grumpy bear. Master Law was the grumpy bear, though Iris kept him smiling more often than not these days. The two of them were good for each other. She kept out of trouble now that she had a steady hand at the wheel, and he couldn't be too serious with Iris around.

Master Asad, of course, was the funny man of the group. Golden retriever energy with the sex drive of a rabbit and a playfully sadistic side that left the submissives panting. He seemed to enjoy defying expectations.

"It's been a good night," Freddy said agreeably. He grinned at Mistress Camille, who smiled back at him.

"A very good night." The warmth in her tone washed over him, almost as good as being called a 'good boy.'

"How's your night going?" he asked, turning back to the others, letting his concern show. "I saw Master Brian leaving."

"Yeah..." Iris' gaze cut to the dance floor. "Rae just came by to introduce her new boyfriend. He stuck around for the introduction, but I don't think he felt like staying for the after show."

Freddy's eyes widened.

"Wait, they're already boyfriend and girlfriend? Not just dating?" Though he shouldn't be too surprised. Master Damian was something of a serial monogamist. He hadn't been to the club for a while after his last breakup, but Freddy hadn't expected him to move quite this fast upon his return... and definitely not with Rae.

Whether she wanted to admit it, Rae was the kind of sub who would thrive with a caretaker or service Dom. A Daddy Dom wasn't that far off from what she needed, and that wasn't Master Damian. He was a good, steady Dom, but his kinks tended more toward someone who took care of themselves outside of the bedroom, with no overlap. It wasn't that he didn't care, but he expected his submissives to handle themselves and behave themselves without oversight from him, which worked for a lot of submissives.

He wasn't sure it would work for Rae, but she would have to figure it out on her own.

"Yup, official as of yesterday." Iris shrugged, but the worry in her dark eyes made it clear she didn't feel confident about this new development either. "She seems happy."

"Well, good." Watching how this all played out would definitely be interesting. The conversation moved on to Domi and Mitch's wedding planning, which led to Master Asad complaining about his need for a fake date for the upcoming wedding. His grumbling had both Mistress Camille and Freddy cracking up.

Apparently, his mom had decided to take matters into her own hands when it came to finding a good match for him, which led to him telling her he had a girlfriend, and *of course,* she'd be at the wedding with him... and that was that. He didn't seem to know that Lexie had picked out Morgan for him, which was interesting, so Freddy kept his mouth shut.

Heading to the bar to get a second drink for himself and Mistress Camille—things were getting a little packed, and he wanted to say hi to Andrew again—Freddy came to a sudden halt when Noelle popped up in front of him. Her wide, imploring eyes met his, and her tongue darted out to lick her lip as if nervous.

"Hi, Freddy... um, I'm Noelle, I'm not sure if you remember me."

"Of course, I do. Is everything okay?" He asked automatically, partly because he couldn't think of any other reason why she would approach him and partly because there was something about her demeanor that made her seem distressed.

She sniffled as tears filled her eyes at his words.

"Well... I've heard you're the person to go to when any of us submissives are having a problem." She paused, looking up at him as though she was waiting for him to respond.

Freddy nodded, not sure where she was going with this, but was very curious. If she did have a problem, he would want to help, though as far as he knew, she hadn't been having trouble with any of the club's Doms. She hadn't played with very many of them, but there hadn't been any complaints or drama. However, he also missed things being at Marquis most of the time.

Her voice lowered. "I'm being bullied."

"You are?" Indignation rose up inside him. No, he didn't particularly like her, and for good reason, but that didn't mean he'd condone bullying, especially not in the club. "Who?"

Her hands twisted in front of her.

"I don't really want to say, I don't want to single anyone out, but... I guess I just want advice on how to handle it. I noticed Doms don't want to scene with me, and subs don't want to be friends with me because... It's people who are popular here and no one wants to go against them."

Freddy frowned. He definitely hadn't heard of anything like that. No one was saying not to be friends with her or not to scene with her, though because of the gossip train, some people knew about how she'd treated Iris and might react accordingly. As far as he knew, everyone had been encouraged not to treat her any differently, and she'd made several friends—including some who were friendly with Iris—and had scened with several Doms. Still, he couldn't dismiss her out of hand since he was a little out of the loop at Stronghold these days.

"If it makes you feel better, I haven't heard of anyone saying anything detrimental about you, and I always end up hearing the gossip. I'll look into it, though, okay? It would help me if you told me who was bothering you." As soon as he said the words, she was shaking her head.

"Oh, no, I can't do that. I don't want to stir anything up, or cause any drama, I just..." She huffed out a breath of air. "I'm glad you haven't heard anything, but I'm worried that maybe no one is saying anything to you because they know how you'll react, and they don't want me to have your protection."

She seemed completely sincere, and if she was anyone else in the club, Freddy would take her words at face value, but because of what he knew about her, it was difficult. On the other hand, he also knew he needed to look into this. There definitely were people who would believe what she said, and it could cause a lot of drama, even if she didn't mean to. Especially if she ended up naming names.

He could guess who she thought was behind any bullying, although he wasn't sure that's what he'd call it, even if there was something going on. So, that's where he'd start.

27

Camille

Sunday morning and Freddy was in her bed after a wonderful night at Stronghold. Even the memory of their interrupted dinner couldn't entirely kill her buzz, though her worry about the consequences of Junior's threat was higher today. No more distractions.

"Good morning." Turned out Freddy was awake, too. "What are you thinking so hard about?" Facing her, head on his pillow, his brilliant blue eyes were both curious and slightly worried.

"Junior and work but also how happy I am to wake up with you here. That definitely outweighs any worry." She grinned as he smiled, delight lighting up his expression.

"Happy to be here. Would you like me to go get started on breakfast? Or... started on breakfast... I'd be happy to distract you."

Oh, well with that kind of offer on the table... Camille was perfectly happy to let Freddy have a first breakfast in bed. As a distraction technique, it was a lovely one. Instead of starting her morning off worrying and letting her anxiety grow, she started it off with Freddy's blond head between her thighs, his wicked tongue eliciting louder and louder moans, until all of her tension was released in a glorious orgasm.

Then they went to the kitchen where he made crepes.

If this wasn't living her best life, she didn't know what was.

"So, what's your plan for dealing with Junior? If you're okay with talking about it," Freddy said, sitting down next to her with his own plate of crepes. He'd made them each one savory and one sweet, and there was more batter if they were still hungry afterwards. "If you're not, please let me know if there's anything I can do to help."

"Honestly, I'm not sure what I'll be able to do until I find out how he spins this to the other partners. I'll tell them the truth, but I'm sure he's already told his dad, and it's spreading around today. I suppose I could reach out to some of them before him, but they'll probably take that as an admission of guilt. Like I'm making a big deal out of it because I have something to hide, not because Junior is."

"Whereas, if he's the one calling around, it's clear he thinks it's a big deal, but you don't and therefore, you're not treating it like it is." Freddy nodded. "I can see that. Though it could backfire since he's going to be coloring their thoughts before they even ask you what's going on."

"Yeah, but there's nothing I can do about that except hope they'll be reasonable, even though he got to them first. If they're not willing to listen to what I have to say because of when I say it, that says an awful lot about them."

"Hmm." He didn't answer right away, and she thought maybe he was savoring a bite of food, but when she looked over, he wasn't chewing, and his eyes were unfocused, as though he was thinking hard about something.

"What?" she asked.

"Just thinking about how that's applicable to Noelle last night," he admitted. On the ride home from Stronghold, he'd told Camille about Noelle's request. She'd bristled at the idea of bullying happening and had absolutely agreed he needed to look into it.

Privately, she'd thought he was maybe being a little too hesitant to give Noelle the full benefit of the doubt because he was starting off from a position of bias against her, but she could see what he was saying. Especially as it applied to herself. Since she didn't know anyone involved in the situation, she was more willing to entertain the idea that perhaps some of the people Freddy was friends with at Stronghold were being unkind to the woman. However, was she being influenced by the fact she'd only heard Noelle's allegations and that she'd heard them first?

Definitely something to think about.

But a different scenario since she already knew the partners would be biased against her and treat Junior's account as the whole truth. Since there was nothing she could do about that, she was trying not to let it ruin her day. She thought attempting to get to them first would make some of them view her even less favorably.

"I can see that," she said. "It's a good reminder not to go in thinking you have the whole story when you've only heard one side of it."

"Which can be hard to remember when you're constantly representing only one side of something." He chuckled. "One of the hazards of our job."

Camille laughed. "Yeah, but sometimes there really is only one side worth considering. I can tell you right now that you did good work with Mrs. Alexander. She deserved much more than she got from that asshole."

"Probably, but I'm not always one hundred percent on the side of the angels, as much as that's where I want to be. When it comes to people I like, whose lives I'm invested in, I don't want to believe they'd behave badly, but that doesn't mean I'm right." He made a face, as if it pained him to make that admission.

"So, you think there's a possibility she's being bullied?"

"I don't know that I would call it bullying," he said slowly. "The more I think about it, the more I think even if people aren't friendly with her or choosing not to scene with her, that doesn't mean that it's bullying. It's not like we force everyone to be friends or hang out together at the club. She didn't say people were actively harassing her or anything, but I'm going to look into it all the same.

"That's all you can do." She'd keep an ear out and check in with Julie and Olivia. Both of them would know better than Freddy what the gossip among the Dominants was and if any of them were avoiding scening with Noelle.

Not that there was much anyone could do if they weren't by their own choice. If they were being told not to, that would be different, but she was having trouble picturing that happening. Even Dominants who liked to follow the rules didn't like to be told what to do outside the necessary structures of the scene. There would always be a few who would buck being told what to do and do the opposite.

Sometimes, Doms looked an awful lot like brats.

Not that she'd ever say so out loud.

Her phone dinged with an email, and she glanced over automatically, freezing when she saw the sender. It was from Murdoch.

"Who is it?" Freddy asked.

"Murdoch... hold on a sec." Dropping her fork, she scrambled to pick up her phone. She had to read the email twice before the message really sank in, then she let out a whoop, throwing her hands in the air—though she kept a tight grip on her phone because she didn't want to accidentally throw that too. "I got the job!"

"You got the job?!" The question was rhetorical and delighted. Freddy jumped to his feet, which inspired her to get onto hers as well. He twirled, showing off his cute butt in the apron, and she did a little dance of happiness, letting it buoy her as she truly celebrated.

Coming close enough to grab him, she pulled him in, and his lips met hers in a joyful kiss. The lingering tension from the night before was gone. It didn't matter what Junior told the other partners now.

Pulling away from the kiss, she didn't let go of him.

"I need to sign the acceptance and get it back to them, then type up my resignation for Donaldson. I got the job!"

"You got the job!"

Both of them laughed, and she squeezed him tightly, resting her head against his shoulder as she fended off relieved tears. It felt good to lean on him, knowing he was here for her and feeling his happiness for her. Having someone to celebrate with was amazing.

Opening up her life to him wasn't easy, neither was being vulnerable and admitting to her feelings, but she wanted him to know how much he was starting to mean to her. She was so glad the job offer had come in while he was around to celebrate with her. Not that not sharing the news would have taken away from how happy it made her, but having him by her side made the moment feel even more complete.

"I'm glad you're here," she admitted, her voice muffled from where she was pressed against his shoulder.

"Me, too."

"Wanna come meet my mom this afternoon?"

He squeezed her a little tighter.

"I would be honored."

FREDDY

Meeting Camille's mother was both a joy and a sadness. He was so glad she wanted him to, but he could also see that the visit made her sad because of how her mother's memory had been affected. Whether Mrs. Sinclair would be able to remember him the next time he came was up in the air, but he was still glad to meet her.

He could see why Camille's job had been so important to her. It was clear the care Mrs. Sinclair was getting was exemplary, and with a disease like dementia, it was important to slowing the effects.

Excusing himself to give them a little privacy for the last bit of Camille's visit, Freddy went down the hall to a small greeting room. No one was using it, so he didn't feel bad taking over one of the armchairs and making a few calls to some of the people who would know if there was any truth to what Noelle said.

Lexie was at the top of his list, followed by Kate, Gina, and finally Sam. He saved the person in Noelle's actual group of friends for last, figuring he'd have more information by then. Unfortunately, he didn't have any.

None of the first three knew of any rumors being spread about Noelle. There had been the initial flurry of discussion when she'd first joined, especially because she'd apparently said a few things in her Introduction Class that had people talking about *Iris*, but that had all been shut down pretty quickly. Iris, on the other hand, had asked everyone to give Noelle a chance.

Kate and Lexie admitted that neither of them was particularly keen on giving Noelle a chance, but that wasn't surprising since they'd both known Iris for a long time, even if she wasn't part of their inner circle. He'd called Gina because she wasn't part of that group, either, and he figured she would have more of an outsider's perspective, but she'd been surprised. She'd never heard anything about it. She did mention a few Doms who weren't interested in scening with Noelle but only because of what they'd heard from Doms who did scene with her.

She was getting a bit of a reputation as someone who liked to play at submission rather than truly submitting, and while some of the Doms were fine with that or even considered her a challenge, it turned others off. Nothing wrong with any of that.

Amy was the first person who had any kind of information for him from Noelle's side of things.

"Yeah, she said it's been getting weird for her at the club lately," Amy said, a note of worry in her voice. "She doesn't think Iris is behind it, but she worries about what Rae and Domi are saying. I don't think they'd be trying to influence anyone, but I know they're also super protective of Iris."

That was true. There had been an incident when he'd had to shut down some nasty talk between the two of them about Morgan, but as far as he knew, they'd never tried to talk to anyone else about her. Afterward, they'd both regretted their words and mended their ways.

He knew some of the issue had been the fact that they didn't know about Morgan's past, so they'd had a very skewed view on why the Doms showed so much interest in her. Didn't help that Rae had been wildly jealous of how much attention Master Brian paid attention to Morgan, even if she wasn't willing to admit it. They'd never said anything directly to Morgan or even where she could hear. It had been pure chance he'd overheard one of their conversations.

That had been over a year ago, and as far as he knew, they'd never said another mean word about her or any other sub. They'd also started working on reaching out and making new friends, which was how they'd become friends with Iris and another sub, Avery. It didn't hurt that Domi's fiancé, Mitch, had a large group of friends they'd been pulled into as well.

He didn't think they'd make trouble for Noelle now but couldn't entirely rule it out.

"Do you know what they're saying?" he asked. "Noelle didn't want to get into specifics."

There was a long moment of silent hesitation, then Amy sighed.

"I'll be honest, I don't know that they're saying anything to anyone. She says they don't like her, which is true, but it's not like they're going around shouting it to the rooftops. She seems really paranoid about it. It doesn't help that Marissa and Caroline smother her in sympathy every time she talks about either. I don't think she realizes that they have their own axe to grind with that group."

"Are you doing okay with all of it?" he asked. "I know you spend a lot of time with Zach, and he's good friends with Mitch…"

"Oh, yeah, they aren't treating me any differently. I don't really spend time with Zach's friends, you know." Almost the moment she finished speaking, Freddy could hear a masculine voice in the background. He couldn't understand what the man was saying, but he sounded angry. Amy's fiancé? "Shoot, Freddy I've gotta go. I'll talk to you later."

She hung up before he could respond, and he frowned. If that was her fiancé, it sounded like trouble in paradise. He hoped he hadn't caused it by bringing up Zach.

"Hey, you ready to go?" Camille appeared in the doorway, a tired smile on her lips. She raised her eyebrows at him. "Everything okay?"

"Yeah. Sounds like Noelle's unhappy, but I can't find anyone who has anything concrete about her being treated badly or even differently, so that's good news." He didn't bring up the end of his call with Amy. He wasn't sure why she'd had to go so quickly and didn't want to spread her business around if she was having trouble with her fiancé. "Anyway, what do you want for your celebration dinner?"

"My celebration dinner?" She laughed as he met her in the doorway, dropping his lips down to hers for a quick kiss.

"Of course. A new job deserves a celebration."

"Alright, you've convinced me." Smiling up at him, he could see the pure happiness in her expression.

Fuck, it was no wonder he was falling so fast.

28

———————

It was official. She wanted Freddy next to her every morning when she woke up. It felt like their relationship was moving fast, but that's because her emotions were moving fast. Lying on her back in the bed alone, wishing he was there, she had to face the fact that she wasn't falling... she'd fallen.

Just in time for Valentine's Day.

Which was in two days.

They'd known each other for a little over a month.

Yeah, but what a month.

Maybe the old saying was true—when you knew, you knew. Didn't matter how long it had been. That's why she'd taken him to meet her mom yesterday. She wasn't sure if he realized what a big deal that was, although he'd seemed like he understood at least a little. He'd also been sensitive enough to know she still wanted a little time alone with her mom.

They should probably talk about it, but it felt like it was too soon. It was too soon, right? She shook her head.

Today, she would be handing in her resignation to Donaldson, so she needed to get her head in the game. She could figure out relationship stuff later. Unlike her job, which was much more pressing.

She wished she felt nothing but relief at handing in her resignation, and she was absolutely thrilled to be moving to a new firm, but there was still a part of her that almost didn't believe it. That worried someone at Donaldson might ruin everything, even though she'd already signed on with Murdoch and had the official offer letter and everything.

Even though Emily Murdoch had reassured her they weren't going to listen to anything anyone at Donaldson had to say about her.

It all felt almost too good to be true. First, Julie reaching out to her and rekindling that friendship, as well as finding new friends. Then meeting Freddy, and him actually wanting to stick around through the Alexander's case, and how amazing he was. Now, the new job she'd been wanting?

It was hard not to be fearful that something terrible was going to happen, as if the universe might balance the scales because too many good things were happening to her. She didn't like to think of herself as superstitious, but it was harder to accept good things happening to her than it was bad. She kept waiting for the other shoe to drop.

Her phone buzzed as she was putting on her coat, indicating an incoming text message. It was from Freddy, of course.

Freddy: *Have a great day and let me know how it goes.*

She smiled.

Their celebration dinner last night had been perfect. Just the two of them, out to dinner, enjoying each other's company. He'd insisted on paying. Despite whatever drama was going on at Stronghold, he'd focused entirely on her for the whole evening. Granted, they'd talked in the car on the way there about what Lexie, Kate, Gina, and Amy had said about the situation because Camille had been curious, but he'd let it go once they got to dinner and only talked about enjoyable topics.

She was still going to check in with Julie and Olivia. She wanted to help and make sure Freddy didn't overload himself. People in the club were going to have to get used to her being a part of things when they asked him for help—and to her occasionally putting her foot down so Freddy wasn't prioritizing everyone else over himself. Right now, it was looking like nothing was actually going on other than a few people not getting along, and she wasn't going to let him run himself ragged trying to navigate someone else's drama.

Camille: *Thank you, I'll talk to you later. Have a good day!*

Freddy: *Have a GREAT day.*

Smiling, feeling a little lighter, the exchange lifting some of her anxiety, she headed out the door. Some of that anxiety returned when she reached the office and Rachel looked up from her computer at the front desk, her expression freezing when she saw it was Camille.

"Good morning," Camille said, pretending to ignore Rachel's reaction. She had no idea what the woman had heard, but Junior must have said something either to her or within her hearing.

"Morning. Um, you're wanted in Conference Room 3 as soon as you arrive." The sympathy in Rachel's eyes would have made Camille quake in her boots on any other day. Now, her resignation letter was burning a hole in her purse.

"Thank you, Rachel," she said calmly, turning to head down the hall to the conference room rather than her office. Behind her, she could hear Rachel picking up the phone and murmuring something, probably a heads up that Camille was on her way.

She was pretty sure the unexpected summons was meant to intimidate her, make her worry about what Junior had told the other partners. When she walked into Conference Room 3 and found herself facing the partners who were in the office, with Junior smirking in the middle of them, she went from pretty sure to completely sure.

It was a room full of old, white men, most looking at her with varying degrees of disapproval. Junior's Uncle Steve was doing something on his phone, and he barely glanced up when she walked in, appearing more indifferent than disapproving.

"Camille, thank you for coming to meet with us. Please sit down." Donaldson Senior sat with his hands folded in front of him, his expression less disapproving than it was serious, but the disapproval was still there.

Deciding to take a seat, Camille sat straight, settling her purse at her side. She wasn't sure whether to be amused or angered at the attempted ambush. What did they actually hope to accomplish?

"Jared came to us with some unsettling news about an encounter he had with you this weekend. Is it true you have been dating the lawyer representing Mrs. Alexander?"

"Yes and no," she replied. "We were not dating while we were representing the Alexanders. As you know, the Alexanders' divorce has been finalized, so there is nothing wrong with us having dinner together this past weekend."

"Can you prove that you weren't dating him while you were representing Mr. Alexander?" Junior asked with a smug expression. He was clearly enjoying himself.

Camille's anger started to stir.

While she could appreciate that the partners wanted to make sure nothing unethical had happened, this was going too far. Not one of them reprimanded him but actually looked at her expectantly.

"Can I prove that something didn't happen?" she asked coolly, raising one eyebrow. "No, I cannot. Not anymore than I can prove Santa Claus doesn't exist or that aliens aren't out there."

Steve chuckled, which caused a few heads to turn toward him, but he was still engrossed in his phone. Whether he was laughing at her response or at whatever he was looking at on his phone was debatable. Since he didn't look up or say anything else, everyone turned away from him after a moment. Camille pressed her lips together to keep from laughing, some of the tension sliding away in favor of relief that she wasn't going to have to put up with this any longer.

She should really put them all out of their misery.

"I hate to break up this interrogation into my personal life, which is none of your business, but it's all a moot point." Several of the partners' jaws dropped, including Donaldson Senior, which was incredibly satisfying. She reached into her purse and pulled out the resignation letter from the side pocket. "Here's my resignation from the firm. I'll work with you to move any of my clients over to new partners during my remaining weeks."

"You're leaving us for him?" Junior sounded outraged, sitting straight up and banging one fist on the table, startling her.

She hadn't thought he would care or if he did, he would be glad to see her go, but instead, he seemed pissed. Then again, he was probably like Mr. Alexander with his desire to be the one to leave any relationship, taking being left as a personal affront.

"No, I'm leaving this job for another one... as people often do. I am very grateful for everything I've learned working here, but it's time for me to move on." Despite the desire to throw a grenade on the bridge and watch it burn, she was going to be a professional. She still had to work here for another month.

Silently, Donaldson Senior reached over to slide the letter closer to him and gave it a quick read through. As he was doing so, Steve Donaldson finally looked up from his phone.

"Where are you going?"

"Murdoch," she said. They'd find out soon enough.

"Ah, good choice." She blinked in surprise, but he was already getting to his feet. "Well, if that's everything, I have actual work to do today. I don't need to be here while Junior has a tantrum about his crush finding a real boyfriend."

Now it was Camille's turn for a jaw drop, and she wasn't the only one. Junior turned bright red and started yelling at his uncle, who ignored him as he made his way out of the room. Deciding no one was going to stop her, Camille followed him, leaving Junior shouting in the room behind her.

A crush? Ew. Ew. Ew.

She didn't bother to try to catch up with Steve, not wanting to know if he'd said it to be a jerk or because he truly believed it. If he truly believed it, she was going to be really grossed out.

She would probably laugh about this later—once she stopped being mortified.

<u>Freddy</u>

Camille: *Wow, do I have a story to tell you later. But my resignation is officially turned in.*

Freddy: *Wait, you're just going to tease me like that?*

Camille: *Yup.*

Freddy: *Rude.*

Camille: *It's too much to type out. And watch your tone.*

Freddy: *Rude, ma'am.*

The laughing emoji she sent back reassured him his text was received in the manner it had been intended.

Camille: *Dinner tonight so I can tell you all about it?*

Freddy: *It's a date.*

Grinning, he put his phone down on his desk. They still hadn't talked about Valentine's Day and if they were doing anything, but he took that she wanted to spend another meal with him as a good sign. They'd spent almost the entire weekend together, though he had slept in his own bed last night.

He'd bring up Valentine's Day tonight and see if she wanted to do anything. Maybe he should get a card asking if she wanted to be his Valentine. That would be cute, right?

Humming happily under his breath, he got to work, staying focused until it was time for him to meet Morgan for lunch. The weather was cold, but not too terrible, so he decided to walk to the restaurant. He was walking up to the entrance when a car pulled up and Morgan got out of the back, waving at the driver. She brightened when she saw him.

"Hey!"

"Hey, let's get you inside where it's warm," he said, frowning at her attire. She was dressed in jeans and a sweater but no coat.

"Oh, I'm fine, I knew I was just going from the car to the restaurant." She let him hustle her inside despite her reassurance, and they nearly ran into the backs of three women who were standing in front of the host desk. Three very familiar women.

Mistress Julie and Mistress Camille turned around to see who had just come in behind them in such a rush, but Mistress Olivia was talking to the host. Freddy's heart rate kicked up in surprised delight, his gaze meeting Camille's.

"Well, hello there," Camille said, eyes brightening with happiness when she saw him. "What are you two doing here?"

"Getting lunch," Morgan replied, smiling at the other three women. She was standing straight and at attention from the moment the three Dominants had noticed her. She wasn't being bratty, just answering the question literally as she often did.

"Is it a special meeting, or would you like to join us?" Olivia asked, looking over her shoulder at them. There was no demand in her voice or anything to push either way. Morgan looked at Freddy. He tilted his head questioningly at her. Her tiny nod and bright eyes were enough for him to answer.

"We'd love to join you," he said. He hadn't noticed any hesitation in Morgan. If anything, she looked excited to be having lunch with the Dommes. Hopefully, she didn't say anything insulting during lunch, even though they'd understand. She'd come a long way from when she'd first come to Stronghold, when she'd had some very odd ideas about Dominants and submissives—especially about Dommes —including what they should 'look' like. None of which was her fault, but it had definitely made for some awkwardness.

It didn't take them long to be shown to a table. Freddy sat with Morgan on one side and Camille on the other. Morgan was practically bouncing in her seat, looking pleased as punch. He might need to encourage the Dommes to spend more time with her. She tended to gravitate towards spending time with men, but obviously, she found something exciting about being around several female Dominants.

Besides, seeing how powerful, confident women acted could only be good for her.

Once they'd ordered their food, Camille told the story of turning in her resignation. Freddy hadn't wanted to ask in case she didn't want to share in front of everyone, but he was thrilled he didn't have to wait until dinner tonight. Though, he was also incensed on her behalf.

"I'm so glad you're not going to be working there anymore," he said, reaching over to take her hand. She squeezed his fingers.

"Me, too. I just have to get through this last month and make sure all my clients are taken care of, but I already feel so much better knowing I have an end date." She sighed with relief and shook her head. "I feel like I've just lost a huge weight from around my neck."

"You did," Olivia said. "They were dragging you down and have been for a while."

"It's true. I don't really want to talk about that, though." Camille laughed. "I'm feeling too good. What else can we talk about that's not a downer or reminiscing on negativity?"

"Lexie wants me to be Master Asad's fake girlfriend, but I'm not sure if I should," Morgan blurted out.

Freddy nearly choked on the water he'd just taken a sip of.

29

———————

Freddy

Morgan's announcement that Lexie wanted to set her up with Master Asad as a fake girlfriend caused a bit of a bombshell. Camille, Freddy, and Olivia all knew about his need for a fake girlfriend to take to his brother's wedding, but Julie had to be brought up to date. Olivia was the only one who'd known Lexie planned on asking Morgan to be the sacrificial victim.

Freddy shook his head.

"You don't think it's a good idea?" Morgan asked, looking worried.

"I think there's several things that could go wrong, but Lexie had good reasons for seeing if you would do it. Have you said yes?"

"Yes." She brightened again. "I was thinking it would be good for me to give Brian some space. He's been very mopey lately, but he won't talk about why. At least, not to me."

Probably because he was moping about Rae and her new boyfriend but didn't want to discuss with it Morgan since in some ways she was part of the problem. Though why Brian hadn't anticipated that when he asked Morgan to move in... but it wasn't like he and Rae had even been flirting when he'd asked Morgan that. The two of them were so busy pretending they weren't into each other, they kept hurting each other.

Both of them were way too stubborn, but it wasn't like either of them were asking for his help, so he stayed out of it. As long as things didn't spill over onto Morgan or anyone else, at least.

"I think it's a great idea," Olivia said, leaning forward. "Just make sure you talk to him about what you are and aren't willing to do that weekend. Going as his fake girlfriend doesn't mean you have to be his real sub."

"Oh, I don't mind being his sub, we've scened together a few times. He's very generous with orgasms." Morgan smiled delightedly. "Hopefully, it will work out."

The look on the server's face as he came up to the table with a tray of food was priceless.

***

Camille

Lunch with Freddy and Morgan was very interesting. She knew they were friends and hadn't been the least bit threatened to find them going out to lunch together, but she couldn't deny she was curious about Morgan as a person. Getting to spend some time with her was both enjoyable and eye-opening. Not in the least because she got a good look at what Freddy was like as an Alpha Submissive.

That wasn't really a thing, but in her head that's what she was starting to think of him as. He was completely submissive to her, but he reacted like a protective Dom when it came to the other submissives, and it was especially clear with Morgan. If he had to go toe-to-toe with another Dom to protect her, he would.

A turn-on for Camille.

Then again, she'd always found confidence sexy, so it wasn't that surprising.

Once they had their food, and their poor server had fled the scene, conversation picked back up.

"Is there any reason you're unsure about being Asad's date?" Julie asked Morgan.

"Well, I wasn't, but then my friend Noelle said she didn't think I should," Morgan said a little hesitantly, glancing at Freddy. His expression went blank, and across the table from Camille, Olivia's jaw tightened as anger flared in her grey eyes, making them look almost molten silver.

"Oh?" Julie asked archly, before anyone else could respond. "Did she say why?"

Looking down at her salad, Morgan pushed one of the croutons to the side of the plate.

"She's worried about me going away for a weekend with a guy I'm not actually with, like I might get attached to him or something." Morgan shrugged her shoulder. "I mean, I like Master Asad... I mean, Asad, but I don't like him that way. I think. I don't know if I'm ready for a relationship again. Faking it for a week seems like a good way to test it out, and I like that it's something I can do for him."

"That makes sense to me." Freddy's grip on Camille's fingers had tightened. He wasn't happy hearing about Noelle trying to talk Morgan out of it. "I don't think it's up to her to know whether you're ready to do something. It's up to you."

"That's pretty much how I felt. I think maybe she's interested in him. She said she could go if I decided not to, but she also scened with Master Dylan this weekend and seemed interested in him, so I don't know." Morgan shook her head.

"Noelle... that's the one who felt like she's being bullied, right?" Camille asked Freddy thoughtfully. She was pretty sure but wanted to be positive. Both Olivia and Julie's eyebrows shot up. Freddy gave her a look, but she didn't care. First of all, if there was bullying, Olivia and Julie were in more authoritative positions, since Olivia managed Marquis and Julie taught the introduction classes, which Noelle had been a part of. Second of all, she wasn't going to let Freddy constantly do things himself. And third of all, it was relevant to the conversation.

For someone who claimed she was having trouble finding scene partners, the fact that she'd clearly found someone over the weekend and now she was trying to set herself up as a fake girlfriend to one of Law and Iris' good friends... well, Camille's sympathy for the woman and her desire to give her the benefit of the doubt were taking some hits.

"Yes, Noelle approached me because she feels people have been... influencing whether or not Doms will scene with her and whether people befriend her at the club." Freddy's careful phrasing left out the bullying part, but that cat was already out of the bag.

Olivia snorted.

"Oddly, the only one I've heard spreading rumors is Noelle herself," Olivia said dryly. "I feel like every other day, I'm having to correct people on something they heard about Iris, and I'm fairly certain most of the misinformation is coming from Noelle. I told Patrick that I think she's going to end up being a problem, but he talked to Iris, who is still insisting she be given a chance. I think she's scared what Noelle will do if we push her out of the club, but if she's not working out... I haven't noticed her lacking for scene partners."

"She doesn't seem to have any more trouble than anyone else with finding someone to scene with," Morgan offered up, her brow wrinkled. From her tone, it seemed like she didn't really understand what Noelle's problem was, despite being friends with her. "I know she takes it really personally when someone tells her no, even though we've tried to explain it's not personal. Not scening with her doesn't mean someone doesn't like her. She says she understands, but then every time she doesn't get to scene with someone she wants to, we end up having the same conversation again. It's weird."

There was that bluntness Freddy had warned her about, and Camille covered her laugh with a cough. Morgan was refreshingly candid, though she could see how that could lead to inadvertent hurt feelings on occasion. Apparently, she didn't always understand what should and should not be said. He blamed it all on her history, but Camille wondered if it was just part of her make-up.

With that kind of open honesty, she could understand why Morgan would have some trouble deciphering a hidden agenda, which she was starting to think Noelle had. That or Noelle was just wildly self-involved and didn't realize how her actions and words appeared to others. Either seemed entirely possible.

"I haven't heard anything from the other Doms, and normally, if there's something going on with or about the new subs, either Law or I hear about it. In this case, considering her history with Iris and Law, I would think people would come to me." Julie was frowning, her fingers tapping on the table, food ignored on her plate.

Camille knew that meant she was thinking hard, probably going through her memories of Noelle to see if she could pick anything out.

"I will say, I get where Patrick is coming from. If he's not going to throw Marissa out for all the things she's blatantly said about Leigh and Jared, he can't throw Noelle out."

"I think he should throw Truckstop out, too," Olivia muttered, stabbing a piece of chicken rather violently.

Wide-eyed, Camille looked at Freddy.

Truckstop? she mouthed.

Freddy just shrugged, suppressing a smile.

"Truckstop?" Morgan asked, wide-eyed. "What does that mean? It sounds awful, but what does it mean?"

Olivia froze as if just remembering that Morgan was there… a submissive, and one who was friends with Marissa. Then she shrugged.

"It's just my nickname for Marissa. It doesn't really mean anything but somehow it fits all of my feelings about her. We don't get along and haven't since she and Jared were together. But please don't allow my opinion of her or her and Jared's relationship to influence you. Everyone gets defensive of the people they love, and I have a very strong opinion when it comes to her, but I don't insist that everyone share it." Olivia's tone was apologetic but accompanied by no actual apology.

Camille had a feeling she wasn't actually sorry for saying it, more so for saying it in front of Morgan, who might take issue with it.

"Oh, that's okay. I know you two don't get along. She's been really nice to me, though."

"Good, but if that ever changes, you know where to find me."

Olivia smiled encouragingly. "Anyway, Noelle has to know that no one can force people to spend time with her or scene with her. If she can't deal with that, I suppose she'll be leaving the club sooner rather than later. Problem solved."

"Maybe. At least I can tell her what she's experiencing is normal and encourage her to scene with the people who are interested in scening with her, especially since there are some." Freddy sighed. Not a conversation he was looking forward to, to be honest.

"Good. If she complains again, maybe you could direct her to Julie since she's the training Domme," Camille said. Freddy shot her a look that was both amused and a little repressive, as if to say 'I know what you're doing.' That was just fine with her. She wasn't trying to be subtle. Freddy didn't need to take care of everyone else's problems, and he needed to know that.

"That's not a bad idea. You're going to need to spend more time focusing on your Domme and less time on all the subs' problems now that you're in a relationship," Olivia said pointedly.

"Oh? Is that what you did?" Freddy smiled like a shark, lobbing the focus back at Olivia, who laughed.

"If they can get up the guts to come talk to me, I know it's serious. You, however, get pulled into everyone's sob story because they know you'll be sympathetic." She grinned at the face he made. "Though I did notice you have a room reserved for Valentine's Day, so you're not totally a lost cause."

"You do?" Camille asked in surprise as Freddy turned beet red, making everyone else at the table look at him curiously.

"I wasn't sure if you wanted to do anything, but I wanted to be prepared if you did... but we don't have to, unless you want to..."

Seeing Freddy knocked off his confident pedestal and turned into a stuttering mess over trying to set up plans for Valentine's Day was surprisingly also a turn-on. She liked that he was sure of himself so often but that *she* made him a little unsure of himself.

"I would love to be your Valentine," she said immediately. "I was hoping we could spend the evening together. I was going to bring it up tonight."

Freddy brightened, sitting straight up again and meeting her gaze. Morgan made a little happy noise as she watched the two of them, and both Olivia and Julie were radiating approval. Nosy Nellies.

"You were?"

"I was. Though I was thinking more about staying in. Going out on Valentine's Day always seemed kind of... hellish to me." The big romance day was always way too hectic with too many people out and about. It didn't feel romantic to her at that point, it felt like a hassle. Though at Marquis, things would be different, but she still wasn't sure she wanted to be out at all. She didn't want to disappoint Freddy, though, after he'd been so thoughtful.

"It's fine. We can stay in. I'll cook for you." He beamed at her, his gaze losing some of its focus, as if he was already starting to plan out the menu in his head.

"That sounds perfect."

Not caring about their audience, she leaned over to plan a kiss on his lips, ignoring the various sounds of approval from everyone. Their approval didn't matter, but it wasn't anything to be embarrassed about. Their friends were happy for them, and that added to her joy.

It was a damn good day.

30

———————

Freddy

Fretting over a menu wasn't the norm for Freddy. He liked to consider himself a pretty decisive person. Right now? He was worried he'd chosen all wrong. Sure, he'd gone over Camille's likes and dislikes with her, but that didn't assuage his anxiety. Why he was stressing so badly he didn't know… maybe the pressure of Valentine's Day.

Which was silly. It was a day like any other day.

Yet here he was.

"Something smells amazing," Camille called from his living room. She'd come over a little early, and he hadn't been quite ready yet. Since he'd wanted to surprise her with the food, she'd been happy to hang out in front of his television with a glass of wine. Work had been a little stressful for her since she'd turned in her resignation—she was getting pressure from the partners to change her mind—but she didn't seem to mind. Knowing she was getting out of there had made her happier than ever, and it showed.

"Hopefully, it tastes amazing," he joked, except he wasn't really joking.

It was too late to change up the whole menu. Sighing, he quickly plated the steaks, oven roasted potatoes, and green beans as artistically as he could. He liked a good presentation. The steak was perfectly cooked, and he'd fanned out thin slices of it atop the potatoes and green beans to show off the perfectly pink centers, though he did cover it up a little when he dripped the red wine reduction sauce over it.

Taking a plate in each hand, he moved to the dining room, where he already had the table set, complete with candles. Since it was Valentine's Day, he'd gone with a red theme—dark red place mats and matching napkins with gold rings and red and gold candles in gold holders. It was really very pretty.

The dining room was open to the television room, unlike the kitchen. Camille looked over as soon as he came into sight, and her smile lit up both rooms. She looked stunning in a creamy pink silk blouse, unbuttoned to show a generous amount of cleavage once she'd gotten in his home. It had been fully buttoned up when she was at work.

Obviously, he liked it better this way.

"Mmm, it looks amazing," she said as she set her wineglass down and slid into her seat. She smiled up at him. "Everything looks amazing. This might be the most romantic thing anyone's ever done for me, including the part where you agreed to stay in. Thank you."

The heartfelt warmth in her voice satisfied every little needy part of him, even the part that was worried about whether or not she would like the food. Regardless of if she did, she was clearly very happy with his efforts, and appreciative, and it made her feel good, which was all *he* wanted.

"It's my pleasure," he replied honestly, placing the plates down in their respective places. "Happy Valentine's Day."

"Happy Valentine's Day." As soon as the plates were on the table, she reached up to grab hold of his collar and pull him down for a kiss. He went eagerly, meeting her lips with his, marveling at the sparks that flew as their lips touched. Everything with Camille got better and better every day.

When the kiss ended, her dark eyes were sparkling.

"We'd better eat, or we might never get around to dinner," she teased.

"You're not wrong."

The little noises of happiness she made as she tasted the food made his heart swell. He didn't need to worry about whether she liked it. She *loved* the meal.

"Everything is so good. What on earth did you put on these potatoes?"

"They're easy." He shrugged nonchalantly even as his chest puffed up with pride. "Just cut the potatoes up, toss them in olive oil, salt, pepper, rosemary, thyme, and dried minced garlic and onion, then throw them in the oven for half an hour at four twenty-five. They get all crispy and the seasonings adds to that."

"They're so good. I can't decide if I like them better with or without the sauce, and I am really loving the sauce, so that's saying something."

Watching her eat was as good as listening to her.

"So, how was your day?" he asked as she ate. "Are they still trying to convince you to stay?"

"Yes, but I think I finally got through to them that I'm done." She shrugged, her expression serene. "They're grumping about it, but they aren't trying to shove more money at me anymore. I think they've figured out they can't pay me enough for me to put up with them any longer. Junior has been avoiding me completely, which has been a blessing. I don't care whether he actually had a crush on me. I could kiss Steve for saying it in front of everyone because even if it's not true, he doesn't want to come anywhere near me anymore. It's made my workday so much better. How about you?"

"Good. Nothing crazy going on at work. I did finally talk to Noelle."

Camille's eyebrows went up. "Oh? How did that go?"

"Surprisingly well. She seemed relieved to hear what she's experiencing is completely normal, and she understood a Dom not wanting to scene with her doesn't necessarily mean someone warned them off. I think she just needed to hear it from an outside party." He shrugged. "I think she was a little paranoid, but not necessarily for no reason. I don't think any of Law's friends will ever scene with her."

"That's a good point. I'm glad it all worked out."

"Me, too. Some of the drama around Stronghold and Marquis can be kind of fun sometimes, but I don't think Noelle and Iris drama would be."

"What's the fun drama?" she asked, laughing. "I'm having trouble picturing fun drama."

"Oh, you know, the drama around people getting together." He grinned and told her the story of Domi and Mitch going from being fuck buddies to engaged, which also led to Andrew and Kate's story by comparison. Of course, that meant he had to include Kate's best friend's 'magic vagina' theory, which Camille got a huge kick out of.

There was something to be said that the Doms who bedhopped the most had been ending up in committed relationships, sometimes without meaning to. Freddy knew Andrew and Kate hadn't been looking for that when they'd hooked up again, even though they'd been in love years before. The whole second chance thing had made all the submissives around the club go swoony, even the ones who had been hung up on Andrew before Kate returned to Maryland.

With Domi and Mitch, pretty much everyone who wasn't them had seen that one coming, even though it had been in slow motion for a while. They'd started off scening with other people when only one of them was at the club, but eventually, they'd only been scening with each other, regardless. That Domi had broken up with Mitch when she'd realized she'd developed feelings for him had only made the story juicier.

That's what he was talking about when he meant fun drama. Not so much fun for the participants as they were going through it, but fun for everyone else who could see where it was going and got to watch.

"I feel a little bad, like we've deprived everyone of gossip." Camille laughed, leaning back in her chair. She'd scraped her plate clean, making Freddy feel particularly pleased. It had been a good dinner, if he did say so himself.

"Oh, trust me, they've been gossiping plenty, especially since we had a night together, then had to pull back because of work." He rolled his eyes. "There was plenty of 'will they, won't they' discussion going on."

She burst out laughing in surprise.

"If you say so. I guess it was a little dramatic, having you walk into the room with Mrs. Alexander."

"Trust me, it felt dramatic when I realized who was on the other side of the table." He laughed along with her. "That was not how I was hoping things were going to go... but it worked out."

"Yes, it did." She extended her hand to him, and he curled his fingers around hers. Their eyes met, and he grinned, unable to keep the goofy smile off of his face when she smiled back.

The moment stretched, the inside of his chest filling with warm happiness. There was nothing awkward about the silence. He was here in the moment with her, and it was perfect.

CAMILLE

As if she needed more proof that Freddy was the perfect man, he lifted her hand to his lips and kissed her knuckles.

"Are you ready for dessert?"

See? Perfect man.

"What's for dessert?" she asked, even though it didn't really matter. She was going to eat whatever it was, regardless. Thankfully, Freddy was a fantastic cook. Clearly, it made him so happy to feed her, she would have faked it even if he wasn't.

"Chocolate mousse."

"You *made* chocolate mousse?" Her voice squeaked, and his smile widened, blue eyes bright with happy pleasure.

"Sure. It's not that difficult. I made it last night, and it's been setting in the fridge since then. Whipped cream on top?" He started to get to his feet, but Camille didn't let go of his hand. Raising his eyebrows questioningly, he looked down at her when he realized he wasn't going anywhere.

"Any objection to having dessert in bed?"

His eyes widened.

"Are you suggesting we bring it back to the bedroom and lick it off each other or that we bring it back to the bedroom and sit in bed to eat it? Either way, yes."

Laughing again—God she loved how much he made her laugh—she let go of his hand.

"Whichever makes you more comfortable. They're your sheets, but I was kind of hoping for Door Number One."

"Door Number One sounds perfect. Sheets are washable and licking chocolate mousse off of you—or vice versa—sounds like the perfect way to end the evening."

Getting to her feet, Camille helped him get the dishes into the kitchen. He looked like he wanted to tell her not to but bit his lip and kept it to himself. The mousse was in the fridge, as he'd said, already in fancy little individual glasses that made her think of old-fashioned ice cream sundaes. Grabbing the whipped cream, Camille winked at him as she sashayed away, heading toward the bedroom and leaving him to follow her.

"So how do you want to do this?" he asked, when they reached the room.

"Well, let's get the covers pulled back, so you only have to wash the sheets and not your comforter." She set her glass of mousse down on the nightstand, Freddy following behind her, before pulling back the navy-blue sheets. If some mousse dripped on the soft cotton, they wouldn't show stains as much. Though she had a feeling Freddy probably had all sorts of tricks for getting stains out, so she wouldn't worry too much about it.

"It's okay if we get messy," he said, like he was reading her mind.

Shaking her head, not to say it wasn't but because he always surprised her with how astute he was, Camille straightened and leaned over to kiss him again, a slow, drugging kiss, intimate rather than passionate, at least initially. Then it heated up quickly.

He tasted like red wine and the quintessential flavor that was Freddy. Her body hummed to life as it pressed against his. Their lips separated and came back together, again and again, as they stripped off each other's clothes. It was more a joint effort than playing with domination and submission, though she was the one leading the way.

Skin touched skin, satiny soft, his body hair rubbing against her sensitive nipples as lips touched again. Camille moaned as his fingers moved over her body, caressing her curves, stroking her with erotic intent. Running her nails lightly across his shoulders and down his chest, she teased his nipples, making him groan in turn.

"Fuck, Mistress..." He gasped out the words when she reached down, cradling his cock and balls in her palm, squeezing them just hard enough to hurt a little. His dick pulsed, jerking in her grip, and she moved her hand up and down the shaft, making him whimper as his head fell back.

"Up on the bed, Freddy. On your back. I want to have my dessert first." He'd been such a good boy, making a lovely dinner for her and dessert, and he deserved a reward. Letting go of his dick, she grabbed her cup of mousse while he got on the bed and rolled onto his back.

"Hands up and grip the headboard." She wasn't going to tie him in place, but she wanted full access while she was playing. Thankfully, he had a very grippable headboard, with lots of vertical bars to wrap his fingers around. Knowing Freddy, he'd probably picked it out on purpose for exactly that reason.

"Yes, Mistress." Stretching out, he arched his back slightly, showing off his muscles as they rippled with his movements. He was stunning, both in appearance and in his submission... and he was all hers.

31

———————

Freddy

Chocolate mousse was *cold*.

Not nearly as cold as ice, but it was still cold. His skin flinched away as Mistress Camille dropped a dollop on his stomach, though she followed immediately with her warm tongue, swiping the dessert from his skin and teasing him.

"Mmmm... that's delicious."

"Glad you like it."

He groaned when she dropped another dollop, this one closer to his groin. Close enough that her breasts brushed against his erection as she leaned over to lick him clean. Her low chuckle of amusement at his sexual frustration made him even harder.

Scooping more mousse up with her spoon, instead of dropping it onto him, she set the spoon on its edge against his stomach and slowly dragged a line of chocolate across his chest and down his stomach to the base of his cock. Leaning over again, she slid her tongue along the same path, licking him clean while he arched beneath her.

Fuck, that felt good.

He shuddered as her mouth moved closer to his cock, her curls brushing against him, followed by her cheek as she lapped up the last of the mousse. The hot, wet sensation of her tongue licking up the cool mousse, the closeness of her head to his dick, was enough to drive a man wild when she kept brushing against it without giving him any more stimulation.

He jerked and cried out when she applied some mousse to his balls. If it felt cold against his skin, it felt even colder on the sensitive sack. His headboard creaked as his muscles flexed. Her warm tongue licked and teased until all the mousse was gone... but she didn't stop there.

Freddy moaned as she sucked his balls into her mouth, rolling them with her tongue, sending the most delicious sensations shooting through him. His toes curling, he panted from the sensations as his cock throbbed with need as her curls brushed over the length.

Cold mousse slid over his shaft, a thick dollop decorating the head. Releasing his balls from her mouth, she slid her tongue up the shaft, lapping at the mousse until she reached the head. Wet heat engulfed the sensitive tip of his dick, her tongue exploring the mushroom head before she slid her lips down the shaft.

"Fuck! Mistress!" He writhed for her, unable to keep completely still as she bobbed her head.

Several long strokes with her mouth, then she pulled away, examining his cock to make sure she'd gotten all her dessert. Then she turned to meet his gaze, her dark eyes gleaming.

"Okay... your turn."

His eagerness to please her, to pleasure her, had grown with every passing moment, and he nearly dropped his glass of mousse on the bed. Taking a deep breath, he managed to get a hold of himself. He wasn't going to impress her by fumbling about.

Mistress Camille laid back on the bed, in nearly the same position as he had but used her hands to prop up her head, not to hold on to the headboard. Despite her hardened nipples, wet pussy, and the heat in her eyes, she looked relaxed—something he was determined to change.

His erection ached and throbbed, still slick from her mouth, but he knew he wouldn't be getting satisfaction there any time soon. He didn't even need it. His first and foremost thought was to give her what she needed.

What she deserved.

"Start with my breasts," she murmured, nodding her head at the bountiful mounds.

"Happily, Mistress."

Her eyes gleamed, lips curving upward as he knelt on the bed beside her and dropped the mousse onto her breasts, using the spoon to ensure a healthy amount covered the hard buds of her nipples. She made a small sound as the cold metal and dessert touched her skin, her eyelashes fluttering at the sensation.

Leaning forward, Freddy began to worship her with his tongue, licking all the mousse from her skin while focusing on giving her as much pleasure as possible. His cock bounced beneath him, heaving, throbbing, and wanting, but it didn't matter. He had a deep need to ensure she came first. In every way.

Sucking the mousse off her nipples took much longer than necessary... but he was just ensuring he got every last bit. She moaned, her fingers threading through his hair, stroking his head in encouragement. Not that he needed any.

This was everything he wanted.

"Now my pussy... but not in it."

Because sugar wasn't good for pussies. Freddy wouldn't have, anyway, but he didn't mind the reminder. He'd been in the scene long enough—and on social media often enough—to know people put all sorts of things inside themselves out of ignorance.

"I can work around that." He winked at her as he shifted on the bed.

She laughed at the terrible but entirely appropriate, pun.

By working around it meant he spread the chocolate mousse all around her opening—across her mound, on her outer labia—worked around both her pussy and her order not to put any inside her vulva. All the while, he teased her, heightening her pleasure as he licked and sucked. Occasionally, his tongue delved between her lips to lap at the sweet moisture there before returning to clean the mousse from her delicate areas.

Once all the mousse was gone, he didn't move away. Pressing in, no longer constrained by where the mousse was, he made her entire pussy his dessert.

"Oh, yes..." Her hips lifted in response, pressing her wet folds more firmly against his mouth, her grip tightening on his hair as he worked his tongue back and forth. Flicking it over her swollen clit, he slid it between her labia and dipped into her hole before doing it all over again.

She undulated, her hips rocking against him, pressing herself against his mouth, until suddenly, her grip on his hair tightened to the point of pain.

"Get up here." She growled the words, tugging at the same time. "I want you inside me."

No argument there. Freddy followed her lead as she pulled him into position, his hands on either side of her, cock pressing against the wet heat of her pussy. She moved her hips up and down, sliding her wetness against him.

"You're going to fuck me hard, and you're not going to cum until I tell you to."

"Yes, Mistress."

Fuck. Freddy's muscles tightened as he thrust forward, burying himself inside her. The slick, wet heat that wrapped around his cock was pure heaven. Being on top wasn't something that happened often, but the truth was, the position didn't matter.

They both knew who was running the show.

***

CAMILLE

Lifting her hips to meet Freddy's thrust, Camille slid her free hand down his side, her other hand still gripping his hair as he moved inside her. Her entire body was humming from all the teasing and his talented tongue. As he moved inside her, stoking her pleasure, building her arousal to higher and higher heights, she could feel her muscles quivering and clenching around him.

"Oh, yes..." Her hand curved over his ass, squeezing as his muscle tightened, his cock driving home inside her. She pressed her finger against the crinkled opening between his cheeks, teasing it and rubbing it, igniting the sensitive nerves, and he cried out as he thrust harder and fast in response.

"Mistress!" He leaned forward, pumping between her thighs, her finger pushing inward despite the lack of lubricant, setting him off his rhythm. He groaned, filling her with his cock and rubbing against her swollen lips and clit, sending her senses soaring.

"Yes... there... right there..." Like a good sub, he kept moving in exactly the way he had been, giving her just what she needed, as ecstasy billowed up and explode through her senses. Just before the passion swallowed her under completely, she managed to gasp out, "You may cum."

Freddy cried out, his hips rocking against her as the waves of her climax rolled through her. She could feel him throbbing inside her, his orgasm joining hers as they moved together. Wrapping her legs around his, she held him close, the hand that had been in his hair moving down to grab hold of his other cheek, as if she could pull him deeper inside her.

Floating on euphoria, she shuddered as the last of her orgasm tightened and released. Her pussy clenching and relaxing, she milked Freddy of his cum until he collapsed atop her. Gentling her grip on his ass, she slid the tip of her finger out of him and used her other hand to stroke her fingers along his spine. Both of them panted for breath as they came back to themselves.

"Fuck..." Freddy pressed his forehead against her shoulder, shuddering again as a mini-orgasm wracked him. He shrank inside her but didn't move away, as if he wanted to be as close to her as possible for as long as possible.

"Happy Valentine's Day," she said, laughing softly when he lifted his head and gave her an incredulous look. Then he shook his head, smiling.

"Happy Valentine's Day." He shook his head again, his blue eyes dancing with happiness. "Is it too soon to say I'm pretty sure I'm falling in love with you?"

Camille's breath felt like it had been sucked away as she stared up at him, completely flabbergasted. That had been one of the last things she'd expected him to say, and her mind went completely blank. His smile faltered, though he pushed it back up, trying to hide his disappointment.

"Ah, too soon, huh?" he joked, except it wasn't really a joke.

"No! I mean, no it's not too soon," she hastily clarified. "I just wasn't expecting it, and I have sex brain right now—you can't ambush me with new information when I'm still on the orgasm cloud."

The sparkle was back in his eyes.

"The orgasm cloud?"

She scowled at him.

"I can still give you a Valentine's Day spanking," she threatened, and he laughed. He started to roll off of her, but she caught him, holding him in place right where he was. "For the record, I'm pretty sure I'm falling in love with you, too."

"Oh, really?"

"Really. How could I not? You're basically perfect for me."

His smile widened.

"Funny, I feel the same way about you. Like my whole life got better when we met."

That made her laugh. It sounded ludicrous—they'd met, then immediately had an issue with their respective clients—but it was true. Her life had gotten better from the moment she met him, and it seemed like the upward trajectory was still going. She'd stopped waiting for the other shoe to drop.

There was no other shoe. There was just her choice to embrace happiness. To give herself permission to be herself and do the things she needed to do. Part of which she'd learned because of him.

Camille pulled him down for another hot kiss. Dessert didn't have to be over yet. It was the perfect way to end Valentine's Day.

Freddy was the happily-ever-after she hadn't thought she would ever get.

EPILOGUE

Looking around Stronghold, Morgan wondered if she could escape the current conversation or if that would cause more drama. She was so tired of hearing Noelle complain that Freddy hadn't taken her complaint of bullying seriously. It didn't help that Carolyn was egging her on, though everyone else seemed to have grown tired of it.

"I'm never going to get taken seriously, not when everyone in charge is friends with Iris or Law," Noelle huffed, crossing her arms across her chest and glaring across the room at the woman in question. Personally, Morgan thought Noelle would be a lot happier if she stopped focusing so much on Iris, but no one was asking her, and she'd learned she wasn't supposed to offer an opinion unless it was requested.

It didn't seem to stop other people from offering opinions, but there were rules around when and how it was okay to do so, and she didn't think she understood them well enough to try.

"You should complain directly to Patrick," Carolyn said, a gleam in her eyes. "Get it on record."

Something about Noelle had brought out a side of her that Morgan hadn't seen before. She didn't like it very much but didn't know what to do. Carolyn was her friend, and that was supposed to mean something, right? She supposed Noelle was her friend now, too, but she was never sure whether she liked Noelle, but since they were all friends with each other, that was another thing she wasn't supposed to say.

"They don't have records like that here. It's not a police station." Amy shook her head.

Morgan tilted her head, trying to figure out why it was okay for Amy to disagree in this instance, but it wouldn't be okay for her to tell Noelle to focus on herself instead of Iris.

Or maybe it would be okay?

But if it wasn't, she could risk her friendships.

Better to stay quiet.

"If they did, I'd never be allowed in," Marissa joked. "Olivia would have a file on me this thick." She held her hands out in front of her, about a foot apart. "Actually, she wouldn't be here, either, if I was allowed to file reports on her. Just let it go. They aren't going to kick you out. If they were going to, they would have already done so."

"But she's making it so I can't scene with some of the Doms," Noelle complained, her gaze darting over to the table where Iris was standing.

"Do you want to scene with one of her friends?" Morgan asked. That seemed like a safe question, and from the way Noelle kept looking over there, she was starting to wonder if Noelle had a crush on one of them.

"I mean, I wouldn't say no to any of them," Noelle said with a smirk. "Especially Connor. He looks like the kind of guy who could throw me around the room, if you know what I mean. But no, I just don't think I should be shut out of things because Iris is trying to get back at me. It's not fair. I'm not going to be bullied into leaving Stronghold."

Amy and Marissa exchanged a glance, which Morgan saw but didn't completely understand. People did that sometimes. They looked at each other and knew what the other one was thinking. She was never part of those glances and was okay with that. She wasn't sure she'd be able to figure out what they were trying to say, anyway.

Navigating relationships on her own was hard.

Worth it, though.

She still remembered when she'd be at play parties with Master Richard and see other subs interacting but wouldn't be allowed to join them. Of course, they might not have liked her. Master Richard had always told her that he was protecting her from their jealousy. She had still been envious, seeing them talking and laughing together. Wanting to be a part of their world.

Now she was and was going to be grateful for it and not risk losing it.

"Master Asad is pretty hot, too," Noelle continued, looking meaningfully at Morgan. This time, she knew what that look meant. Noelle kept offering to take Morgan's place as Master Asad's fake date since she'd told her friends that Lexie had asked her if she'd be interested.

"He is."

If Noelle had a thing for him, she would have turned Lexie down, but it seemed Noelle just wanted any of Master Law's friends. Morgan didn't understand why. There were plenty of other Doms willing to scene with her, and it only made sense that his closest friends wouldn't. Not while there was still an issue between her and Iris, and there definitely was.

"I'm supposed to talk to him tonight about being his wedding date. Well, I guess Lexie and Master Patrick will be doing most of the talking, but they wanted to tell him tonight."

"Are you sure you don't want me to take your place? You don't have to do this if you're not ready. It can be hard faking a relationship for someone's family." Noelle's expression had changed to earnestness.

"You've faked a relationship for someone's family before?" Carolyn asked. Her attention had wandered while Noelle and Morgan had been talking, but it snapped back with laser focus.

"Well, not exactly... but I'm a good actress."

"I want to do it." Morgan glanced over her shoulder to where

Master Brian was talking to some submissives. As always when they were in the club, he seemed completely attuned to her. His gaze lifted to meet hers. He tilted his head, raising his eyebrows. When she'd asked him, he'd told her that meant he was wondering if she needed him. She smiled and shook her head, turning back to her friends before her smile faded.

"I need to show Brian and the other Doms that I'm okay on my own. I don't need them hovering over me all the time."

It was starting to make her wonder if she really was okay. She was starting to feel stifled. Not in the same way her parents had made her feel, exactly, but... it was bringing up some old emotions. Mistress Julie thought it was a good idea, and since she was a Domme, as well as being Morgan's therapist, she put a lot of weight on Mistress Julie's opinion.

"Just know that I'm here for you if you change your mind." Noelle reached out and took Morgan's hand, giving it a brief squeeze before letting it drop.

Morgan smiled at her. Despite her faults, Noelle could be very generous and sweet. She could probably use a few sessions with Mistress Julie to help her get over her insecurities around Iris, but Morgan wasn't brave enough to make that suggestion, either. Besides, if Mistress Julie didn't want to treat her because she was friends with Master Law, that would only make things with Noelle even worse.

"Oooh, here comes Master Patrick," Amy said, and immediately all of them sat up. The man had that effect.

A lot of the Doms did, though Morgan had noticed that she and Amy were more likely to have that reaction, whereas Carolyn and Noelle rarely jumped to attention. Marissa fell somewhere in between. But everyone was on their best behavior for Master Patrick, and not just because he owned the club. He just had the kind of presence that demanded attention—and respect.

"Hello, ladies." He smiled, white teeth flashing against dark skin, his gaze glancing over all of them before settling on Morgan. "Morgan, do you have a minute?"

"Yes, Master Patrick." She stood, resisting the urge to put her arms behind her back in the position she'd been taught to use when on her feet before a Dom. That wasn't necessary here, and it would make both Master Patrick and Lexie uncomfortable.

"Great, come with me, please."

She looked over at the table where Master Asad had been talking to his friends, but he wasn't there anymore, and she realized Master Patrick was leading her to his office. Apparently, he didn't want to have the discussion with an audience, which made sense.

The gossip at Stronghold and Marquis ran rampant most days.

A little bubble of excitement ran through her. She was going to be leaving Maryland and all the people at Stronghold for the first time since she'd been rescued. And with a Dom who knew her limits and boundaries... Maybe they'd even be able to go to the Outlands. She knew the wedding was in Pittsburgh, and she would love to visit another club.

Best of all, she was going somewhere no one had any preconceived notions of her.

She couldn't wait.

<hr>

ASAD

"So you're clear on the rules, right?" Lexie asked as they waited for Patrick to return with Morgan.

Asad did his best not to scowl at her. It was becoming a little insulting how little they thought he was paying attention. Though he supposed that was partly his own fault.

He might be a bit of a manwhore, and he absolutely did not want the responsibility of a submissive, but he wasn't a total jerk. He didn't want to lead Morgan on or damage her. He just needed a date for his brother's wedding, so his mom wouldn't try to set him up with every woman there, and... okay, if he was going to be completely honest, he didn't want to go solo because he didn't want to be alone. He loved his family, but spending time with them was hard.

"Rule Number One, no fucking the gorgeous submissive. Rule

Number Two, no fucking the gorgeous submissive. Rule Number Three—"

"As long as you follow it, you don't need to repeat it a bunch of times," Lexie said with a threatening scowl. "Don't make me regret suggesting Morgan as your date."

"It'll be fine. All of you are far too protective of her. How is she ever going to grow if everyone keeps swathing her in bubble wrap?"

Lexie sighed.

"This is why I'm worried but also think you might be the perfect person for her to go with." She shook her head. "You might think we're a little too protective, but I think you're a little too cavalier. You need to take care of her."

The words made him start to sweat, hitting a little too close to home as he heard his mom's voice in his head. *You need to take care of him.* His brother was fine now. He was in remission, all grown up, and getting married. What Lexie was asking of him and what his parents had asked of him were two wildly different things. All he had to do was take care of a perfectly healthy, if emotionally vulnerable, grown submissive for a week.

He could handle that.

Probably.

Though he would have liked to have gone with someone with a little more confidence in themselves and without all the emotional baggage, he had to admit Morgan was otherwise perfect. She was gorgeous, smart, funny, and not at all needy. Some subs tried to manipulate extra aftercare out of him, but Morgan never had. She didn't want a boyfriend, probably because her last one had been an abusive tool, and that worked for Asad. He could deal with a little emotional baggage since she worked well in every other respect.

That she didn't want a boyfriend and definitely wouldn't be trying to use this as an excuse to get close to him were the biggest points in her favor.

The door opened and Asad sat up straighter in his chair as Patrick escorted Morgan in. She looked nervous yet excited as she gave him a little wave.

"Okay," Patrick said from where he was by the door. "You two are going to talk about what you need from each other. You can change your mind at any time. You have the use of my office for as long as you want."

"Wait, we aren't staying?" Lexie pouted.

"Come here, Pixie. Let them have their privacy. They need to work this out for themselves." Patrick shot Asad a warning look over Morgan's head.

Asad gave him a thumbs-up, which made Morgan glance over her shoulder, and Patrick's expression immediately shifted back to a smile.

"Unless you want us to stay, Morgan?"

"No," she said immediately, shaking her head. "I want to do this for myself."

Lexie sighed but got to her feet and met Patrick at the door. He gave her a swift swat on the ass to get her moving past him, then shot Asad another warning look.

Asad was starting to feel like a Bond villain or something. If they didn't trust him, why were they sending Morgan with him?

Nah, they trusted him or else they wouldn't have chosen her to go with him. But Patrick was a control freak, so he had to do what he could to put his stamp all over the situation. Asad could live with that. He was surrounded by control freaks at the clubs and was a bit of one himself.

"So, I'm going to be your fake girlfriend?" Morgan asked, sounding excited.

She was pretty darn cute when she got like this.

Asad flashed her a grin.

"Looks like it."

Master Asad and Morgan will return in *Shallow Submission!*

ACKNOWLEDGMENTS

As always, a huge thank you to my beta readers. Candida, Marie, Marta, Annie, Karen, and Katherine - these books would not be the same without you. I am so blessed to have such amazing supporters.

Thank you to Sandy, from Personal Touch Editing, whose work always makes my own so much better.

A huge thank you to my husband, whose support is so integral to my own success.

Thank you to everyone who reached out, asking for a story about Freddy. He's been a fan favorite for so long and while I never intended to write a story for him, I'm so glad I got the chance to, and it was largely because he heard how much all of you wanted him to have one (Yes, my characters are that real to me).

And, finally, thank you to you, all of you. I never had any idea that Venus Rising would lead to Stronghold or that there would be another series following it. But as long as you keep reading, I'll keep writing!

Stay Sassy,
Angel

ABOUT THE AUTHOR

Golden Angel is a USA Today best-selling author and self-described bibliophile with a "kinky" bent who loves to write stories for the characters in her head. If she didn't get them out, she's pretty sure she'd go just a little crazy.

She is happily married, old enough to know better but still too young to care, and a big fan of happily-ever-afters, strong heroes and heroines, and sizzling chemistry.

When she's not writing, she can often be found on the couch reading, in front of her sewing machine making a new cosplay, hanging out with her friends, or wandering the Maryland Renaissance Fair.

www.goldenangelromance.com

BB bookbub.com/authors/golden-angel
g goodreads.com/goldeniangel
f facebook.com/GoldenAngelAuthor
instagram.com/goldeniangel

OTHER BOOKS BY GOLDEN ANGEL

Contemporary BDSM Romance

Venus Rising Series (MFM Romance)

The Venus School

Venus Aspiring

Venus Desiring

Venus Transcendent

Venus Wedding

Venus Rising Box Set

Stronghold Doms Series

The Sassy Submissive

Taming the Tease

Mastering Lexie

Pieces of Stronghold

Breaking the Chain

Bound to the Past

Stripping the Sub

Tempting the Domme

Hardcore Vanilla

Steamy Stocking Stuffers

Entering Stronghold Box Set

Nights at Stronghold Box Set

Stronghold: Closing Time Box Set

Masters of Marquis Series

Bondage Buddies

Master Chef

Law & Disorder

Switch Play

Legally Bound

Shallow Submission

Dungeons & Doms Series

Dungeon Master

Dungeon Daddy

Dungeon Showdown

Daddies Everywhere

Chef Daddy

Foosball Daddies

Taco Daddy

Little Villain

Historical Spanking Romance

Domestic Discipline Quartet

Birching His Bride

Dealing With Discipline

Punishing His Ward

Claiming His Wife

The Domestic Discipline Quartet Box Set

Bridal Discipline Series

Philip's Rules

Gabrielle's Discipline

Lydia's Penance

Benedict's Commands

Arabella's Taming

Pride and Punishment Box Set

Commands and Consequences Box Set

Deception and Discipline

A Season for Treason

A Season for Scandal

A Season for Smugglers

A Season for Spies

Bridgewater Brides

Their Harlot Bride

Standalone

Marriage Training

The Duke's Pursuit

Rogue Booty

Sci-fi Romance

Tsenturion Masters Series with Lee Savino

Alien Captive

Alien Tribute

Alien Abduction

Standalone

Mated on Hades

Shifter Romance

Big Bad Bunnies Series

Chasing His Bunny

Chasing His Squirrel

Chasing His Puma

Chasing His Polar Bear

Chasing His Honey Badger

Chasing Her Lion

Night of the Wild Stags

Chasing Tail Box Set

Chasing Tail... Again Box Set

www.ingramcontent.com/pod-product-compliance
Lightning Source LLC
Chambersburg PA
CBHW070452200726
48293CB00007B/2176